A Publisher's Note

To my dearest readers:

Triple Crown Publications provides you with the best reads in hip-hop fiction. Each novel is hand-selected in its purest form with you, the reader, in mind. *Let That Be the Reason*, an insta-classic, pioneered the hip-hop genre. Always innovative, you can count on Triple Crown's growth: manuscript notes — published books — audio — film.

Triple Crown has also gone international, with novels distributed around the globe. In Tokyo, the books have been translated into Japanese. Triple Crown's revolutionary brand has garnered attention from prominent news media, with features in ABC News, The New York Times, Newsweek, MTV, Publisher's Weekly, The Boston Globe, Vibe, Essence, Entrepreneur Magazine, Inc Magazine, Black Enterprise Magazine, The Washington Post, Millionaire Blueprints Magazine and Writer's Digest, just to name a few. I recently earned Ball State University's Ascent Award for Entrepreneurial Business Excellence and was named by Book Magazine as one of publishing's 50 most influential women. Those prestigious honors have taken me from street corner to boardroom accreditation.

Undisputedly, Triple Crown is the leader of the urban fiction renaissance, boasting more than one million sizzling books sold and counting…

Without you, our readers, there is no us,

Vickie Stringer
Publisher

Hood Richest

By Michelle Monay

Triple Crown Publications
PO Box 247378
Columbus, Ohio 43224
www.TripleCrownPublications.com

Library of Congress Control Number: 2010920097
ISBN 13: 978-0-9825888-7-1

Author: Michelle Monay
Graphics Design: Valerie Thompson, Leap Graphics
Photography: Treagen Kier
Editor-in-Chief: Vickie Stringer
Editor: Matthew Allan Roberson
Editorial Assistant: Christina Carter

First Trade Paperback Edition Printing 2010

10 9 8 7 6 5 4 3 2 1

Printed in the United States of America

Acknowledgements

Dear Father God:

Words can never describe how much I want to thank you. I can't envision myself thanking or acknowledging anyone before you, Father. I solely thank you, from the bottom of my heart to deep inside my soul, for this precious gift that you've instilled in me. The gift you have given me with my imagination is beyond certainty that you are a living God, full of promises and purpose in life. You make a way when there's no way. And I exclusively believe you're able to do everything that you said you would do. You fulfill your children's dreams, and with Faith, I believe I will be everything that I'm destined to become, and that you've called me to become Lord. I will conquer all of my desires and wishes, and it will all be because of you. And I want you to know, without you, there is no me, and all praise goes to you, My Heavenly Father.

People have doubted me when you've encouraged me through the spirit, while others that I needed close were hesitant and uncertain. Some have left me who I wouldn't ever have abandoned. Many have unfulfilled promise towards me that at the time benefited them, which turned into utter lies once circumstances changed over. Many that I have helped to extreme measures didn't think twice about helping me when I needed them, and not just in a monetary way, but in an inspiring and heartening manner. People that I've lent a hand to smacked mine down without appreciation and a mere thanks. And many have used me up, which I can only blame myself for my own stupidity, Father. But as I have learned, the flesh is truly unappreciative, ungrateful and selfish. But the good news is, Father, you've never left my side, not even for a nanosecond. And now, I have learned to never depend on a human, because they will fail me every time. Also, because I have you, and with you, I cannot lose. Because you already have my accomplishments and success written in the Heavens. Know that I will never ever be able to express my gratitude for all the things you do, done and is gonna do, Father God. You are definitely My Rock and You Completes Me. Again, I thank you, with great thanks, Father, for being Highly Favored by you. Glory to God!

I can never forget about My Lord and Savior, Jesus Christ. You was sent to help the ones who may fall short in this earthly world. I know I don't do everything the way things were intended, but I know you will continue this walk with me, because you know my heart. I know you and the Father are ones of understanding, and I'm so grateful for you saving me. I can never give enough or say enough on how much I appreciate you for your blood. I have been forgiven aplenty, so I forgive everyone that has struck against me and everyone that has done me wrong in the past. Everything happens for a reason. God Bless you all, no grudges held. And people, know that I am the perfect example of knowing that Jesus is the Son of God. Thank you, God, for sending your only begotten son!

I want to give a Special shout out to my wonderful mother, Tonya Cole. I love you for all that you've done and all that you do, my love. You're the best! To my two lovely and supportive sisters, Jha'quanna and Denise, my father Mike (remember what I told you when I was 10? Lol), my bad, spoiled nephews Dana and Boo Boo, my dear friend Destinee, who told me that I should become a writer years before I penned anything, thanks for the encouragement. To my family, friends and my pastor, Paul Mitchell, you're the best! That's why they call you the hood pastor! Lol.

A special thanks to the TCP staff for making this wonderful project possible for me. Thank you all for the help and the diligent work you all put in. I really appreciate you guys very much, thanks Christina and Matthew. Thanks Vickie for believing in others and allowing the start of my dreams to come true. God touched your heart for me, without a mistake, so may this be the beginning of a beautiful thing between us. Could only be God's work manifesting, magnificently and miraculously. You are truly heaven sent, Vickie! Know for you, I'll always be in debt.

Lastly, I would like to greatly thank all the authors that paved a way for me. I really appreciate you all's hard work. Blessings upon blessings!

I truly love you all and I hope everyone enjoys my debut novel. God bless!

Dedication

I would like to dedicate this book to all the Dream Chaser's out here. Never give up on your dreams or get discouraged. Keep God first, have faith, and the rest is history if you merely follow the Lord's plan. And to my lil cousin, Pooder. I love you boy, and I see you lil nigga. Just know I know you want different, but some circumstances is a distraction.

And lastly, a special dedication to my homeboy Ryan Daniels, RIP. Out of everybody, I never thought it would have been you fam'. You were really a good person and laid back. I hate that your time had to reach its demise for foolishness. But know I will always remember what you told me the last time I saw you when I was parked outside the barbershop on Salem and Hillcrest. Saying that really made me feel good, because you always saw the greatness and the different route in me. How ironic I receive the book deal call on your birthday. I know for a fact that you are God's Angel looking down on me. I just wanna say I will always love you and you will forever be missed family. I'ma do it for you, too, since you can't anymore. I love you Friend, forever and ever.

RIP Ryan Joseph Daniels
Sunrise 12-3-1987
Sunset 7-8-2009

Chapter One

Introducing Jayah Carter!

All bitches are good for is hatin', that's my core reason for not fucking with 'em. You might catch me with a few broads, but believe me, not many bitches. Bitches ain't real! Hoes these days either hatin' on me because their best friend like my swag or their nigga digging me. Let's not forget about the niggas! You better know it when I say this. All niggas are good for is giving up that cake and taking a bitch like me on trips and shopping sprees. Nothing else matters to me but that paper! I'm the perfect example of a real money go-getta. I really don't understand why a bitch gotta trip over some dick. I see it like this, M.O.E. Money over everythang. It's certain that I'ma get to the money. Hell, that's why I breathe. Needless to say, these chicks need to catch up, because I'm already 10 steps ahead of them all.

It all begun my freshman year of high school. The niggas at school start geekin' my head up, saying I was gorgeous, bad, thick, all kind of shit. Papers would go around the entire school asking who the finest girl was, and I'd always got the most votes. That shit was real crazy. I was the most popular girl at Miami Central and I had just gotten there. Not one senior liked me because, of

course, I was the captain of the varsity cheerleading squad. The seniors couldn't take that from a freshman. I wasn't mad by far. I don't like dealing with females anyway, so the shit was easier for me.

That's when shit really started popping off for me though. I transformed and blossomed into a beautiful young lady. I was unstoppable and untouchable. My ass was fat, rounded nicely and went damn good with my shape. My 34 C cups sat up just right, too. The size seven jeans complimented my waist line. I stood at 5 foot 4, meaning I had the most perfect body, weighing 125 pounds flat. Not to mention, my caramel complexion and almond-shaped, hazel eyes caught everybody's attention. To complete my beauty, my long black hair framed high cheek bones and a smile that would brighten anybody's day. Also, there was no bitch fucking with me on the dressing level. I donned elite designers from the top of my head to the bottom of my feet. It was only right to have the outfit, bag, frames and shoes to match. I had give it to myself, I was America's baddest bitch.

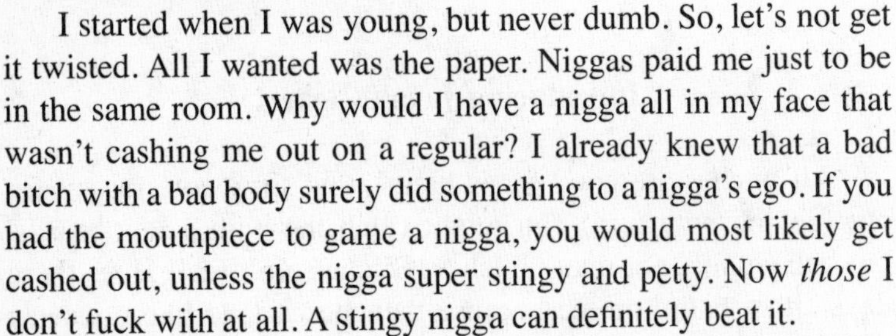

I started when I was young, but never dumb. So, let's not get it twisted. All I wanted was the paper. Niggas paid me just to be in the same room. Why would I have a nigga all in my face that wasn't cashing me out on a regular? I already knew that a bad bitch with a bad body surely did something to a nigga's ego. If you had the mouthpiece to game a nigga, you would most likely get cashed out, unless the nigga super stingy and petty. Now *those* I don't fuck with at all. A stingy nigga can definitely beat it.

Bitches always say use what you got to get what you want. Who the fuck came up with that saying!? Fuck that. Shit, if you a boss, you gonna get shit done without fucking a nigga. My shit get done according to Jayah. Fuck what a nigga conversing about! I only fucked a nigga if I wanted to, not to get something. The dough was comin' at me regardless of whether I was gonna fuck a nigga or not.

When I hit senior year, it was really on. My body and face were starting to mature. I was now curvaceous. And that's when shit settled for me. I knew I had to get it. Meaning that the nigga had to have a lot of benjis and certainly financially support me more than my daddy, which was a significant amount. So, either play the game, or get out of it. That's just how I felt.

Just imagine, I had niggas digging me hard from jump, so when I aged, it was over for Miami. I was the shit, and nobody could tell me otherwise. Niggas from all over the city wanted to get at me or Donteice, my sister from another mother. Hoes wasn't nearly hurting Miami like we were. Me and Tee was the hottest chicks that walked the streets of South Beach, and most definitely the flyest bitches that entered Dade County.

We knew each other since before I could remember. Our fathers were best friends. Donteice father got killed in a shootout nine years ago. My father treated Tee like his very own, so our standards of living were equivalent. We like blood sisters, real close. Most of the time, when you seen me, you seen her. Bitches hated us, too. We stayed upgrading our style and their niggas stayed on that cop shit, straight tryna cuff a bitch. Honestly? It was money to be made, and these cats had ta cut the check like that one man Jerry Maguire would say, show me the money!

Fuck niggas and get money, that was my motto. My dad always told me if a chick fucks with a nigga that's gettin' street money, it's only expected that he's gonna have bitches. That's what came along with street niggas. So, either you gonna accept the infidelity, or don't fall in love. My mom, on the other hand, wasn't having that shit. My mother and father was together until I was seven years old. She really wasn't on all the drama that surrounded my father's life, such as the bitches, the feds and I can't forget the jack boys. Every city got them, yeah, the stick-up kids. She loathed all the activities that came along with my father and the dope game, so she wound up leaving him alone. Shortly after they separated, she got involved with a traveling doctor. Yes, moms bounced back quickly. They always gone out of the country though, so I barely got the chance to have a mother and daughter face-to-face conversation. The seeing was scarce, but she called all the time to check up on me, so it was all good.

Now, Jay, my lovely father, was a different story. I fucked with him on the daily. I have always been a daddy's girl. My daddy married this Indian and African American therapist when I was 11. She was truly down for the nigga. Didn't matter how many bitches he had or how many feds was after him. I guess she was what you can call a real down-ass bitch. Honestly, I felt that she was gonna need a therapist herself fucking with Jay Carter. Although he had chicks in the streets, he made sure that chicks respected her and never once approached her. My father wasn't dumb and made certain that he chose a bad, independent bitch. And Amelia was the epitome of that. She's very wealthy and her

family had that Donald Trump type cash. He knew exactly what he was doing when he'd chosen that prize.

My dad was my heart. That nigga was my soul. My parents had me when they were young, my daddy was only 16 and my mother was 19. As my father had that amazing cash, it didn't help any. And he'd swept her right off her feet. I guess the apple didn't fall far from the tree. Like mother, like daughter.

It was amazing how me and my daddy were so close though. We were more like sister and brother instead of father and daughter. People never understood how a father and daughter could be so close and so cool. Most fathers are strict and annoying, not Jay. He already knew what I was capable of doing, so there wasn't any need to keep secrets. We confided in each other, discussing everything from bitches to niggas, to the drugs and to the money. There was never nothing that we kept from each other. He just did a jail bid a couple years back because some hatin'-ass niggas tried to snitch him out. But daddy got that money. It wasn't nothing to get them niggas out the way and only have to serve a few months instead of a few years. He paid the judge to knock off some charges and did that little petty time for a probation violation. He promised that he wasn't gonna miss his princess graduate for nothing in the world. That's when he started being in and out of town like crazy. So a nigga, or the feds, wouldn't catch him slipping for shit.

Being raised in Miami was a good thing. Shit, all the parties, car shows and the events, we had jumped for real. Miami was always alive and truly the party city. There is something constantly popping off and I always had something to do. That's right, I don't got no weeping, miserable, depressing-ass story to tell about growing up not having shit, and the struggle. Although I didn't live in the hood, I knew the hood very well and was straight hood-bound, being there on a daily basis. That's where Donteice mother resided. Her mother had three kids, Tee and her two older sisters. Ms. Laura was cool as hell. Mecia and Keycia were also cool, and they didn't play when it came to me and Tee. They weren't gonna play with a bitch. The twins were five years older than us and would fuck a bitch up. They stood at 5 feet 10 inches and weighed 265 pounds each. They were big and knew how to fight. Those twins had that work, fuck what you heard. But, real shit, Miami was the place to have fun. There was always crazy mothafuckas living in that world, so shit went down frequently.

My granny lived over there as well. She was the type that

never wanted to leave the hood. She loved it, and all the ballers over there loved her, bringing her money on a daily basis. 'Cause she wasn't one of them old-ass ladies complaining to the law. Some niggas even used to keep stashes over there because she's all they trusted. I loved my granny so much, she was so nice and sweet, but ghetto-fabulous. She was 52 years young and looked younger than my mother. People thought they were sisters instead of mother and daughter. All in all, Granny was cool as fuck.

I remember this one day, some fine-ass nigga name Cheno came in the house to put 30 G's in his safe that he stored there. He was a nigga that had that amazing cake and was only in his early 20s. Some even looked at him as the upcoming Jay Carter. Why did I have to see his sexy, fine ass that day? I had a crush on Cheno, but no one ever knew it, not even Tee. I had known him from being around the hood since I was a youngster.

"Hey Chen," my granny greeted him as he entered the kitchen.

"Hey ma' dukes, you good?" Cheno inquired, making sure her cash was right.

"Yeah, I'm fine, but when you get the chance, I wanna holla at you about something."

"What might that be, G?" He asked, flashing a concerned facial expression.

"Something that I'm gonna get with you on later." She cocked her head back, hating having to repeat herself.

"Damn, mom dukes, alright," he laughed, darting to the basement.

See, Cheno was that nigga, real talk, and getting galore money. I needed to be all parts of him so he could cake me off some real money. Fuck a few hundred. I needed top dollars, baby. If I had only known what I would be getting myself into. He was fine as fuck though, and well worth it all. Cheno. Bronze skin was smoother than a newborn baby's bottom. He was middle built, reaching just an inch from 6 feet, weighing a buck eighty with black hair and some stern fishes swimming in the sea. A bitch got sea sick, all them damn waves he had.

His hood rich attire complimented his swagger to the max. He was dressed impeccably for the nice weather. The white and royal blue Coogi button-down shirt that was left open, revealing his white T-shirt and Coogi shorts with the brand stitched across the back. On his feet sat a brand spanking new pair of white Air

Force 1s that were obviously fresh out the box. They looked more of the color pearl than white. A set of 6-carat blue diamond earrings glistened from his ears. The light mated pleasantly with the shimmer from the chain that laid flat on his white T-shirt. A frostbit Jacob the Jeweler watch adorned his right wrist. It was no mistaking that the nigga looked like new money. *That nigga can get it, he is absolutely gorgeous*, was all I could think as he emerged.

"Bye Cheno," I said, cheerfully.

It was too late though, because the nigga was already out the door. *Damn! Something gotta shake with that nigga*. My cell phone rang, knocking me out of my lustful thoughts.

"Hello?" I answered.

"What's up, bitch? You going down to the beach today?" Tee asked, amped.

"And you know it. Although I do need to be studying for my Algebra 2 test. You know I gotta get at least a B to cheer the final game. You know what that game means to me," I whined.

"Girl, bye," Tee smacked her lips. "You know that's all you get is A's. I'm the one who need to study." She giggled. "I definitely gotta cheer that game. Its gon' be cranking with all the niggas that's getting that stupid dough. You know we got to get-get-get it," Tee said, laughing.

"You silly, man," I exploded into laughter. "Ay, Tee who does the Chen nigga fuck with?" I wanted to know.

"Girl you should say who don't that nigga fuck with? Everybody is the answer to your question. He is a male whore. They say he got a main bitch, her name Teika. But I guess she low low, he keeps her out the way. Oh, but girl, he fucked dirty-ass Veronica though, and had her and Tyiesha fighting over him. And Veronica got the dirty look to her man, yuck!" She sighed, loudly. "The bitch can put on some name brand shit and still look filthy. And the Tyiesha chick is a slut. She fucks all type of niggas just for the fuckin' fun of it. That girl be straight foolin'. But ain't that some shit, 'cause ain't neither one of the lame-ass hoes his wifey, so what the fuck was they on?"

"Damn, he on that. I know if he fucked with them tacks I know I can get some fuck with," I replied in an arrogant tone.

"You mean he fucked them, he never fucked with them losers like that." Tee replied.

"Man, I gotta see what's up with dude." We made plans to

meet at the beach.

Why did I tell her ass that? She was already fuckin' with his best friend J.P., so she would certainly make it her business to hook that up.

As I was cruising down to the beach in my Charger Hemi, the one my daddy purchased for me with the condo on my 17th birthday, my mind was stuck on Cheno. I just couldn't get the thought of the nigga out of my head. He was what I'd been waiting on, a money go-getta, good-looking brotha and a well-dressed nigga who had a bitch, so he really wouldn't be focused on me like that. I would still be able to do me. It would all be good if I started fucking with him because I would most certainly be able to cut ugly-ass Jay Jay off, cause fuck a pair of Maxes and a Roc outfit. I can get my daddy to get that little shit. Hell, I could've got the shit myself on the real. I was about to be 18 that May and like I said, I was on shopping sprees and trips. Shit, why bitches were fucking for free? I was tryna get rich. Plus, his hatin'-ass bitch Chassidy Brown be on some other sucka type shit.

That's the definition of a true hater. I assure you that her picture will soon be located next to Jayah's number one hater, I promise. I know I'ma have to end up beating that hoe's ass one day. She talked entirely too much shit.

In all honesty, if your cash wasn't right, then Jayah wasn't right, and it was critical that I stayed laced. Fat Attack was getting cut the fuck off too. All his fat ass wanted to do for a bitch was go out and eat at some fancy restaurant. Don't get it mistaken, because a bitch do love to eat, especially at five star restaurants, but damn, the nigga used to give me six or seven hundred. Now it was always, "Bye, and maybe next time you'll stop playing with that pussy."

I always would tell that fat fucker, "I think not, nigga. You already know what it is my way." He would always just laugh with his fat, sweaty neck self.

When I finally got to the beach, some nigga was watching me. "Damn baby!" He said as I was getting out of the car. *Man what clown is this?* I turned around and was pleasantly surprised when I saw a fine, well-built, peanut butter brown nigga with a perfectly trimmed goatee and mustache. He was hairy all over, but sexy as could be. He threw me in a trance for a second, snapping me out of my daze by asking was I okay.

"Oh, yeah, I'm good."

"So, what's up with you? You are so beautiful," he complimented me in a raspy, deep, sexy voice.

"Well thanks," I beamed. *Where in the hell did he come from?*

"So, do you got a man? 'Cause my girl wouldn't be at the beach by herself." He rubbed his hands together as he spoke.

"Nope, I don't really do the relationship thing. Do you have a woman?"

"Naw, I haven't found one that's right for me, but I think I found her now." He smiled, slyly.

Who do he think he gaming, man. I been had the game. He a real clown, but damn...I just knew someone as sexy as him had a bitch. He could of got some play, but he look like he can be on the crazy, stalking a bitch side. I'm cool.

But me being me, I played along. "Shid, maybe you have." I winked.

"Baby, give me yo' number and I'ma give you a call later 'cause I'm here on business."

Ooohh shit, change of plans. I'm gonna give the nigga some fuck with. Why wouldn't I? I mean, he from out of town, too. Oh yeah, that's a must.

As I gave him my number, he handed me $1,000 in cash, because I was so gorgeous. It was obvious that dude was letting me know that he wasn't a broke nigga. Truth be told, it wasn't shit for real. But, I did start questioning myself. Like damn, he don't even know me. Now, let's not get confused, because I done got stacks out of niggas. But either he thought he could fuck me or I'd been dating the nigga for a while. It had never been a first time encounter. I just was imagining what he would do for me if I put this virgin little pussy on 'em. Yeah, homie was that appealing.

Before he walked off he told me. "My name is Maine, so be expecting my call, shorty."

"Jayah." Tee yelled as she walked up behind me, throwing me out of my deep thoughts. I was on a whole nother planet pondering about what the nigga had just done. *He must really have that cake for real, he can surely break me off some bans flat-out, keep that dough coming, keep it coming*. I told Donteice what he did and she was more excited than I was.

The beach was jumping like we thought it would be. The sky was beautiful and the air was fresh with a light breeze. Sixty-five degrees, that was what the weatherman reported. Everybody was there, including the Cheno nigga. And I just couldn't get my mind off him, even though a flock of chicks was all over him like ants on a sour lollipop. All different type of bitches was coming up to the homie. I didn't give a fuck cause I really was digging his swagg, so fuck them bitches.

Tee knew me too well and noticed that the shit was bothering me. So, my bitch went over there and gave him my number. The girl wasn't gonna back down from shit. She gonna get it done with or without your consent. I was so salty. She was straight up clowning. I could have slapped the piss out of her ass because the nigga looked like he wasn't even paying her ass any attention.

By that time, I was frustrated and I didn't even wanna stay there. Needless to say, I bounced and went to my condo. *Fuck him*, I had to study for a test the following day. My coach was a hater, and she didn't allow anything to slide. The grade C was like an F in her vision. As I was finishing up my last bit of deep studying, I was snapped out of it by the phone ringing.

"Who the hell is this callin' me private?" I said, irritated. Some clown was calling me block, and if I didn't despise anything else, I certainly hated a restricted call.

"Is this Jayah?" The caller asked.

"Yeah! Who this?" I asked as my stomach started forming butterflies. I just knew it was the Maine nigga, but I realized I didn't even tell him my name.

"Who you want it to be?" The familiar voice spoke.

"Man quit playing on my phone, you clown-ass nigga, whoever you are tryin' to play games and shit," I yelled with much attitude.

"Damn, calm down. This Cheno. Man, what's up? Didn't you want me to call you?"

Dang! Do the nigga gotta put it like that? I mean, I want the fine nigga, but fuck! Does he got to be that damn confident in his self? Tee could of just made that shit up. I laughed. He must've felt how I was lookin' at him when I was over at Granny's today.

"Yeah, I was just wondering what be up with you, and just thought since you be over my granny's house often, I would just holla at you from time to time," I said, lying down on my stomach with my eyes to the ceiling. I could tell I sounded so lame.

"Oh... a'ight, that's what's up. Well, do you wanna go get some breakfast in the morning before you go to school?" Chen asked.

"Yeah, that's cool, just call me in the morning and let me know where we going and I gotta be at school at nine so you better be up and ready to go by like seven, okay?" I said, seriously.

"Okay, baby."

The conversation ended. I lay there thinking. *Man I'm about to be on my grown woman and play my hand right, and just keep my game face on at all times*. Hell, I had to do something, because it wasn't no telling when the hatin'-ass feds was gonna try to target my father again. I had to get this money myself. Real money, so I really had to cut the lame, little money-getting niggas completely off. I devised a good strategy. It's always best to plan ahead and you might just come out on top, if you know how to play your cards right.

By the time I was 22, I was determined to have at least $2.5 million. I knew if I got a few ballers on my team, I mean, championship ballers, and switched them up every year after I done raped their pockets dry, I was sure to be good. That gave me a little less than five years, and if everything worked out accordingly, I would be straight. My daddy already gave me $20,000 each month to get by. He'd been doing that since I was a freshman. And the money did not stop when he was incarcerated. He gave that to me and the same to Tee. Mine went all to the bank though, because my mother had me all the way together. She suggested that I put the money that I received from my father inside my bank account and didn't touch it until I turned 21. And that was a good idea to me, 'cause I knew once it added up, I would have some shit. Fuck it, it was game time and I had to take all the losers off my team, cause they were only in the way.

Chapter Two

Yo, I'm jumpin'!

The following morning, the sunlight poured into my room. I opened my eyes, allowing them to adjust to the light. Swinging my foot around to the floor, it settled on my bearskin rug. I remained standing and stretched my back, neck and shoulders, then ambled to my oversized balcony window. Pulling back my drapes, I allowed the room to become brighter. I strolled from the window over to my closet.

What the hell am I about to put on? I got two walk-in closets full of clothes. Just gotta find the right attire to blow this nigga way back so he can know that I'ma hot commodity. Oooh! I forgot all about this Coco Chanel fit.

I spotted the clothes among all the gear in my closet by the sparkle. New, with the tags still attached. It was just the right apparel for that day, a red and white short sleeve blazer with the huge Coco Chanel symbol in white representing on the back, and a light pair of Chanel skinny jeans that matched perfectly. The designer's name was embossed in white lettering on the back pocket area. To set it off, I threw on my checkerboard red and white Chanel pumps. For embellishment, I grabbed my white Chanel shoulder bag and glasses, not forgetting the classy white accessories. My hair fell from a cute, neatly loose ponytail, draping down my back.

Once I was cleaned and refreshed, it was already seven. The clown still hadn't called. *Oh no, I know I didn't go all out for this clown-ass muthaf…* yep, my phone rang before I could finish the thought.

"Yeah, what up?" I answered dryly, as if I wasn't waiting for him to call.

"What's good, baby? Where we going, you ready?" He inquired, fully awake.

"Yeah I'm ready, meet me at the Breakfast Club on 109th street."

"That's cool I will be there in like 15 minutes."

"Yup."

It was about a quarter to eight when I arrived at the Breakfast Club, located in a semi-nice neighborhood on the north side. I parked directly on the side street and walked in, spotting him in the VIP booth awaiting my arrival.

I ordered my food as soon as I sat down. Once that was done, the nigga instantaneously started tripping. He thought he was some kinda king or something. Dude was acting like he was already Jay Carter, or some shit, please.

"Damn, where was you at taking all damn day?" Cheno asked, very rudely.

I furrowed my brow. "Nigga, you know I live in white peoples land. I hope you didn't think I would be doing 140 miles just to get here!" I exclaimed, cocking my neck back and rolled my eyes. "Oh, or maybe you thought I would, but I'm not Teika, Veronica, Tyiesha or none of them lame-ass hoes you fuck with that say how high when you say jump, alright?" I shot with an attitude.

He flashed a friendly smile. "Baby, I like that in you. I love a challenge. I can see that I can't run over you, you gonna give a nigga a run for his money." He laughed like shit was funny.

"You damn skippy. Boy I don't play them kind of games." I flared my nose up, acting like a snobbish bitch. Not knowing how he would react towards me if I kept talking shit to him. *Fuck it*.

"A'ight man, what's good? Our first date we arguing, that is not a good sign. You cool, baby?" He grabbed my hands.

"Yea, I'm straight."

"So, who you fuck with?" He asked, gazing into my eyes.

This nigga gon' have the audacity to ask me that and he fuck with the whole city. I called him on his own shit.

"Naw, nigga, who you fuck with is the question? Fuck it, it would be better if I said who you don't fuck with," I said, laughing at him.

"Oh, you on that ma?" He laughed like I was giving him shade. "I mean, I don't fuck with no bitch. I fucks bitches, but ain't none of them hoes wifey. You feel me?"

"Whatever, what about the girl Teika?"

"Shid, what about her? She my daughter mom and she look out for me when shit get fucked up, and when everything good I look out for her. But other than that, it ain't nothing like you thinking."

Damn, Tee had her shit all fucked up. I thought he had a main. Fuck, I can't win for losing, but fuck it, he still a winner.

"Oh really, so it shouldn't be any problems if we fucked around, huh?" I simply asked.

"None at all. So, that's what we gon' do, fuck around?"

"I guess we gon' talk. But shid, you can have friends that don't bother me, just keep your bitches in check, don't try to shit on me or nothing. Just respect me and we good, babe." I spoke, sternly.

He chuckled. "Look at you trying to be hard, but that's what's up. I got you ma."

"Whatever, so what is your real name?" I wanted to know.

"Cheno."

I sucked my teeth. "Boy, don't play with me. What's your government name? You know, the one that's on your birth certificate, not yo' street name fool," I playfully rolled my eyes.

"It's Cheno, real talk, everybody thinks that's my nickname, but it's not."

"So Cheno… what?"

"Cheno Tate, babe. Damn, you the police?" He laughed.

"Ha ha, real cute, but I'm just asking," I said while playing with my ponytail.

We ate and talked, getting to know each other better. To my surprise, he was interested in my schooling and loved how I was so hoodish, but still adored how I spoke highly on my education. I told him how I made honor roll each year and was number one in my class. He was pleased, and you could tell that he admired my

all around humor. We laughed and joked, enjoying each other's company. Time flew pass. I didn't even notice that I had to be in school in 10 minutes. I hated being late.

"Well it's almost nine and I have to be at school, so I'ma get with you as soon as I get out alright babe?"

He grabbed a blue box that was in a bag next to him. "Here baby, this you."

He clamped a diamond bracelet around my wrist. I was surprised he got it for me before he came there, and he knew I would be expensive because Jay Carter my pops. He said I was gon' be good and he would love to spoil me because I wasn't one of those thirsty, broke-ass bitches gold digging.

"Thanks. This is really nice. You really didn't have to." Yeah I'm far from broke and thirsty, but I do gotta get this money.

♛ ♛ ♛ ♛ ♛ ♛ ♛ ♛ ♛ ♛ ♛ ♛ ♛ ♛ ♛ ♛ ♛

I was sitting in class waiting on the teacher to pass me my test. I was anxious to see what I got. The teacher was taking all damn day, so I carried on a conversation with Tee about what had happened with Cheno at breakfast. Tee was my homie homie. We were what you called true friends because we never hated on each other. She was happy for me and we always loved to hear good stuff about the other.

"Girl, that's what's up, but what you gon' do about Dajuan?" She giggled.

"Fuck that nigga. He keep being on all these hoes on the low low anyway. Plus, Dajuan is a schoolboy. He can't do nothing for me. He will get the picture one way or another, ya dig?" I shrugged.

Donteice burst out in laughter.

The teacher handed me my test. Looking at that A+, I didn't even know why I panicked. Real polish bitches aren't just fab stars, they're fabulous with brains, the total and complete package.

"Damn, my phone keep vibrating. I don't know who this is callin' my phone from a 404 area code," I said to Donteice, eyeing my screen with confusion.

"Shid, ain't no telling So, bitch the game is on Friday, what are you wearing to the after party?" Tee said, dancing around in her seat, all hyped up like always.

"Umm — this Ed Hardy white and black outfit with the tiger

print throughout the shirt, pants, and track jacket with them J's that came out on Saturday, the ones Daddy got us. I mean, why wouldn't I step out on them fresh. This is the last game to see who going to state!"

"You silly, Jayah," Tee giggled. "I wanna wear some Ed Hardy, too." She playfully pouted, folding her arms cross.

"Go get the tiger outfit I got, just get the one that got mostly black in it, because mine is mostly white."

"We gon' be shittin' on bitches. But bitch, I ain't getting the track jacket cause it's gonna be hot. We only live in Miami," Tee said, sarcastically.

"You right, but you know it's always chilly in February girl. On Friday it's only gon' be 58 degrees with a windy breeze. So, you can get that off."

"Yeah you right, so we can go get it after school."

"Bet," I said as the lunch bell rang.

It was time for me to go though. I only had three classes in the morning and after that I could leave. I passed almost all my required classes junior year, so I was good.

Let me see who this is callin' me from this weird-ass number, I thought, popping inside my whip.

"What's up, baby?" The unfamiliar voice said as he picked up his phone.

"Who is this?" I slowly asked, curiously.

"This Maine, baby. What's up? Can I see you?"

"Hey, what you doing?" I inquired, smiling from ear to ear.

"Nothing. Thinking about yo' sexy ass,"

"Oh really," I blushed. "So, what are you gettin' into today?"

"Hopefully seeing you. That's what I wanna do."

"We can make that work, what time you tryna' see me?"

"A Sap." We both started laughing.

"Well, meet me at the Bal Harbour Mall in like 30 minutes because that's where I'm headed." I said.

"Yeah I'ma call your phone when I get there."

"Cool." I hung up the phone and got ready for some serious shopping.

♛ ♛ ♛ ♛ ♛ ♛ ♛ ♛ ♛ ♛ ♛ ♛ ♛ ♛ ♛ ♛ ♛

Rushing home from the mall was all I could do. The nigga got me so fitted, I had to get home and try on the shit. Everything I got

was on some classy grown woman type shit. It was ridiculous. I mean, a bitch had the hottest shit out, I had no mercy on the malls, but today, that nigga took dressing to a whole different attire. He got me this Marc Jacobs short trench and printed ottoman dress for four grand. Not to mention the Vera Wang Chinese dress that cost damn near ten bans. I got the works. He had to have spent at least fifteen stacks on nothing more than a couple fits and handbags. The Maine nigga was so far away from petty, and that was certainly my type of brotha. He was a cool-ass nigga though, because when we were leaving, he gave me a stack of hundreds. Dude didn't have a problem with throwing that cash. He didn't want to leave with me or nothing. I just knew he would want this little pussy after he copped me that Vera Wang shit, but hey, real niggas do real thangs, and I learned that shit from Jay Carter.

I was in my house looking on how shit just work out. Life was the shit, and why wouldn't it be? I was the shit. Bitches hated me and all the niggas loved me. My great day finally ended. Hearing a rattling sound at the door, I realized it was the sound of keys. I knew it either had to be my dad or Tee. I was lounging on my white leather sectional sofa with my legs propped up on the glass table looking to see which one it was. Tee entered, hyped as hell.

"Bitch! Why you haven't been answering your phone all day? Yo, some shit went the fuck down. Girl, first let me tell you about your boy Cheno. He came up to the school checking for you, asking everybody about you, where you at and all kind of shit," she took a deep breath and continued. "Then I'm in the hood, chillin' and shit right. That hood rat bitch Veronica had the nerve to come up to me why I'm on the block kickin' rocks with J.P. I mean, me and the nigga was kickin' shit real hard you hear me," she paused to catch her breath again. "Yo, we was just 'bout to go for a ride. We was waiting on his lil brother to pull back up. This bitch pops her ugly ass out like she related to the Ali's and had the balls to ask where that ugly fuck bitch friend of mine was at. I asked that clown-ass bitch who she thought she was talking to. She said she was talking to me and asking about your jiggy ass, girl," she stopped her story to see my reaction. I couldn't believe this hoe was tryna start some shit. Tee continued when she saw I wanted to know what happened. "I told her she got me fucked up, disrespecting fam' like that. That bitch didn't believe me, until I cracked her ass dead in her mouth, letting her know how we really get down. I'm beating the bitch-ass. I kept hitting that bitch in her face, and got the skank-ass hoe on the ground quick. Yo, her cat got salty and stole on me from the side. So I instantly stop fighting her and get to beatin' the fuck out of her cat."

"This is some shit that went down Tee. Thanks for having my back though." I would have done the same for Tee.

"Yeah, real talk, you're my fam', and when it comes to fam', I can beat a bitch down. The entire time, all she was doing was pulling the fuck out of my hair, with both of her hands though. Where the FUCK they do that at? Hair pulling bitches! That's that weak, can't fight shit." She rubbed her fingers through her hair. "Man, my shit gone – "

"Let's go back to the hood!" I interrupted, mad as hell. "Let's go back!"

"Man, let me finish telling you! So, I'm fucking this bitch up on some G shit doe, kneeing her in her shit, her shit was bleeding bad, literally leaking. After that, I hear this one bitch in my ear like get off my cat, this and that, right? So that's when I surmise Veronica got up and her and the other girl started jumping me. I'm giving these bitches a run for their money. I'm stepping back and running in stealing on these hoes. Finally, J.P. and his niggas broke it up."

"Man, what the fuck! Them bitches got me fucked up. I know this weak-ass bitch didn't," my voice cracked. "I'ma beat the fuck out of each of the hatin' losers. Did you tell Keycia and Mecia?" I asked as tears of anger fell from my face.

"You know it, we couldn't find them anywhere. Believe me, it's going all the way down Friday night after the game and they already said it, so be ready and we gon' be dummy deep cause Keycia already done called all their project cousins. You know they rough, some straight goonz. So they better beware, 'cause soon as I see her I'm punching, looking or not looking. Call it sneaking if you want to, but I'm stealing on bitches. Oh yeah, and I'm calling Daddy so he can be right there just in case they wanna bring some niggas or something."

I took a deep breath in utter disbelief. "I can't believe she going around looking for me over this nigga and I only talked to him for one day!" I yelled, boiling hot inside. I snatched my cell phone from the table and dialed Chen number so quick, he answered on the first ring like shit was sweet.

"What's good, baby? I been looking for you all damn day, you got yo' phone off and shit."

"Fuck that, yo' bitch Veronica was out looking for me and her and Donteice got into a fight and they start jumping her! Fuck you and don't ever call my phone again." I roared in anger.

Click, was all Cheno heard.

♛ ♛ ♛ ♛ ♛ ♛ ♛ ♛ ♛ ♛ ♛ ♛ ♛ ♛ ♛ ♛ ♛

"Donteice, why this nigga keep calling? Didn't I tell him to stop calling this Sprint phone? Damn lame, I'm good." I spoke as I was answering the phone. Not giving him a chance to respond, I hung up again.

Fuck him, because if he on some shit now, it's really gon' be a problem in the future. So fuck that nigga, real talk. I decided to give Maine a call and dialed his number.

"What up? This Maine?" I asked, seductively.

"Yeah babe, what up?"

"Oh, I was just callin' to tell you thanks for the things you got me earlier."

"Babe, you welcome. That lil shit ain't nothin'. That's just light shopping. I really wanna take you to Italy or somewhere major like that. You deserve the best, so when will you be ready to go?"

I sat there flabbergasted. *Damn, this nigga for real! I'm already living the good life, but he really wanna welcome a bitch to the good good life. That's some real shit, Italy. Damn, I can't turn that down at all, but then again, I know my daddy ain't having that. Not out the country. Hell nah.*

"Hello? Babe? What you think about that?" Maine asked.

"For real, I would love to go, but that's like out of the country and my dad gon' be like hell no, ain't gon' happen. So I don't know about Italy, but maybe New York or Cali."

"Yo' dad can go with us. I just wanna show you out of the country. I'm sure you won't be excited to be in New York or Cali like you would to be in Italy. Just discuss it with cha old man, and let me know, and tell him it's on me. Is that fair enough, baby?"

"Yeah it is, I'm gonna holla at him about it soon 'cause we go on spring break in a month. That'd be tight if he say yeah."

"It would be though. But I'm gon' miss you, 'cause you know I'm going back home tonight."

Damn. Got niggas missing me already, that's professional work baby.

"I know, but why so soon? You only got to kick it with me for a few hours, that's it." I said in my fake caring tone.

"Babe, I know, but I'ma busy man and my time always booked up for at least three weeks."

"So basically you are saying I got to put my time in, huh?" I spoke in a child-like tone.

"Naw, not like that. You making shit more than it is."

"Rigggght!" I said, sarcastically.

"For real, you is. Just see if you can go on this trip with me and we will spend one whole week together. If not, I'm still gon' fuck with you when you on spring break. Is that cool with you shorty?" Maine asked, sincerely.

"It sounds like a plan, yeah that's cool."

"Well, I'ma holla at you when I touch down in my city, alright baby?"

"Okay, bye." I closed my phone.

I was telling Tee what he said and she was on it. Her loud butt wanted to go to Italy too. I thought if dad gave his permission, it'd be on and poppin' for real.

"Damn, Tee. You didn't even get to get your outfit today." I said.

"I can just grab it tomorrow." Tee replied. She was getting ready to leave because J.P. kept blowing her phone up. "But, I'm up sis." She informed me right before heading out the door.

Cheno wouldn't stop calling my phone for shit. I turned it off for about 30 minutes and he was still calling back to back. I had four voicemails and two text messages. He was saying all kinda shit. He had beaten the bitch up and he was sorry for her ignorance, so I finally decided to answer.

"What is it that you want with me? I don't wanna fuck with you at all," I began. "As a matter of fact, I never even fucked with you anyway. We was just cool, and that's that playa, so why do you insist on calling my phone? I'm good, man!"

"Baby, just let me come where you are. I don't fuck with that girl, she's a stalker! I only fucked her once, and she sucked my dick twice and that's it. I don't know why she thinks she's my bitch or close to it. 'Cause she's not and I just choked her out, 'cause she got me fucked up. I'm tryna' fuck with you, wife you up, and that bitch on some straight sucka shit. She does that shit all the time. Tryna fight chicks who I fuck wit'. But Jayah, baby, the bad thing about all this is I fucked her about four months ago and she still on a nigga dick." He sighed. "So, baby, you gon' let me come see you for a minute?"

"Boy, whatever! Me and my bitches don't be on that sucka hatin' type shit. That bitch need to gone wit' the bullshit. But one thing you better believe is I'm gonna beat the fuck out of that bitch Friday after my game, bitch better put her 3-D shades on. She think I'ma punk 'cause I'm little and I'm cute, but I'm gonna show this bitch how a little bitty bitch get down, watch me!"

"You crazy babe. So, will you let a nigga come over and holla at you?"

"Nope," I yelled into the phone.

"Why?"

"'Cause I still ain't fuckin' with you like that." I said right before hanging up the phone.

Not even two seconds later, my phone had rang..

"Babe, why you on that petty shit? Just give me one more chance and I bet you won't have no more problems with no bitch after this, for real, ma." He sounded earnest.

"Alright, but you can't come over because I'm 'bout to go to sleep. I got class in the morning, so I will holla at you when I get out of school."

"Nah, why can't we go to breakfast again in the morning before you go to school?"

"That'll be fine, same spot same time."

"Yeah, a'ight Jayah."

Chapter Three

The game!

It was the end of the game and score was 98 to 97. We were leading and the other team had the ball with seven seconds on the clock. We had to make 'em miss it.

Coach called for a timeout and we had to perform our last cheer on the floor. We rushed to the middle and I showed my ass off extra hard, because, of course, I seen my baby Cheno. That bitch Veronica was watching him, but I wasn't worried, because he was watching me. At the end of the cheer, I did 10 toe-touches straight. When I was done, I read his lips and he mouthed. "Damn, baby, I gotta have you." The two teams started back playing. The dude from the other team shot the ball and missed it "YYeeeaahhhh!" was all you heard.

I looked at Cheno and started laughing. Me and Tee instantly scurried off to the locker room to change into our fighting gear. Once we were outside, all of our peoples was waiting. It was about 50 chicks and 50 niggas.

My daddy didn't hesitate. "Point the bitches out that jumped you, Tee." I followed Tee's finger to this ugly bald chick and she just stole on her ass. Yep, and I came right behind her. We got to beatin' the fuck out of the chick and Mecia began stealing on any random chick that was surrounded by the other girls, knocking hoes down and straight placing them onto their backs. She didn't give a fuck if they jumped in or not. Hell, they shouldn't have been standing there. Before we knew it, the whole squad just was banging. It was a war for real because they had about the same amount of chicks we had, but their crew was filled with weak and lame hoes.

I stopped fighting and started surveying the crowd for Veronica, and then I spotted her tussling with Na'daijah, my god sister. She was 15 and was Donteice sister on her father side. They was banging, going blow-for-blow, but Veronica was tryna use her weight on Daijah so Veronica was getting the best of her. Instantaneously, I jumped in that fight and got to working her ass something terrible. Next thing I know, I had Veronica on the ground and was pounding her face in. I started sitting on her hands and was beatin' my hand up with her face.

Before I noticed, my dad pried in and swooped me up from off of her and yelled, "Jayah, she feel you, don't kill her though. You got her, baby. She will know not to be out looking for you no more, believe that." My father's words wasn't even out of his mouth good enough before this one bold-ass chick stole on me from the side when my daddy was grabbing me up. My dad instantly dropped her ass.

"Bitch, don't try to steal on my baby while I'm grabbing her away from the fight. Dumb little bitch," my daddy roared out. "Lil Jay, get her mothafucka ass."

That's all I needed to hear. I pulled her up onto her feet and the girl caught a fist to her right eye, which she was already fucked up from my daddy dropping her like she was a nigga.

The police wound up coming. So we all jumped in our whips and headed to the gas station because we all wanted to fight some more. We was all definitely going hard that night, fuck what you heard.

Pulling up at the gas station, we popped out of our whips and they got out their cars. These bitches start pulling out bats and swords. I doubled over in laughter, my dad shouted. "Haven't y'all been taught never bring bullshit to a gun fight!" He pulled out two 9 mm pistols and his main man Big Tommy pulled out this big-ass shot gun. He ordered them in the most stern and aggressive tone.

"Put that little shit up. Y'all 'bout to fight one on one. Now, who wanna go first, go pick their candidate, and then the second person who wanna fight, pick. Then y'all two can swap it out. And then after that, two more people can go."

"That's what's up," Me and Tee said in unison, clapping hands.

"Shid, I want Veronica," I bounced around like I was in a boxing match. "And the other two bitches that jumped my right hand."

"What's up, who want it with me? Bitches is dumb, what's up," Tee called them out while pounding her fist with her hand. "I'm ready for whoever, the beastiest one. That's who I want. I'ma fucking beast what's jumping." Tee voiced, irritated and ready to bang.

The bitches were acting scary, so my daddy called Veronica out. "Come out Veronica. You want to fight her, right? My daughter right here now so you don't gotta try to find her or nothing. She's here, so step in the center sweetie." He said as he backed the crowd up. "So y'all can fight. That's what y'all wanted to do, right? What's good? Let's get to it." He laughed. "I already know my daughters gonna put their mans down, believe that. I put five stacks on both of their head, what's up, get out here baby girl." He demanded.

"Right, come out here bitch! You want me, right? What's jumping!" I screamed. Of course, she tried to play hard and came to the center slightly squaring up with me.

"I ain't scary, what up?" She said, boldly. But I saw that Veronica was stuntin' and didn't really want to fight me one-on-one by the look in her eyes.

"Oh, alright, that's what I want you to do, come out here and get embarrassed right in front of Cheno." I jumped around with my killers up, ready for war.

So we both squared up like some beast. But I decided to end the circling and I just ran in, never tryna give the chick a chance to hit me first. All I heard was, "Damn Jayah got work. Damn." *Whop, whop, whop*. I was throwing nothing but hard blows. I know I punched her with at least an eight-piece dark crispy. Then that's when Keycia just grabbed her ass up and body slammed her to the ground, hard as hell though. Then I just stole on the bitch in the pink just because she was standing there looking retarded.

Tee worked the girl that pulled out her hair and she pulled all hers out too. Fuck it, tit for tat. We all shifted to our left and noticed that Na'daijah working this chick name Joy, who was about 24. The chick was Veronica's older sister. Daijah was manhandling her without a problem. At the time, we didn't think Daijah had that much work, but she was throwing blows to her ass. Straight face shots though, and they all were connecting swiftly. After a while, we all started jumping in and stomped Joy out. Like always, my daddy said that it was enough and he made us all leave.

Twenty minutes later, we were sauntering into the crammed house party like superstars, ambushed by the greetings of so many.

"Damn, Jayah. We beat them bitches down, they couldn't see us, fam'," my cousin D'vena said.

"That's all I'm saying. We made sure we put our mans down tonight." I laughed with excitement.

"Girl, they are so dumb. Why would they try to bring weapons and shit? Like our people gon' let that go down." We burst into laughter.

"Riiight, they just silly and must be crazy because they know my daddy ain't gon' play!"

"You right cuz, but that one girl Veronica can bang, I ain't gon' lie." D'vena snickered.

"Yeah, she can though. I give props when they're due and she got hands." I nodded, keeping it all the way one hunnid. "Them other chicks she had fight too wildly for me though, wind milling and shit. Where they do that at? She need a new squad some shit."

Vena chuckled. "Hell yeah, but Veronica didn't have shit coming when it came to you. She was trying to hang, but ole girl ain't quick enough."

"You silly." I giggled. "You were beastin' hoes too."

"Yeah you right, but I gotta give it to Daijah. I didn't think she could fight, but she proved me wrong."

"You silly cuz." I said smiling as we started dancing rhythmically to the beat, enjoying ourselves.

♛ ♛ ♛ ♛ ♛ ♛ ♛ ♛ ♛ ♛ ♛ ♛ ♛ ♛ ♛ ♛ ♛

When I awoke the following morning, my body was aching terribly. *Damn, I can't believe we was banging them bitches like that, but I bet they will learn to RESPECT me 'cause I ain't gon' play with 'em. My gooniez ain't playing. We ready for whatever and whoever.* I laughed to myself.

My phone had 15 miss calls and nine of them were from Cheno. Briefly, I debated if I should return his call or not. After a short minute thinking, I decided to call him back.

"Hello, what's up?" I asked when he picked up.

"Shid, you baby, you cool. I just wanna see you so fuckin' bad." He began that little sincere talk. "I couldn't sleep last night. I kept thinkin' about you cheering. Then I kept picturing you beatin' them hoes asses." He laughed.

"Oh, I'm most definitely cool. It wasn't shit, I got two scratches on my face, but that's about it, babe. Those weak hoes didn't do any type of damage to none of my people."

"I'm happy to hear that, but why don't you let me pamper you up for the day since you was fighting some haters on my account. That way we can give 'em a reason to hate, for real now." Cheno said, hoping to convince me.

"Why not? I guess it is because of you that the bitches hatin' on me."

"You silly, Jayah. But a nigga really loving your swagger, you hood and classy, yo."

"So, where are we going?"

"Where ever you wanna go. The world is yours, baby."

I liked how he was starting out. "For real, it doesn't even matter."

"Well, I'm sure you will come up with something by the time you get ready. How long will it take you?" He was eager.

"I prolly be ready like around five."

"Damn." He sounded off loudly. "It's only 11 and I said the whole day, not half."

"Okay, babe. I will meet you at my granny's at 1:30 then. Is that fine?"

"Yeah that's better." He said. "See you then, ugly."

"Okay," I said right before answering my other line. "Hello?"

"Bitch, you fighting over niggas now?" Some clown screamed through my phone.

"Who the fuck is this?" I yelled, slightly offended.

"Dajuan, bitch, who else would it be?"

"Boy, you better kick rocks and stop calling my phone. I don't fuck with you nigga." I spat, snottily.

"Bitch, you a hoe." Dajuan said, angrily.

"And you are a fuckin' hater. Just like these bitches and you wish I was a hoe." I snickered. "Pussssh. Not neva!"

"Fucking whore." He sighed, like he was agitated or some shit.

"I could never be a hoe. If I was, you sure didn't fuck. So, what it mean to me?"

"I could've."

"Doubt it. You ain't got enough money to fuck me, my nigga." I cracked up laughing.

"So, you a prostitute, fucking for money now?"

"Nah, not yet, because I haven't fucked nobody. But I'll be soon, and I will let you know when a boss nigga take my V card from me?"

"Fuck you, you fucking whore bag."

"You wish, and call me out my name one more time and I will have my daddy at yo' pussy." I said, now irritated. The nigga was calling me a hoe, but actually he was burnt that he didn't get the pussy.

"So what, girl. I don't give a fuck about that nigga."

"You don't have to, but call me out my name again BITCH and you will feel us, word to my daddy and you know that's from the heart." I spoke calmly and very clearly.

"Alright. Fuck you." He said, hanging up his phone.

These folks sure do have a lot of hate in their blood. Got you hatin' cause I'm the baddest in the city. Broke bitches need to get their money up and these broke-ass niggas need to get their money up and hustle a lil harder or something, damn. 'Cause they be straight hatin' on a G.

It was a quarter to two when I pulled up at my granny's dressed fly, rocking my turquoise Coogi authentic sweater dress with some Giuseppe Zanotti turquoise and silver patchwork peep toe pumps. My hair laid in a flat wrap parted down the middle, I was accessorized in silver Tiffany jewelry. I must say I was looking too cute for this nigga. Glancing in the mirror to make sure I was intact, I then climbed out of my vehicle.

"Damn, babe. You looking good." Cheno said, greeting me

"You like it?" I asked, blushing.

"Yeah, I like the dress, but I'm loving you period."

"Really?" I beamed even harder.

"Yeah, so you know where you wanna go now?" He asked.

"No you can decide that 'cause it really doesn't matter." I told him.

"Alright, we can go shopping, then go get something to eat, and later we can go to the Mansion."

"Okay, that's fine. But I'm about to go holla at Granny for a few minutes."

As I was walking inside the house Cheno called out my name, I looked back and he blew me a kiss. I was geeked up because there was a lot of people outside. As I turned the corner to enter my granny's living room, I saw she was excited to see me. Her eyes glowed, and she immediately started discussing the fight. My granny was so damn hood.

"Them bitches better be glad I didn't come because it would have been trouble. But everybody told me that you handle yo' self real well." She nodded and smiled proudly. "Word is you and Tee was beastin' and even lil Daijah was getting down and dirty." She puckered her lips up. "But your hatin'-ass cousin Tamera said that she heard y'all lost, but I knew that was just a little of that hate in that child blood." She said, filing her nails down.

"Yeah, Granny, we was all surprised at Daijah because she was dogging a grown lady. I mean whooping her and all of her punches were connecting. They say the girl Daijah took down can fight real good. But she didn't have nothing on Daijah." I paused briefly. "And forget what your granddaughter talking about, she need to worry about other things and keep me off her mind."

"I will never understand why you and your own family can't get along."

"That's her, Granny. She's a hater. I can't help that her mother's a dopefiend and can't provide for her like my parents provide for me. It's not my fault that her momma don't know who her father is and mines do. There's nothing I can do about that, and if she wasn't so much of a hater, we'd prolly be cool. But that'd never be the case, 'cause that's all she know how to do, is hate."

"I guess I'll never know why y'all children don't like each other, for god sake y'all are first cousins." I rolled my eyes. She continued. "I'm glad that you and Chen back cool because I was gon' fuck Cheno up. But he ended up chocking up that girl that night they jumped on Tee anyway."

"I know he told me and we 'bout to go to the mall and spend the day together so I will holla at you later, Granny." I kissed her cheek and strutted out the door.

Smack dead in my face was my hatin'-ass cousin, Tamera. "Bitch, you need to watch where the fuck you goin'." She barked as she purposely bumped me while I stepped off the porch.

"Ay, my nigga, you be straight clowning, I think you need to watch where the fuck you goin', since you the one pleading to be seen. 'Cause I don't pay your hatin' ass no damn attention. Is that what you mad for, though? Gotta be, 'cause I simply just don't understand all the fuckin' hatin' you be doing, my nigga."

"Hate on you for what?" she jerked her neck back. "You ain't nobody for me to be hatin' on. Please! Wouldn't give you the satisfaction."

"Evidently it's something, 'cause you be beggin' for me to beat the fuck up outta ya." I put my hands on my waist, letting my own family know she could get it too. "Jealous-ass bum bitches, man."

"What the hell is goin' on out here?" Granny asked, pushing the screen door open.

We both turned in her direction and then our eyes landed back on each other.

"I'm good, it's your envious grandchild that must got somethin' heavy on her chest." I said, my voice filled with disdain.

"Both of y'all need to quit the bickering, y'all family," my granny came at us with the same line.

"Granny, like I said, I'm good, that's her. But, I'ma need to be goin' now. You know I gotta give 'em a reason to keep hatin' on da G." I laughed, tossing my hair that nearly brushed against Tamera's face as a turned around and walked towards my car with a swagger that I knew was killing her inside.

Cheno popped in the car with me and we headed towards the Bal Harbour Mall. Simply put, it was time for him to spend some serious cash on me.

As soon as we reached the mall entrance, my phone began ringing and the nigga gonna have the audacity to pick it up and looked at the screen and inquired, "Who the fuck is Maine?" He looked seriously, waiting on my response.

"A friend." I replied, quite frankly.

"Really, a friend, Jayah?"

"Yep, a friend nigga." I rolled my eyes. "Don't you have friends?" I asked annoyed, pulling up into a parking space.

"Yeah, but they all already know about you."

"Okay, what that suppose to mean?" I cut my eyes.

"Exactly what it sounds like, they all know you my bitch."

"Do they?" I asked, shocked. "How in the hell is they gon' know that? I don't even know that."

"Oh, so you wanna act funny, like I ain't yo' nigga now?" He asked, solemnly.

"What? Boy, you clowning for real. We already established that we fuck with each other and we also can talk to other people we just gon' respect each other."

"That's before I start catching feelings for you." Cheno admitted just like any other nigga. He wanted to do him, but wanted me all to himself.

"Boy, how you catching feelings for me and you got bitches? Please Cheno, run that game on a chick that don't know any better, okay?" I told him.

"Those chicks don't matter, you me now. So I'm gon' give you a few weeks to cut all these niggas off, a'ight?" He demanded.

I smacked me lips, and folded my arms firmly. "Ain't no sense in us getting out this car then. I can take you right back where you was because I'm gonna talk to whoever I want to, and when I want to boy! So what you gon' do?" I turned and focused my attention towards him.

"Damn, you can't do that for me?" Cheno whined, jealously.

"Sure can't, Chen. You got bitches and you sure ain't about to get me involved with the grimy shit you be on." I rolled my eyes. "I'm not about to fall for the games that you play on these lame-ass bitches, a'ight? So we can fuck around or we can just throw the deuces up when we see each other, it won't make me a difference."

"A'ight, that's cool, we cool. Let's go in this mall, babe. I ain't gon' beg you." He shot, arrogantly.

"Good, now give me my phone." I snatched it from his hand, and headed towards the open-air shopping mall stores

Chapter Four

Wifey material!

"Baby lets go in this jewelry store and cop you the matching diamond necklace and earring set to match your diamond tennis bracelet that I got you the other day."

"A'ight." I said, walking beside him into Cartier.

The jeweler politely greeted us. "May I help you with something?"

"Yeah, I came in here the other day and I bought this bracelet. Now I wanna buy the other two pieces to match." He requested, showing her my wrist.

"Okay, but you know that it has the matching ring also." She retrieved the set from its glass case.

"Aw, that's fine ma'am. Throw that in with it." Cheno told her.

"Will that be all sir?" Chen turned towards me to make sure. "Will that be all?"

Me, being the boss that I am, hell nah! I want all this shit.

"Can I get this canary yellow diamond watch?" I asked in a kiddy tone.

"Yeah babe, you can have the whole canary yellow diamond set if you want it."

The lady standing beside us couldn't help but smile. "Aww, that's so nice. How long have y'all been together?"

"We're just friends, that's it." I did not want to give him no reasons to think we were together.

Her faced wrinkled. "Wow, y'all must be really good friends to be getting all of this." The Caucasian woman said with another friendly smile.

"Yeah, we are." I smiled back.

After the jeweler rung the items up, she gave us the total. "That will be $76,000."

"That's cool." Cheno stated, excusing himself from the store to count the money.

He returned and handed the lady an envelope full of money.

I'm not gonna lie, I was utterly enthused. He was certainly tryna show me that he wanted me for real. *Shit, keep that money flowing and we might make something work.*

"So do you wanna shop for anything else or you just wanna go straight to the dealership?"

"Huh?" I asked, perplexed. "What you mean?"

He laughed. "I said you wanna go get a new car."

"From where?"

"Where every your lil heart desire, ma." He pulled me close to his chest.

"Can we go to the Benz lot?" I asked, excitedly.

"Sure. That's what you want, a new Benz?"

"Yeah, I do, I really do," I replied, full of energy.

"Okay that's what's up, that's where we heading after I grab us something to wear tonight to Mansion."

"Alright," I said ecstatic, knowing that in less than an hour I would be pushing a Benz. *Them bitches didn't do shit but get me some new shit, they helped me upgrade. I needed to upgrade anyway. I should call them hoes and tell 'em thanks for the new vehicle.*

Pulling up to the Mercedes-Benz dealership was such an rush. I was really starting to think he was serious. Dude was trying so hard to reel me in his world.

"Hello, how are you guys doing? Is there something particular that I can help you find?" The car sales rep asked.

"Not really. We're just searching for the new cars that have just reached stock. We want two cars though." He paused as he went into deep thought, and continued rubbing his chin. "Different colors. Maybe… a white one and a black one."

I looked at him and smiled. "Not a matching Benz, you are so crazy." I playfully prodded him in the arm.

The lady was talking to us when I noticed a pearl white CL550. It was beautiful and I knew that I had to have it. "Excuse me miss, but how much is that?" I pointed to the one that was showcased in the middle of the showroom floor.

She laughed as if I was joking. "Oh sweetie, that will be $100,000 plus." She paused for a second.

"She will take it, and I will also take this black one right here." Cheno said, irritated at the woman's assumption that $100,000 was too high for us.

The car sales associate looked startled, but she quickly regained her composure. "Let's go over the paperwork and see if you will be approved to get this car."

"Oh, this is being paid with cash." Cheno told the saleswoman.

She flashed a huge smile. "Well then, let's get down to business." She changed up her act real quick at the sound of that much cake.

"That's all I'm saying." Cheno said, seemingly mad because the woman tried to play him. "Let's get to it." Cheno used a real rude tone because of how the woman treated him before she knew how much dollars he was gonna leave in her pocket.

Damn. Do he do this for everyone, or is this something new? I really don't give a fuck, because I'm not tryna be with him or nothing like that.

I called Donteice and asked her to get dropped off so she could drive my car back to my place. Everything was all happening too fast. He had me pushing a new whip, laced me with the best without hesitation, and only in one day. Shit, that's what I wanted, so that's what I got. Hell, I thought the lil shit Maine had gotten me was something, but Cheno was really tryna' compete with Jay Carter for real.

♛ ♛ ♛ ♛ ♛ ♛ ♛ ♛ ♛ ♛ ♛ ♛ ♛ ♛ ♛ ♛ ♛

Back in my exquisite condo after shopping, I pulled up as Cheno parked his new ride alongside mine. I popped the trunk, grabbed all the bags that I'd accumulated and headed for my door. Once I entered, I turned off the alarm. Then, I sat the Gucci, Coogi and Chanel bags on the sofa. Cheno followed behind me, placing his Coogi bag next to mine. This nigga do have the nerve to convince me to get the matching Coogi outfits, and my dumb ass just went right along with it. I didn't know that the nigga wanted me to wear it to the Mansion that night. Ain't that something? It was obvious that he was tryna stamp and label me as his bitch.

"Baby, where your towels and rags at?"

"Upstairs in the closet. Where else would they be, silly." I said with sarcasm.

"You crazy. We gon' have to work on the smart remarks."

"Riiight..."

After I checked my machine, I took my clothes to my room and placed the items inside the closet. Suddenly, Cheno came from out of nowhere, tryna touch on my pussy, grabbing on my breast, and started tryna kiss all on my neck.

"What in the hell are you doing?" I jumped back.

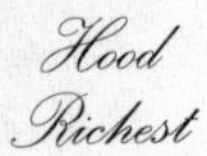

"You know exactly what I'm doing. I want you to feel me." He had a naughty look on his face.

"Really, well it won't be today," I said, growing frustrated.

"C'mon, baby, you know you want it. And I'ma give it to you like you never had it before."

"Is you really?" I smacked my lips.

"Yeah. You ain't gon' want to fuck nobody again after this, ma."

"Well, I never had sex before, so what you mean?" I shifted my eyes and spoke truthfully.

"Yeah, right," he said, letting me go and looking me in my eyes to see if he could read me.

"I haven't," I whispered.

He paused for a few minutes and finally spoke. "Okay, baby. Well, let me just kiss my pussy, therefore I can know that it's mine?" He smiled, licking his sexy lips.

"You crazy, Chen, for real. Why do you want to do that to me?" I asked, seductively.

"'Cause I just want you to know what it is." He leaned in kissing my lips and led me towards my bed. He started pulling off my pants and kissing me all over my body.

This rare feeling just came over me. I was horny as fuck. Although I really wasn't trying to fuck him, but when those hormones start jumping, a person will do any- and everything.

"So, put it in?" I whispered to him.

He got excited and hurried up and took his pants off in a split second. The nigga wasn't gon' play.

"Where is the condom?" I asked.

"I don't have one, but I'm gonna pull out."

"Nigga, I hope you don't got nothing."

"Come on now, I'm cleaner than Mr. Clean." He laughed.

"But you were fucking Tyiesha, my nigga, and that bitch nasty, that's a nasty bitch."

"Yeah, I did, but I strapped up securely with a condom."

"You silly, but no glove, no love."

"Come on. I just got checked like a week ago, and I'ma pull out. I promise." He begged and pleaded. For some odd reason, I trusted him and let loose.

He slowly started putting his big, black, erect dick in me. It was hurting so damn bad, and the penis wasn't even halfway in. I was trying to hold it in, but a tear fell from my face. He asked if I wanted him to stop. I said yeah, because it was too damn painful. He slid it out and started kissing me. He told me that he loved me while kissing all over my stomach and he started playing with my pussy, circling around my clitoris. It was feeling so damn good. I had never experienced a feeling like that, not ever.

"Baby, yo' pussy so damn wet, like the Atlantic Ocean."

This nigga was crazy. Next thing I knew he eating the fuck out of my pussy. All I know was my legs started feeling funny. I felt relaxed and it felt like I had to release something. And before I knew it, I was experiencing my very first orgasm. I moaned as I called out his name for the umpteenth time. He kissed me on the forehead without one word being said, and we just lay in the bed, both speechless. Before I knew it, I was in a blissful, tranquil slumber.

Truth be told, I thought it was all a dream, until I woke up to his smooth face next to mine. It was 10 at night, and I was in need of getting dress 'cause I had to hit up Mansion by midnight. It was a chance that we wouldn't have been getting in, 'cause the club be over capacity the majority of the time

Parking our Benzes in VIP, we popped out and walked inside, dressed exactly alike. We both donned yellow Coogi collar shirts accented with Coogi lettering, a pair of light Coogi jeans that had Coogi written on the pocket area. To complete the look, we rocked the brand new yellow and white Air Max 95s. Canary yellow diamond jewels glimmered from our hands, wrists, ears and necks.

We were shittin' on bitches. Hoes were coming from everywhere looking at us. But I didn't give a fuck, long as the hoes stayed glued to the sideline cheerleading, I was cool. Just don't interfere in the game by stepping out on the court.

Once inside the club, I adjusted my eyes around the dimly lit room and surveyed the crowd for Tee. I rushed over to her and immediately told her what happened at the house.

"What? Bitch, you playing?"

"Nah, I ain't ,and Tee, it was feeling good."

"You ain't got to tell me. I told you that's the best feeling ever." She laughed, rotating her hips to the beat.

"But who you in here with?" She questioned.

"Cheno, girl," I said, excitedly.

"Oh really? So y'all together?"

"Yeah. We came here together, but we not a couple. Tee, you know I ain't gon' do nothing like that." I tilted my head to the side, shaking it.

"You so crazy. But I guess we both came with some boss ass niggas 'cause I'm here with J.P."

"Really."

"Yeah. I told him that you and Chen got matching Benzes and he rushed to the Jaguar dealership and got us matching Jags."

"Aww, that was nice." I was happy J.P. was treating Tee like she deserved.

We bopping on these bitches, these hoes wish they were us.

"Hey, sweet thing, you are so beautiful," this fine-ass Cuban commented in his thick accent.

"Well thanks. You not bad yourself." I flashed my perfect pearly whites.

"I saw you when you walked in with your boyfriend."

"That's just a friend."

"Oh, so that means I can have you number, sweetie."

"Sure, why not." I told him, giving him my number without thought.

I skimmed the crowd, making sure Chen wasn't in sight. He wasn't nowhere in my view, and I didn't know where he'd disappeared off to. But that was good, because I'd gotten five additional niggas' numbers following the young Cuban guy.

I smiled at my flesh that was reflecting from the mirror in front of me. I was dancing, watching myself belly dance in the mirror. Minutes later, Tee came up. "Girl, did you see Chen all in that girl's face?"

"Nah, I didn't, and truthfully I don't care." I continued rocking my hips and mid-section to the hip-hop tunes.

"I think it's the girl, Teika."

"Okay, that's his baby momma. He can talk to her if he wants."

"Nah, it was more like, why the fuck you in here and leave, for he show his true color in this mu'fucka."

"Tee, what you want me to do about it? That ain't my man." I showed my irritation.

"You right, but it's about respect."

Listening to this bitch as always, I walked over there, asking sternly. "Like, what is this?" I glared into Cheno's eyes.

"Oh, baby this ain't nothing. I'm just tryna find out where this hoe got my daughter at, why she in the club, that's it."

"HOE." She bellowed. "I got yo' hoe." The girl yelled as she threw her drink on him.

He instantly grabbed her by her neck and got to choking the living daylights out his baby mother. I felt really bad for her. I even tried to interfere and break them apart, but I stopped because I wasn't trying to have him turn against me out of anger.

Abruptly, a huge guy weighing well over 300 pounds came through the crowd and hit Cheno upside the head with a Moët bottle. Cheno started stumbling all over the place and J.P. came from Lord knows where and pulled out his gun and start busing heat, instantly.

I snatched Tee up in a swift moment and we scampered to the door. I turned around to see where Chen was and the nigga was lying on the ground, bleeding to death.

I noticed that J.P. had pulled him over his shoulder and ran out the club with him. He put him in the backseat and skidded off hastily. Rushing to the hospital, I knew that all he could do was pray that he hadn't killed his nigga.

I was sitting in the parking lot looking at the coroners bringing out a dead body. It belonged to the dude that'd hit Cheno with the bottle. I didn't understand what had happened or why it had happened. It just all seemed to have occurred too fast for my eyes to have caught and actually register the reasons. I was just hoping and wishing that Cheno was alive and stable.

"Donteice, why? Why tonight? Man, why did I have to go over there? It's all my fault. I can't believe this shit has happened. Over some bullshit! It wasn't worth it. I hope Cheno okay, I really do." My sobs came faster and soon I was crying hysterically.

"No it's not, and he gon' be okay. Let's just go to the hospital and make sure he cool. I know he gon' be fine, Jayah." She assured me the entire trip to the hospital.

Chapter Five

He got me open!

Seeing Cheno wide awake in the hospital bed made me feel so much better I rushed over to his bedside. The anxiety disappeared once I learned that he'd gotten shot in the shoulder and was gonna recover quickly. And once they ran a few more tests on him, he would be able to go home no later than the morning.

"Baby, hey, how you feel?" I inquired, pleasantly.

"I'm good as long as you alright. I'm fine, baby."

"That's so sweet, but I didn't know what I was gon' do if something was to happen to you."

"Oh, so where did the I don't give two fucks Jayah go?" Cheno said, half smiling.

"I'm still here. I'm gon' be me at all times," I said, cracking a smile. I had to admit my true feelings to him though. "But honestly Chen, I am really catching feelings for you. You did almost take my virginity, and you was the first person that ever touched this pussy, so don't you think I would have been devastated if something bad had happened to your black ass?"

"Yeah I know, but I was just hoping that you was straight,

because you were right there the whole time."

"I know." I spoke sadly, head down.

"But, the bad thing about this is that J.P., dumb-ass, shot me. The nigga was too trigger happy and was tryna shoot something."

"He is so dumb," I swayed my head. "But you better know that he killed that nigga that hit you with the Moët bottle. They were bringing the nigga out in a black body bag."

"Word!?"

"Yep, that was crazy. I just wanna look past that night."

"Me too, baby. But that dude had to be somebody that my baby momma messes with. Because he was salty about me choking the bitch up and shit."

"That's all I was thinking, you think she gon' tell?" I asked concerned.

"No way, we got a good strong bond and no matter what, she ain't gon' do nothing like that."

"That's good." I said, growing restless.

That was one crazy-ass night over nothing, though. If the nigga just would have minded his own business, he would've still been here. But that was one thing that I couldn't worry about. Hell, shit happens.

Waking up at the hospital was something that I dreaded, but I had to stay there because Chen would've had a serious attitude. So, I just decided to stay until morning.

♛ ♛ ♛ ♛ ♛ ♛ ♛ ♛ ♛ ♛ ♛ ♛ ♛ ♛ ♛ ♛ ♛

As soon as I got home from the hospital, I indulged myself with a relaxing bath. I was relieved that Chen was okay, and really mad that the situation happened because it showed how much I really liked dude.

Soon as I'd exited the bathroom, my phone was ringing.

"Hello?"

"Damn, you getting shot at now?"

"What, who the fuck is this?" *Damn! Who is calling me about my business?*

"Fat Attack."

"Boy, get lost. Why you calling my phone?" I started in on this fat mothafucka. "You ain't got no money for me, so it ain't no need for you to even keep calling me. So, I'll holla at you." I yelled through the phone. I was mad as hell because the lame-ass didn't even know what he was even talking about.

The second I hung up my phone had rang right back.

"Hello?" I screamed into the phone.

"What's up babe?"

"Who dis?" I asked, impolitely.

"This Maine, shorty, who you expecting to call?"

"You crazy." I laughed, playing it off.

"What's up with you though, shorty?"

"Shit, just got in."

"Damn, you must have had a good time last night." I could tell he was jealous.

"It was cool." I said, nonchalantly. I wanted to see how bad he was trippin'.

Maine let it go and just started talking about the trip to Italy almost instantly. I still hadn't even talked to my daddy about the vacation, but I was going to soon. The right time makes all the difference because daddy be on some other shit when it comes down to serious shit like giving me my passport and leaving out of the country. That's a no in Jay Carter's world, most definitely. While we was talking, my phone beeped, indicating that someone was on the other line

I interrupted him. "Hold on, babe." I clicked right over. "Hello?"

"Is this Jayah?" The caller had spoken with an accent.

"Who this?"

"Rico." He replied.

Oh, alrrighhttt, I thought to myself. I'm jumping. This Cuban gotta cake me off some bans.

"Oh hey, how you doing?"

"I'm fine, but I would be better if I had you around, so when can we hang?"

"I don't know because I gotta do a lot today so maybe tomorrow when I get out of school."

"Do you want me to just pick you up from school?"

"Nah, I got my own ride." I replied, proudly.

"What are you driving, sweetie?"

"A Charger and a Benz CL550." I spoke, knowing I had every right to be cocky about my rides.

"So, would your boyfriend like me talking to you?" He seemed to have Cheno on his mind more than me, damn.

"I told you, I don't have a boyfriend."

"Really. I can't believe that, because you were all on that one guy last night that had on the yellow, as you had on, too."

"That don't mean he my man, we just cool. What does it matter to you for anyway?"

"It don't."

"Okay then."

"You feisty." He laughed. "All I want to do is to be around you. We don't have to do anything or nothing and I will pay you whatever just to spend a day with you. Have a lil fun, you know, 'cause you are so gorgeous."

Bingo! My sheet is covered That's all it better be, a lil fun, and I'ma kick it with him. I'ma need some stacks. He better know it's game time and I'm in the game the long way. So it's a must that I win.

"That's fine just holla at me tomorrow and we can kick it. Talk to you then." I hung up.

This is a crazy dude, because he sure don't know what he getting his self involved in, but that's another story. I laughed.

I most definitely had to call the Maine nigga back. Dude was wondering if I could come and visit him the following weekend just to kick it. How could I refuse?

Chapter Six

Daddy and daughter day!

Sauntering into my daddy's store, my eyes instantaneously grew wide. I'd seen some superb clothing gear in my days, but the merchandise that he had that day in particular was so major and grand. *This nigga must have got a new shipment yesterday or something*, I mouthed in admiration.

"What's up, Dad?" I said after walking through the dual doors.

"Hey, sweetie, who got you the fly ride that you pulled up in?" He asked, placing his new merchandise on the racks.

"Oh, just the Cheno nigga." I said, blushing.

"Word."

"Yeah I think I deserved it, all the fighting we did Friday night." I said, laughing.

"You right." He didn't hesitate and got straight to what the streets was chatting about "But tell me, what happened last night?" He wanted to know.

As I was telling my daddy the story, some hood rat bitch stormed into my daddy clothing shop that's located on 88th St.

The chick walked right up to my daddy and demanded money, I stood confused and had to tune in. "Let me get five hunnet." We both looked at this bitch as if she was crazy. She had the audacity to say. "Yeah I'm gon' need that because I have your 5-week-old child at home." At that point I was tripping. I just knew my daddy didn't stoop down that low and fucked that rat bitch. I'ma keep it real, she wasn't ugly, she was just a true hood bitch and a lil rough around the edges.

"Girl, bye. I fucked you like a year ago, so it ain't even possible." He waved her off.

"Don't play dumb, Jay." She stood with her hands on her hip. "Nigga, it was like eleven months ago, and now our daughter is a month, so what's up?" She said, motioning her hands in the air.

"Nah, don't come in here with that shit now. You should have been told my daddy if that's the case." I interjected, angrily.

"Lil-ass girl, stay in a child's place," she voiced snottily, flaring up her nose.

"Lil girl," I giggled, mad-like. "Really, but I got big girl money though." I said real fly to the bum-ass bitch.

"So, and what is that suppose to mean, you're a whore?"She had her hands on her hips thinking she was all that.

"Man," I shook my head, disgusted. "Bitches always hatin', you wish I was a hoe, I can't help that I got niggas on my team. But believe, if I was a hoe, I would be a paid hoe." I glared and continued on. "Bitch, you up here beggin' my daddy for $500. Get real, bitch. I blow that shit daily. What the fuck!" I popped.

"Man, Tasha. Get your bum-ass out of my store and go find your baby daddy."

"Nigga, you know this yo' baby. Why else would you give me money for an abortion? Get to that." She clutched her jaws together, fumingly.

"Because you already had four, hoe." I knew my daddy and I knew he was frustrated with her presence. "I was tryna help you out, but I surmise yo' bum-ass spent the money, so you shit out of luck." My daddy was a good nigga at heart, with certain people. But that chick better be lucky my flesh was present because he would have probably floored her ass.

"Nah, weak-ass, deadbeat mothafucka. I'm just gon' get a DNA test." She said in a teasing tone. "Yeah, you gon' be doing something anyways. So, if you wanna get the white mothafucka's involved, that's cool too. We can do that, we sure can," she nodded.

I couldn't do nothing but spit on this bitch because she had me fucked up. That was one disrespectful chick. Who she thought I was, some kind of weak-ass bitch or something? She could've never thought I was just gonna sit there and allow her to kick shit to my dad like that. The bitch had lost her mind. After the spit landed on her face, my daddy pushed me to the back and my dad's main man Big Tommy put her outta the store.

"Daddy, who is that girl?" I asked, really concerned.

"Man, punkin' that's some hoe name Tasha that I fucked last year, and I only fucked her a few times and that was it."

"Really, so did you fuck her raw?"

"Hell no, but one time, the condom did break."

"So, that mean the baby could be yours?"

"She fucks so many niggas though. I really don't know."

"So, you gon' get a blood test?"

"Do you want me to?"

"Yeah, I do because I don't wanna have to fuck that bitch up," I said, smiling. He knew I really would fuck that hoe up, too. Especially 'cause she was disrespecting, and I've never allowed a chick to play my pops performing in that state of affair.

"Jayah, you are so crazy, spitting on that girl like that."

"She was just steppin' too out of line, for real, Daddy."

"You wild, man." He just laughed.

"So Daddy, what we doing today?"

"What you wanna do?"

He always let me pick when we did shit together like this. "I just wanna chill on the yacht and talk to you about everything."

"First we gotta eat, a nigga hungry." He said, rubbing his belly.

♛ ♛ ♛ ♛ ♛ ♛ ♛ ♛ ♛ ♛ ♛ ♛ ♛ ♛ ♛ ♛ ♛

As usual, our dinner was extraordinary. We ate by the beach at a Caribbean restaurant and had a casual conversation while enjoying our meal on the deck. Once finished, we headed to my daddy's yacht on the coast. I had to tell him about Saturday night when I almost lost my virginity. I used to tell my old man everything, so I felt I had to let him in. I had a dire feeling in my stomach, it was crazy butterflies. I don't know if it was because I was scared or nervous, 'cause he'd told me not to have sexual involvements until I really found somebody that I'd made a serious commitment with.

It wasn't as bad as I thought it was gonna be. All he told me was to protect myself, because niggas are extremely nasty. Don't be fucking all type of niggas. And not to get pregnant because I have a whole successful life ahead of me and I have plenty of time to have a baby.

I was cool with that. I thought he was gonna trip a little bit and had almost forgot to ask him about the trip to Italy, but you know I didn't though. I'd just up and got the courage to ask.

"Daddy, it's this dude that I met, his name Maine. He from the A and he wants to take me to Italy, so can I go?"

"What you think I'm gon' say princess?" He gave me a dumbfounded look.

"I don't know, that's why I'm asking you, 'cause you know I'm gonna respect your mind. So, whatever you say, that's the answer. But I told him I had to ask you, and he was saying that's fine, he can go also."

"Word?"

"Yeah, and he said he gonna take care of all the expenses." I informed him with a smile across my face.

"Oh yeah, we going on that free trip, babe." He cracked up laughing. "Black folk don't turn down a free trip."

I jumped on my daddy and told him thanks. In, like a month, I was sure I'd be chillin' in Italy. I couldn't wait until I told Tee that daddy gave his permission. I knew she would be delighted. At the time, I hadn't even told Maine that she'd be tagging along, but oh well, he'd eventually find out.

"Thanks, Dad," I repeated.

"You good, I guess me and Amelia will be going, 'cause that can be the time I tell her about the girl Tasha and her child that supposed to be mine."

"Right, I guess. So, it's gon' be a fun experience. And Daddy, I'm going to the A this weekend just to kick it with him and get to know him a lil better."

"Okay, Tee going with you?" He probed.

"And you know it."

"A'ight."

I glanced at the clock, it was almost 11 and I certainly needed to be in bed because I had school the following day. When the yacht docked, I checked my phone and Cheno had texted me. He was saying all kinda shit like he wanted to spend the night, he wanted me to take care of him and all type of shit. But I wasn't on that. I was sleepy as shit. I did decide to call and see what was up. Dialing his number, the voicemail came straight on, on the first ring though.

We all know what that means! He's with a bitch, but hey, what it mean to me? Nothing! He just didn't need to be texting me, and blowing my phone up all the damn time. Because what was understood didn't need to be explained. It really didn't. Or did it?

♛ ♛ ♛ ♛ ♛ ♛ ♛ ♛ ♛ ♛ ♛ ♛ ♛ ♛ ♛ ♛ ♛

Navigating through the school parking lot in my brand new Benz had heads spinning. I saw so many people observing, marveling in amazement of who I might be. Especially when I turned to park and the people in front of the school saw my license plates. That read: CHENO outlined in diamond cuts. You know bitches really didn't like me after they seen that whip. If I was them, I probably would've hated me too.

Climbing out of my fresh-ass, cool whip, I spotted the Veronica bitch and a few of her bitches. Including my hater cousin Tamera. It was sad to say, but a lot people didn't even know we were blood cousins because all she did was hate on me all the fucking time. My daddy had told me to get over it. Family or not, fuck her. And to never trust that bitch.

"Ugh, that hoe thinks she's all that 'cause she got a Benz. Ain't no tellin' how many dicks she sucked to get that muthafucka." Tamera said as I was approaching the front of the school building. "Stupid bitch got Cheno on her license plate looking like a complete fool. He fucking everythang and she claiming this nigga."

"I know right. Yo' cousin's a gotdamn fool," one of her friends added.

"She just stupid like that." Tamera continued to hate. "One day, that bitch gon' get hers."

I didn't give a fuck about them haters, because I stayed stepping out on the exclusive side, which was why they hated on me so much. That day in particular, I was rocking a pair of True Religion jeans with fuchsia rhinestones outlining the front pockets, a fitted fuchsia Armani Collezioni button-down blouse and suede fuchsia Prada moccasins with the matching knapsack that came from

Xclusive Swagg (my daddy's store). I'd gotten five outfits that no other store had that season. So, I could definitely understand why they continued to hate, 'cause I was that bitch. But, nothing they said even mattered to me while on school grounds. *I'm polished and boss bitches doesn't fight at school get to that*, I said to myself not paying the labeled down haters any form of attention as a strutted straight pass them in my cocky, don diva stride.

"Jayaaaaah!" I heard someone call out, knocking me out of my thoughts. All I could think about was who was calling my damn name like I was wanted by the law some shit. Turning around, it was Donteice. I should have known it was her loudmouth self.

"Sup, babe?" Tee greeted.

"Shit, and you?"

"Nothing, girl, about to go into this lunch area and grab some super donuts."

"You so silly. Did you see them hatin' bitches over there?" I asked.

"Yeah, but they know what's best for 'em, so they ain't gonna do a mothafuckin' thang."

"We already know them bitches all bark and no bite. They hatin' too hard too. Talkin' shit 'cause they know I don't bring the beef to the place where I get my education. Bitches steady worried 'bout how I do this shit, need to worry 'bout passing that FCAT test. Dumb-ass bitches."

"Right. They know you won't say too much of nothing at school because you don't wanna get kicked off none of the school academic committees, and most certainly not the student council. I don't understand why they always hatin' on the next bitch."

"Right, where they do that at? That's that corny, lame shit."

We walked to the outside lunch area and I saw the Dajuan nigga. Of course, he was hatin'. I could see it in his eyes. He despised me. I knew it too. But I didn't give a fuck because he lame anyway. I couldn't do nothing but think about Rico, he was majorly on my mind because I knew he had bank.

By the time my last class came, there were about 30 hoes that had come up to me inquiring about me and Cheno's status. Broads were informing me who he was messing with, what Veronica was bumping her dick sucker's about. And now her and Tyiesha both were supposedly pregnant by him and they'd become the best of friends. Just some wack hearsay, something that didn't excite a diva like me.

I had to bounce because I wasn't on that bullshit at all. I decided to call up Rico 'cause I wanted to kick it with him. The phone had rung like 10 times and I got no answer. *Okay, the Cuban nigga got his spinner shoes on.*

It was around 2 in the afternoon when he returned my phone call. He said he was busy and sort of still busy, but I could pick up some money just for having me waiting.

You know that was cool with me, I didn't have a problem with that at all. I went over there and he gave me a few bans, and that was tight because I was only there for approximately three minutes flat.

When I pulled off, I immediately called my beautician Fiona up. I knew she stayed booked up because all she had was permanent clients that'd schedule for the same time each week. I needed to get in on that Friday, not the usual Thursdays that I went because my hair had to have a fresh body wrap. This Cuban lady wasn't gonna play with the hair. She was the hottest stylist in Miami for the individuals that rocked natural hair. She'd have your hair looking so silky, like you was Cuban yourself. Ole girl was a beast. Of course, I got in because she knows I tip her very well.

A couple days had passed, and Friday came quickly. The shop was packed as usual. It was this light-skinned girl name Candace in there. She had been coming to the shop for a few weeks now, and each time her dude came up there to bring her food and shit. And me being the bitch that I am was straight up looking at him. He was a sexy, dark skinned brotha. Usually, if I saw a dark nigga, I would turn the other way, but there was something about this cat, it really was.

As bitches do, she was up there gossiping to the beauticians about all of her business, like a fucking plum fool. Speaking on certain things that gave bitches like me the urge to wanna fuck with dude. Far as saying, he was a good nigga and all the bitches wanted him, but he would never holla back at them because she was all he wanted. In addition to that, the nigga was given her back massages and caking her off something terrible.

A'ight. I knew I was gonna try to get that nigga and I certainly made a mental note to do just that. I made it my business to get him.

Why wouldn't I? To me, I was in my prime, so it was definitely snatching bitches' niggas up season. I knew how to move a bitch all the way out the way, and that was what I intended to do.

All that week, Cheno wasn't answering his phone and I knew he was alright because Tee had mentioned that he was with J.P. So, that meant that I would have to really play him now, because even if I did dig a nigga, I still would never sweat over him. It was about to be on and poppin'.

♛ ♛ ♛ ♛ ♛ ♛ ♛ ♛ ♛ ♛ ♛ ♛ ♛ ♛ ♛ ♛ ♛

Arriving in Atlanta was truly an excitement; it felt good to be in a new city for a change. Maine had informed me to meet him at the Lenox-Sqaure Mall. So I'd already knew what time it was. As I was exiting the escalator, I turned to the right and saw Maine with some dude, which was good because he could get with Donteice. While I crept up behind him, he sensed someone and turned around.

"What's up, girl? Don't be tryna creep up on a nigga like that." But Maine's smile let me know he wasn't really mad.

"Shut up, I was just about to call you. I didn't think you was here yet." I really did think me and Tee were gonna be waiting. It was a pleasant surprise not to.

"Come on now, you know I'm gon' be on time to see you ma."

"A'ight, whatever." I playfully rolled my eyes.

We were conversing for a minute, and his nigga just interrupted us. "Umm." He cleared his throat. "Damn, y'all some rude mothafuckas." Main's dude jokingly said, showcasing his mouth full of platinum teeth

"What's good? I'm Jamar, but just Mar to you fine-ass ladies." He extended his hand.

"Hey, I'm Donteice."

"Don who?" Jamar obviously never heard such a name.

"Donteice, nigga, but you can call me Tee for short."

"Yeah that's what I will call you, Tee." Everyone just started cracking up.

"So what's on the agenda for today?" I asked.

"I'm gonna let y'all grab what y'all want out of here, then we can head in the direction of getting something to eat and I guess chill back at my crib." Maine spoke with a grin spread across his face.

"That's cool." We replied, simultaneously.

Shopping was something me and Tee both enjoyed, so you know we got so many outfits and handbags. One bag in particular that we both had gotten was $7,000. It was an alligator Fendi bag and we both dug how generous these set of guys were. Long as they kept the cake coming, things were a'ight.

Parking in Maine's driveway, me and Tee was so sick. We'd seen some big houses. As a matter of fact, my mother lived in a $900,000 home and my daddy lived in a $4.8 million mansion. The house we pulled up to was a whole nother ball game though. It was so humongous. It had to be worth like at least $10 million. The house was better than a lot of famous people's houses that I'd seen on MTV cribs.

"Damn! You see this house Jayah?" Tee asked in her excitement.

"How could I miss it, bitch?" I countered.

"He got mad money for real."

"I knew he had it, but not like this," I muttered.

"I know, giving you money before even kicking it with you, and then taking you shopping and not wanting any. Not to mention, the shit we got today, his friend can get it fo'sho today," Donteice said serious as a heart attack.

I chuckled. "Man, you silly girl."

Donteice and I walked inside the enormous house to put our things away. The mansion was even more beautiful inside. The crib was plushed out from marble flooring, to glass cabinets, to stainless steel appliances and flat screen TVs that were built inside the walls, decorated by the most exquisite paintings known to my eyes. It was gorgeous. As soon as I was on my way down the stairs, my phone rang.

"Who the hell is this calling me private, damn?" I said aggravated because I really hate it when people don't let their number show up, that just makes my skin crawl.

"Who you want it to be?" Cheno's slippery voice came from the other end of the line.

"Ed McMan with a lot of money?"

"That's me."

I could hear the smile in his voice. "Beat it boy, it's just egg McMuffin with a lot of beef." We both chuckled.

"Nah, but what's jumpin' baby? I miss you," he tried sounding

so sincere. So fake.

"Nah, you don't. If you did, you would have called me," I smacked my lips.

"I was over my momma's house. You know can't nobody take care of you like moms can."

"Boy, tell that to somebody that a give a fuck, 'cause it sure ain't me. I can care less who you were with or what you was doing. I told you we ain't together, so you just do you and I'ma do me." I spat, hitting my the power switch to turn the phone off.

I dashed downstairs only not to find Tee there. But I did see Maine's hairy ass lying on the couch with one leg propped up on the table. My pussy instantly got wet. I eased my way to the couch he was on, wondering if I should make a move or not. I didn't though. I just sat there waiting on him to say something. He finally did after about 10 minutes.

"Do you want something to drink on shorty?"

"I'm really not a drinker, so you can just get me what you drinking."

"That's cool, do you smoke?"

"Not all the time, but occasionally."

"Do you know how to roll up?" I looked at him giving him a "duh" look.

"Of course I do. I stay rolling my dad's purp up."

"Yeah, well roll this up." He said, passing the purp and a blunt wrap. He went to pour us a glass of Grey Goose.

We had set there just chopping shit up, blowing purp and drinking. He was telling me how his mother and dad had played their connect and they had gotten killed right in front of him when he was 12 years old, and the connect was tryna kill him, too. And they thought they had shot him in the head but he was only grazed. Instead of giving them the chance to kill him, he merely lay there and played possum. I felt so sorry for dude because I knew that that event replayed in his mind very often. That was some deep and sad shit.

He informed me that he'd dreaded selling drugs, but that was the only way to have a better life. He hated the way he lived, but he had to take care of his family and that's exactly what he did. Basically, that's what he lived for and that was all that mattered to Maine.

"C'mere Jayah." He said.

I replied in a relaxed tone. "Why, what's up?"

"Just come over here." He demanded.

Maine couldn't resist me as I snuggled my body against his. He just couldn't help himself and began kissing my neck, nibbling on my earlobes and passionately tongued me down.

"Let's go upstairs." He said pulling me upstairs.

Once we entered the room, he laid me down on the bed. He took off my shoes then peeled off all my garments one by one. He started caressing my entire body. I almost climaxed from the presence of him. I was so wet and turned on, it shocked me. My hormones was surely showing out at something as simple as his touch. He traced my body down with his soft kisses.

Abruptly, he got up without saying a word, and walked out of the room. I didn't know what he was doing. I jus wished that he would hurry the hell up. I was so turned on and just wanted to feel him inside of me. I was hoping and wishing that he wasn't big like Cheno, because I desperately wanted to know what it felt like to have a dick inside that didn't hurt. The thought immediately passed when he reentered the room with nothing but a condom on. At that moment, I knew it wouldn't hurt at all. It was barely half the size of Cheno's. Even though Maine was right in front of my eyes, I thought about Chen.

Damn! How did Chen dick get that huge? I just don't understand, that nigga got a pole dick or something. It gotta be like 10 inches, and this nigga might be a good six inches, but it's cool, he can break me in because it is kinda fat.

He climbed onto the bed and started gliding his tongue across my breast as cool chills was sent up my spine. He slowly penetrated me separating my legs a part and entered at a slow and gentle pace.

"Baby, you cool? Do it hurt?"

"Yeah it does," I said truthfully because it was hurting, badly.

"Why, you ain't did it in a while?" He asked moaning and slowing stroking his dick in and out of me.

"Actually, I never did it at all," I replied with an attitude because I wanted him to stop talking to me. Damn.

"So, I'm your first?" He paused, in the motioning.

"Yeah boy," I said, irritated.

"A'ight, I'm gonna take it slow." It was written all over his face that he was overjoyed as shit, being the only nigga that ever went inside of me. Technically, Chen was, but he didn't have to know that.

Once he finally was able to get it in all the way, he continued to take slow and gentle strokes in and out of my wet juice box. He was making sure that he wasn't hurting me. The pain quickly subsided and it had begun to feel real good to me. We both were feeling really good.

"Damn, baby, who pussy is this?" He groaned.

"Yours," I said, throwing my pussy back at him.

"Do you want this dick?" Maine asked stroking me harder, speeding up a couple of notches.

"Yes I want it." I softly moaned.

"Jayah, I'ma give it to you, baby." He moaned, sliding in and out of my wetness with his eyes rolling in the back of his head. I guess I was getting the job done well, even for a rookie.

"Give it to me, oh yeah, shit Maine. Fuck me!" I cried out.

"Damn, baby, this my pussy," He said, pounding harder, reaching his climax.

Collapsing down on me, he said. "I think I love you."

I didn't know what to say, so I just ignored.

I got up to go to the bathroom and as I was wiping myself, I had a little bit of blood on the tissue. Returning back to the room, I looked on the bed to see if it was some blood on it, but there wasn't any.

"Damn, baby, I had some blood on the condom."

I stared at him. "Really, that suppose to happen when you first do it silly," I said, jokingly.

"You right."

I returned back to the bathroom and showered. After I showered, I massaged my body down with some massage cream. I sat on the edge of the bed pondering if I did something that I would regret because I didn't even know dude like that. *Maybe I should have known him a lil while longer.* Those thoughts quickly vanished. I knew what I was doing and that was that, so fuck what a hater thought about Jayah Carter.

I was wondering where Tee had disappeared off to. I picked up the phone and dialed her number to see where she was. She answered on the second ring.

"What's jumpin' baby girl?" Tee said fully charged.

"Really, you that geeked up?" I asked.

"Yeah, girl this nigga just fucked the shit out of me."

"Bitch, beat it."

"Nah, real talk dude got work and got a bad-ass neck game, you hear me family?" Tee said laughing at herself.

"Girl, anyways, where you at?" I rolled my eyes to the ceiling.

"Down the street at Mar's crib."

"Oh, alright well just call me in the morning, that's when we leaving." I told her.

"Okay, and why Cheno called my phone looking for you furious. Talking about tell that bitch I'm gonna kill her and she ain't slick."

"Who do he think he is? Looking for me like he my nigga. That clown better check with that bitch he was with all damn week." I spat. "Bye Tee, I will see you in the morning."

Chapter Seven

Back home!

Here I was on my way to meet the clown-ass nigga Cheno. For some reason, my plan was only working halfway. I was definitely getting the cash, that was the main thing, but I was also starting to catch mad feeling for the nigga and that certainly wasn't the deal. I was supposed to fuck with him for a while, no feelings attached, then leave him alone. But no, not how it went down. Even after the shit he pulled while I was in Atlanta, I just had to start digging him. I couldn't believe I was actually falling for him like a sucka. That wasn't even my character. Fuck niggas, get money. *Only the money Jayah, nothing else*. I reiterate the thought over and over in my head.

It was about a quarter to four when I arrived to my hood in Liberty City. I parked in front of the main trap house where there was so much activity taking place. Niggas had so many dice games going on, it was ridiculous. Shooting the regular two-dice game and some was playing c-lo with three dice. Niggas that was tired of losing their money to J.P. were either pissed or tryna win their money back in one of the seven games that was occurring. J.P.

was the king of craps. I just didn't fathom why people still played against him. It was obvious that he was the best. Hell, dude never lost a game. I guess it was the niggas' pride that allowed them to continue giving J.P. their money.

Some folks were sitting inside their cars with the music blasting, allowing the good music from each vehicle to collide making the rap songs sound so raggedy. Majority of the audience was chick's tryna get up on a dude or spy on a nigga that they thought was theirs. I applied some Chanel lip gloss to my lips before I hopped out my Benz. I was simply dressed, wearing a pink and gold Versace T-shirt, a pair of faded, ripped, wide-leg Hudson jeans, and a pair of gold Versace jeweled sandals. I wasn't even clear out of the car yet before this nigga began running his mouth.

"Man, where in the fuck have you been, Jayah?" Cheno asked, angrily.

"You ain't my nigga. Why?" I cocked my head back, walking onto the sidewalk.

"Jayah, you better stop fuckin' playing with me," he demanded.

"Boy, bye, what you mean? Where the fuck was you all last week, since you wanna play Mr. Questionnaire," I spat with an attitude.

"Man, don't make me embarrass you out here Jayah."

"You ain't a damn fool," I replied with as much sass as I could.

"So, you ain't gonna tell me where you was at?" He questioned me again.

"For what my nigga? You ain't gon' tell me, so why tell you?" I yelled, now growing very agitated.

"Damn, I told you I was over my mommas. You can call and ask her right now." He retrieved his phone from his Polo jogging pants, extending his hand for me to grab his phone. Everybody know that was the oldest trick of them all.

"Ain't no sense in it. As a matter a fact, ain't no sense in this whole conversation, 'cause we are not together, so you ain't got to explain shit to me," I giggled. "And I sure don't have to explain shit to you, and that's that." I finished, knowing I really cared, but had to play it off.

"Damn, lil Jay, calm down. You ain't gotta play my nigga like that," J.P. interrupted, flipping through a wad of money he probably won. "You can kill the noise, too. I told both of y'all it ain't shit, so shut up."

"A'ight man, what's good, you cool baby?" Cheno asked, still fuming, and I could tell he had something for my ass.

"Yeah, I'm good."

Finally, after the interrogation ceased, we were cool. We all sat around laughing, cracking jokes and chilling. Unexpectedly, a woman drove a huge, extended gray van up with roughly 10 kids crammed inside. Out of nowhere, the unknown woman motioned for me to come to her. But I wasn't going to a car that I didn't know nobody in. I gestured with my right hand to block the sunbeam, but I still couldn't see the face because the sun was shining down on that big, raggedy van. I yelled back at the chick and waved, motioning for her to come holla at me. She instantly popped out. I still didn't recognize who she was until she fully approached me.

"What's up, man? You cool?" I mugged, handing Cheno my Kooba handbag.

"Nah, don't think I'm coming over here to fight you or nothing." The woman that stormed into my daddy's store demanding money seemed like a whole nother person compared to this momma out with her kids.

"Oh, babe, I ain't worried, I ain't worried at all." I folded my arms.

"I just want you to come to the car so you can see my daughter. Everybody says that she looks just like you, and seeing you close up the other day, I was tripping."

I thought about it for a minute and decided not to be selfish. I grabbed my bag from Cheno, threw it on my shoulder and walked over to the van. I looked in the front seat, knowing that the baby wouldn't look shit like me. Oh boy, wasn't that a surprise that smacked me dead in my face. The lil girl looked dead on me as if I had spit her out myself. I just sat there in disbelief. She was really the splitting image of me. That was crazy.

Damn, this gotta be his daughter. She looks too much like us. I feel so bad for spitting on her. Ain't that something. I truly felt terrible.

"So, what do you think?" Tasha asked, wanting to know what was in my head.

I smiled, still staring at the baby. "Man, that's crazy, and I'm so sorry for spitting on you, but I am very ignorant when it comes down to my daddy," I continued looking at my baby sister.

"Nah, that was my fault. I completely understand. I should have approached y'all like a grown woman."

"I think that is so crazy though. She is my twin and she only a baby," I said, amazed. She was just as happy as she wanted to be.

"That's what I said." Tash laughed.

I felt so bad and didn't hesitate. "So, how much money you needed again?" I asked, pulling my Gucci wallet out of my bag.

She paused for a second, I could tell she probably was embarrassed. "Five hunnet." She dropped her head. "Because I'm 'bout to get evicted out my house 'cause some lame-ass bitch name Ashley stole my rent money."

I bucked my eyes. "Lil Ashley that be with my God sister, Na'daijah?" I asked in a high-pitch tone.

"Yeah, that is yo lil sister, ain't it?" She didn't wait for me to respond and continued. "Ashley told me that when she found out I was pregnant by Jay. She sure did tell me Daijah is Jay Goddaughter and that's her best friend."

"Yeah that's my sissy, but they ain't best friends." I gnashed my teeth, that information there naturally bothered me. "They just cool 'cause their mommas grow up together. That's it, babe."

"I kinda figured that she was stuntin' 'cause she is pathological liar, and she be dogging her and hatin' on her big time."

"Really?" I asked with my hands on my hip and my head tilted to the side.

"Yup, she once told me that y'all steals all y'all clothes and y'all daddy a jackboy."

"I'ma slap the fuck out of that hoe when I see her," I exclaimed, motioning my hands while I was talking.

"You wild girl," Tasha cracked up laughing.

"Nah, I ain't. I'm me." I formed a half-smile, but was so serious cause I hate hatin'-ass bitches. I grabbed some crisp bills out my wallet and handed her 20 \$100 bills. "But here you go, and an extra fifteen hunnet to spend on your kids. Don't worry about my twin, I got her all the way." I smiled after handing her the money.

"Thanks, I really appreciate it. And by the way, her name is Jaylah," Tasha grinned.

"Are you serious?"

"Yeah, I am."

"Aw, that is so cute. Do you mind if I take her with me for a lil while?"

"Girl, I don't care. You can have her whenever you want to. She is an excellent baby, too. She don't even cry." She gathered her things, we exchanged numbers and she bounced.

The first thing on my mind was to take this baby to my daddy so he could see her. I wasn't gonna tell him who baby it was. He so petty, if I told him I was about to bring the baby over, he would already have it embedded in his skull to say that Jaylah didn't look like me or him. And in actuality, she looked dead on us because we look just alike. So, my plan was to fake it, like she was one of my friends kids, until he admitted that she could almost pass for my child.

I told Cheno I would get with him later,and I left, heading straight to my daddy's shop.

Walking inside the store, I just so happened to run into the one bitch nigga. Yeah, the sexy-ass dark nigga that was coming up to the beauty shop Artistic's for the Candace broad.

Alright, this the perfect time to get at him. But what I'm I gon' say? How am I gonna say it? Damn. He looked at me and asked, "Is that your baby? She's real pretty, just like her mom."

"She is pretty, but this isn't my daughter. I don't have any kids. But thanks, you don't look too bad yourself." I said, sitting Jaylah's seat on the floor.

He just laughed at my humor.

"So what's up?" I asked.

"Shit, tryna find me a Coogi fit to wear to the club tonight."

"Is that right?"

"Yeah, you tryna hit the club with me shorty?" He flashed his two gold open-face fronts.

I thought he knew better, but the nigga is very flirtatious. He didn't even know me for five seconds and tryna get at me. I laughed inside. Bitches are dumb.

"Damn, nigga. You wanna hit the club with me, but you got a main bitch."

"And who might that be?" he asked sternly and confused.

"The Candace girl." I folded my arms.

"What that suppose to mean?"

"Exactly what it sounds like." I paused for a second. "You got a bitch, so why you want me to go to the club with you?"

"Girl, you fooling. That ain't my girl. I fucks with her and fuck her, but she ain't worth settling down with."

"Ok, Mr. I wanna play Mr. Honesty." I said, sarcastically.

"Real talk, she already know what it is."

Damn I could have sworn she said he knows what it is. I merely kept my thought to myself because hatin' is something Jayah doesn't do.

"Nah, we can't go to a club, but we can eat somewhere or go to the movies." I wasn't tryna be seen with the nigga now. That was just a bit much.

"That's cool. Call me though, the name is Brian." He said, and we exchanged numbers.

My daddy laughed his ass off once dude left out of the store. "You sure know how to choose 'em, don't you?"

"Yeah daddy, I ain't gon' play with 'em."

"Punkin' pie, you crazy. But who pretty ass baby is that? She is a beauty," he complimented Jaylah.

"This girl? I know," I held in my laugh.

"Damn, she is gorgeous, and she looks just like you. I know you ain't snuck around and had a baby on me!" He kidded me, laughing. "That's weird though."

"Not really, because it's my sister," I blurted out.

"Shut up. When yo momma have a baby?" My dad replied, getting paranoid. His facial expression gave him away almost instantly. He was salty. He already knew what I was about to say next.

"Nah Daddy, don't play. This Tasha baby."

"Fo' real, damn." That was all he could say, because he'd remember the first time he seen me and he had the same feeling about this baby. I could feel it through him. He knew that was his damn daughter.

"She looks just like us, doesn't she?" I asked gently.

"She do though," He responded in a low tone. "Damn, I'm trippin', 'cause this lil girl looks just like you did when you was a baby, and she looks just like you now. This shit crazy. What the fuck is Amelia gon' think of this shit?" He said, shaking his head. "Call Tasha phone for me." He told me, grabbing the baby out of her punkin seat.

After dialing the number for the tenth time, she finally answered.

"Hello?" she answered out of breath.

"Ay, Tash, my daddy wanna holla at you."

She hesitated for a moment. "A'ight, put him on." I turned on the speakerphone and passed him the phone.

Soon as I handed him the phone he spoke. “Damn, Tash, my bad for playin’ you like that. I really didn’t know she looked like us.” I could tell he was saddened.

“You cool. It’s really my fault. I should have told you I didn’t get that abortion.”

“Nah, I should’ve just stepped up,” he said, sitting down on the sofa that sat in the middle of the floor, and placed the phone atop the glass table. “She is very gorgeous, and I’m sorry for missing her being born.” He smiled with the baby on his lap and her head in his hands.

“You cool.”

“But I’ma send that money you wanted with Jayah and a lil extra.” He leaned in to kiss the baby on the cheek. I was light way getting jealous, I admit.

“You don’t have to. Jayah gave me the five and extras to get the kids some clothes and that’s what I’m doing now at the Dadeland Mall.”

“Word.” He kissed Jaylah on her lil brown forehead. “I’m still gon’ send her with some more money so you can find you somewhere better to live.” The nigga had the biggest smile on his face. “I’ma have you and Jayah go out and pick out some furniture and new beds for you and the kids.”

“Oh, Jay I really thank you for that, you is indeed a real-ass nigga,” I could hear the huge smile in her voice. She must have had a huge grin on her face.

“You straight, and my baby girl gon’ be cool, so don’t worry about nothing.” He said implying for me to get the phone with his head motion.

“Yeah, hello?” I took her off speakerphone.

“All, y’all are so sweet. Y’all do have a heart after all,” Tasha teased. We both started cracking up laughing.

“You crazy, but I’m grabbin’ her some clothes from here. Then I’ma head to the mall and get her some more stuff. After that I’ll be there to drop her and the money off.”

“A’ight, girlie, just call me.”

We were silent after hanging up with Tasha, sitting there staring a hole into the baby. She was so damn pretty. She had smooth brown skin and some pretty, straight silky hair. Baby sis was indeed the shit, just like her big sister.

“Jayah what is her name?”

While laughing I told him. “Jaylah.”

"Bullshit, no it ain't?"

"That's what I said. That's tight. She got the JC initials, like us.

I had to call and tell my momma that new information. She gon' tell me my daddy wasn't shit. That's all she had to say, with her hatin' ass. I love her, even though she a hater when it comes down to my father. I know it was because she still secretly loved him.

♛ ♛ ♛ ♛ ♛ ♛ ♛ ♛ ♛ ♛ ♛ ♛ ♛ ♛ ♛ ♛ ♛

Everything was going wonderful. When I got home, Donteice called and told me that Daijah and the girl Ashley was around at her house. That was music to my ears. Tee only lived around the corner from me. I could have walked, but it would have took a few minutes and my adrenaline pump was working, I bolted out the door.

I popped in my car, put the accelerator to the floor and arrived in 30 seconds tops, not even checking to see if I'd parked my car correctly. Jumping out of the car hastily, I aimed for the door. They were all chillin' on the red sofa, lollygagging.

"What the fuck is you doin' over here, Ashley?" I asked, skimming over her.

"What you mean I'm with Daijah," she responded.

"Are you really? Fo'real? Is you really here with Daijah? Or you here to find another reason to hate?" I asked, snottily.

"Girl wha---"

I cut her off mid-sentence so fast and continued with what I had to say. "So what's this shit that you talkin' about my daddy suppose to be a jackboy?" I walked up on her.

"What the fuck you talking about, I ain't never said no shit like that. I got too much love for y'all," she said, rolling her eyes.

"Bitch, quit lying hoe. And you ain't got love for none of us." I pointed at me and my sisters.

"Girl, Daijah and Tee, y'all better get y'all sister." She scrunched up her face, folding her arms.

"Bitch, they ain't better get a mothafuckin' thang," I yelled as my hands just freely slapped the shit out of this bitch.

Tee immediately snatched me away, because she knew Ashley didn't have shit coming with me. She sat me down on her barstool.

She tried jumping up like she was tough and gangster. "Oh, bitch you will regret ever putting your hands on my face." Ashley said, threateningly.

"Man, listen to this," I sighed. "I don't give a fuck who you get, or what you try to do." I swayed my head side to side. "You bitches ain't got shit on me, and ain't gon' do a mothafuckin' thang coming my way. You're a fuckin' clown." I laughed, knowing that I was getting to her. "And bitch, me and my sisters hood rich, what the fuck we look like stealing? That's what you broke, faking bitches do. We got money the long way and stay cashin' out for all our clothes. So what is you saying, bum-ass bitch!?"

"Lil Jay, what you talking about?" Daijah asked concerned.

"This bitch that be in your fuckin' face all the time biting on all of our pussy, she was dogging us." I shook my head because that's the main reason why I didn't fuck with bitches. The hoe bloodline had to be filled with hate. The chick's blood type, I know, was Type H, meaning 100 percent hater. "Talking about we steal our clothes and we fuck bitches, and all kinda hatin' shit. This bitch y'all got here is straight play, and full of bullshit."

"Did she?" Tee asked, stunned. I guess the bitch was surely fooling the hell out of them.

"Yup, she was telling this girl Tasha all this bogus-ass shit."

"Girl, one thing about me is I can never be a fuck bitch," Tee said, angrily.

"What the fuck ever, no I didn't." She pouted. "She just saying that 'cause she don't like me." Ashley said with teary eyes. That was just a dead give a way there.

"I wouldn't like you neither, you stole her rent money," I shouted.

"Whatever." She stood, tapping her feet on the floor.

"Tee, I'm 'bout to get up for I beat the living shit out this bitch." I rose walking towards the door. I turned around. "But I know one thing, you better keep me and my peoples name out your mouth hoe, and that's that. I'm up and out. You be careful, my cat." I mugged, walking out the door.

Chapter Eight

My Lo Lo!

I spent the next couple of weeks with Brian, the sexy-ass nigga that said the Candace girl wasn't his main bitch. We were kickin' shit real hard. He was over all the time. It was as if we were inseparable. We was always going somewhere out of town, to the mall, bowling. I even had dude taking me out to eat ice cream. He really wasn't a big fan of the lame-ass shit I had him engaging in, but he said he was starting to really feel me intensely, so it was all good. He began playing the Candace girl real hard. Me, on the other hand, really wasn't feeling him on that level. But I did think he was cool to hang out and kick it with, just to have a little fun. One thing I did like about him was that he hadn't pressured me into being sexually involved, even though he was caking me off something real lovely. I was happy about that 'cause I knew I couldn't get into him sexually. There was something that I didn't like about his swagger, so I was cool on the sexual level.

As the weeks passed, I hadn't been in contact with Maine or Cheno. *Shit, the niggas hadn't called me so why call them? Fuck it*. The same tune that played in my head.

I did want to call Maine though, 'cause a bitch did want to visit Italy, and spring break was beginning the following week, for two weeks. *But shit, if he wanted to talk he would have called me, so fuck it. I guess he just wanted to fuck, but that's cool too 'cause I got like 45 bans out of him, so what the fuck. So what.*

The nigga Cheno was really clowning though. He hadn't bothered to call or nothing. I seen him, he didn't even speak. I started to clown his pussy-eating ass, but I just played it cool. Fuck it, have a sucka attack? For what? That was something that I wasn't gonna act on.

Thinking of all that, I just had to give his phone a dial. He answered on the first ring.

"What's up?" I said.

"Shit." Cheno spoke dryly.

"What were you doing?"

"Shit."

"Where you been at?"

"Chillin'."

"Damn, nigga, why you short answering me? Is it that serious?" I asked, concerned.

"Yeah, it's that serious, you be on some clown-ass shit, and I heard you been kickin' it hard with the B nigga." He laughed.

"Okay, who the fuck told you that?" I said, very aggravated. I didn't understand why lames were always in my fucking business.

"Man, it don't even matter who told me. Do you?" He asked again.

"I mean, we cool, if that's what you asking."

"Jayah, quit fucking playin' with me. Did you fuck the nigga?"

"No I did not. But would it matter to you? I haven't talked to you in damn near a month, so what?" I said with an attitude.

"Really," he said, sarcastically.

"You know what, I don't even know why I called yo bitch-ass. Bye!" I screamed, pissed off as I slammed my phone shut.

Before I knew it, he was calling my phone right back.

"What do you want?" I yelled.

"It's like that?"

"Yup."

"Man, shut up. I'm on my way over there."

"Boy, I'm on my way to the salon."

"Well come to the hood and get me when you leave there. You know what's up."

"A'ight." I said smiling from ear to ear. I loved the bomb head that he gave me.

♛ ♛ ♛ ♛ ♛ ♛ ♛ ♛ ♛ ♛ ♛ ♛ ♛ ♛ ♛ ♛ ♛

I arrived at the shop at three o' clock, and it was deep, of course, but it was something a little different today. Fiona snatched me up soon as I walked through the door. She led me to the shampoo bowl and was about to start my shampoo.

"What you getting today?"

"A straight wrap."

"Okay. Girl, you know those girls over there with Candace looking for you." She informed me.

"Are they really? I walked straight pass and nobody said anything."

"Girl, you know they childish, so they probably tryna get the courage to come up to you." She laughed as she dried my hair with the dark blue towel.

"I can make it better for them watch this Fee." There wasn't any fear in my blood and I walked straight up to them.

"Are y'all looking for me?' I asked snottily, hands on my hips.

"Who are you?" Said this big, black, ugly, fat-ass hood rat.

"Dig this, if ANY OF YOU BITCHES LOOKING FOR ME, HERE I GO! WHAT'S UP, MAN?" I threw my hands in the air. They had me fucked up.

"Girl, ain't nobody looking for you. I just wanna know if you mess with my baby daddy, B?" Candace asked.

"Beat it, don't ask me nothing. Ask that nigga," I raised my voice a bit.

"It ain't that serious honey," she rolled her neck and eyes.

"It must be." I sounded off with a yell. "You questioning me like we know each other, babe. And one thing I don't do is explain myself to another bitch, for what!?" I said as Fee was pulling on me to start rolling my hair up.

"Fee, please, spare me. And you don't have to grab her, 'cause the bitch ain't tough. And you lucky, bitch, we in the hair salon, 'cause I would beat the fuck out of you." The bitch thought she was puttin' up a good front.

"Really, would you?" I said, laughing my ass off.

"Sure I would, you jiggy-ass bitch."

"Could never be a jig hater hoe. I just get this money and that's the reason all y'all jealous bitches hate me so much. Because my breed is rare and you hoes wish you could do this shit like Jayah Carter." I chortled, unnecessarily loud. "And your nigga sure didn't fuck me, so I could neva be a jig. He just ate it and caked me off with some stacks. You mad 'cause yo' baby daddy trick with me, hoe." I continued to laugh at the miserable broad. "And we only been kickin' it for three weeks, so get to that." I threw up three fingers with a smirk on my face. I know she was furious.

"I doubt that." She replied very certain.

"You shouldn't, 'cause all I got to do is let you read these text and you'll be too salty."

"Well let me read 'em," she smacked her lips.

"Like I told you hoe, I explain to no bitch."

"You lying, you ain't gotta stunt." She tried frontin' on me.

"Oh, don't doubt me, baby girl." I said as I pulled out my phone and let Fee read all the text messages out loud. Yo, the broad wasn't only infuriated, she was mortified, too. Every text said something nice, relating to him tricking in some way. I'm at the mall you want something, or I'm on my way to bring you some money, all kind of shit. Needless to say, she was hurting and her heart was crushed.

She stormed out the shop in tears. The entire shop went on and on about her being so stupid. We joked and laughed at the clown, until it was time for me to bounce. As I was leaving the shop, Tee called hyped as hell, which never fails. I swear, she be fully charged and ready to hang, party or whatever. That hoe used to try to kick it when hurricanes was about to destroy the city, she didn't care.

"Damn, Jayah, why you ain't been answering the phone?"

"Bitch, I was at Artistic, getting my wig split."

"Well the reason why we haven't talked to Maine and them, is because they got caught with a truck load full of bricks, bra." She sounded saltier than me. "Ain't that crazy, they about to do some major time," she sighed.

"Word, damn, bricks…that's crazy…that is fucked up, yo."

"I know, I'm so mad though. I really wanted to go to Italy."

"Me too, girl."

"Maine called my phone, too. The nigga said call Jayah and

tell her to come up here and visit me. I just sat there. I know good and well that you ain't visiting nobody that's in jail except your daddy."

"You damn right, girl. Hey, fuck it, maybe I can have someone else take us. He was a cool nigga while it lasted. But what the hell can he do for me while he in the cage, except tell me where that money at. 'Cause I need, I need, I need cash man." I quoted one of our hometown artist songs.

Tee burst out laughing "Yeah I'm tryna see what that be like."

"You so crazy, but you wanna go out tonight?"

"Yeah why not." She said. I told her to meet me at my house and we hung up.

Tee was already at the house waiting on me. She was sitting on the sofa with her legs propped up on my table on the phone with J.P., of course. They were truly inseparable. The duo had become very close, and they started really liking each other. Of course, they didn't stop talking to other people. They hadn't gotten that far, but for some strange reason, I felt that Tee was on her way to falling in love with the nigga. But I knew J.P. wouldn't be on that. I didn't care though, because I rarely involved myself in her business. Hell, I knew I would be pimpin' for a long while and that was all that matter. Hanging up with him, Tee asked. "So are you dressing up or dressing down?"

"Bitch, you know I'm straight hood. I'm dressing down." I laughed. "Nah, but I ain't up for no heels tonight."

"You silly. So what are you wearing?"

"My light Hollister cut-up jeans, fitted purple and pink Hollister tee, the pink collar shirt underneath, my pink glittery belt and pink accessories. I'm rocking my pink and purple Dooney large top handle bag and my white, pink and purple Air Max 90s, that's it. I'ma keep it simple on the haters tonight." I said, grabbing my peach soda out if the fridge.

"Alright, I guess I'm gon' wear my yellow and orange Abercrombie stuff."

We didn't give a fuck. We'd dress classy, hood, sexy, whatever. Our shopping only took place everywhere that was polished and expensive.

My phone rang. I glanced at my caller ID screen. An unknown number displayed and I instantly got pissed off.

"Hellllooooo?" I screamed through the phone.

"What's up niece?"

"Who the hell is this?" I asked, stormily.

"This yo' Aunt JoAnne."

"Hey Auntie, I miss you," I said, immediately getting excited.

"I miss you too niece."

"When y'all coming down here to see me?" I asked.

"That's what I was calling you for. You know me and Steve getting married, we want you and your daddy to come to the wedding."

"All that's so sweet. When is it?"

"Next Saturday."

"Dang, Auntie why you call and tell us at the last minute?"

"I just got your number from your cousin Jazzman. She just found it she said."

"Oh, well, we coming 'cause on Monday we gon' be on spring break for two weeks. So we just might come down there Wednesday or Thursday and stay for a week."

"That'll be fine but after the wedding we going on our honeymoon but y'all still can stay," she said, proudly.

"Okay, Auntie, we will be down there, and Donteice coming too."

"Okay love you sweetie, can't wait to see yall." She voiced the kissing sound through the phone.

"Love you, too," I said right before hanging up the phone.

"Tee, Aunt JoAnne and Uncle Steve finally getting married girl."

"All that's tight."

"Yeah and we going."

"Umm...to Dayton Ohio!?" Tee screamed. She hated going to Dayton. She told me once before it was pure torture. Tee was so silly and extra at times.

"Yeah, that's only where they getting married at." I looked at her like she turned retarded.

The room was quiet because Donteice really loathed going to Dayton. She felt that it was too small and the city really didn't excite her one bit. Last time we went down there, it was so boring. Nothing was going on, and there girls are some true haters. That's the shit that always came out her mouth when Dayton came up in conversation.

I, on the other hand, really didn't care. I already knew that it was a boring place, especially because we were so used to our sexy partying city. But I also knew if you went anywhere and knew the right people, you would have fun, and my favorite cousin Jazzman knew the right people, so it would be fun.,to me anyways. Hell, Dayton wasn't that bad, being that it was the size of just our entire west side of town.

I told her sternly. "Donteice you don't gotta go if you don't want to."

"I know, but if you go I'm going, so that's that."

"Well stop frowning if you know you going." I spat.

"Shut up." She yelled. "Let's just get dressed."

"Okay where we going?"

"To the Level."

Sitting in VIP alone wasn't enjoyable. Donteice and J.P. were buying up the picture booth. I was slightly envious of their bond because I wanted Cheno to be there taking pictures with me.

The club was thumping and that night was special because a lot of rappers were performing, but I wasn't on them. I was waiting on Cheno to strut through the front entrance. His swagg was so mean. I was digging him so much, it was crazy. And I just couldn't believe myself.

As soon as I stop thinking about him he walked in. This nigga gon' have the nerve to walk in with a bitch. *Oh, okay.* I was pissed, I'm not gonna even lie. And, I continued to look as he slithered through the crowd. I then realize it was the bitch Candace. I laughed. *Oh, they mad, but that's cool too. I'm about to play'em both like I don't give a fuck.* Even though I did care, because I was the bitch looking the dumbest. I was still riding in the Benz with his name on the plates, and I didn't even fuck with him no more. How stupid did that make me look? Once I saw that, I just knew I wasn't fuckin' with him again. He was too damn disrespectful. I really wasn't mad at the bitch though, because she was suffering from a broken heart and was just tryna play get back. She was an asshole though, because I knew with certainty that Cheno hadn't purchased her a Benz freshly of the dealer's lot. *And she called me a fuck bitch. Come to think of it, that bitch was the one who hated on me. Bitches kill me, hatin' on another chick, for what, that is so lame. It is cool, I'm just about to take this Goose to the*

head and say fuck 'em. And the Goose make me loose. I feel so sorry for them.

Walking to the dance floor with my drink in my hand, I bopped to Young Jeezy shit. His shit was hot in our clubs, so it was on. I chanted along with him word for word without missing a beat.

Last time I checked I was the man on these streets
They call me residue, I leave blow on these beats
Got diarrhea flow, man I shit on niggaz
Even when I'm constipated I still shit on niggaz
(let's get it)...

It was something about that deep voice that had me hype and I didn't give a fuck about shit. That nigga wasn't gon' play he had the whole crowd amped as shit. People were going bananas.

An hour had passed and I was drunk as fuck, on some clown ass shit. Staggering over to Donteice, I finally reached her and allowed my entire body to drape on her.

"Tee." I said with a slur.

"What, girl?" Donteice mad because she knew I was drunk and she also knew it had a lot to do with Cheno being in the club with Candace.

"Damn, I am a lil tipsy, not drunk, so you don't gotta try to play me. Damn."

"Okay, sup babe? You good?"

"Yeah, I'm straight." I shook my body and stood in a straight goon stance, throwing my two fists in the air. "Ready to go beat that Candace bitch up? 'Cause she hated on me." I informed her. "To try to get my nigga. What kinda weak shit is that? But it's cool, 'cause I got her faded, I'm gon' beat the fuck out of her Tee, real talk."

Tee sighed and rolled her eyes. "Man, ain't nobody on that bullshit all the time. Girl, fuck him. You don't like him anyway, do you?"

"Here you go, tryna' play cool 'cause you with J.P. I'm gon' clown, it's simple. Just 'cause I got this Goose in me," I nodded, drunkenly. "Yup I'm gon' straight clown. Just wait," I warned as I walked away.

Donteice, not knowing what to do, she came, and grabbed me and told me she was ready to bounce. That was cool with me because I really wasn't tryna have a sucka attack and I was just ready to go before the crowd got any hyper anyway. So *fuck it*, I thought. That was a mistake. Why did Donteice have me depart at that particular moment? I'd noticed Candace and Cheno getting inside his Benz. Yeah, the one like he got me. It was only right for me to clown on his ass.

"Tee, I know this bitch ain't in the driver seat?" I asked, facing Tee.

"Yeah, she is Lil Jay," Tee replied, covering her mouth.

"I'm 'bout to show the fuck out." I threw my head back and trotted over there like the dead guy Bernie did in the movie "Weekend at Bernie's."

I didn't say shit. I reached down, grabbed a brick that was on the side of the curb, didn't even bother mulling it over and threw it hard at the windshield. Glass shattered everywhere. Cheno jumped out of the car hastily.

"Man, Jayah, what the fuck is up with you? We ain't together, what you trippin' for? Damn, you said we wasn't together when I saw you earlier today."

"You damn right I said that shit, but I also said, you bitch-ass nigga, to never disrespect me or make me out to be the fool."

"Yo, I should beat the fuck out of you bra." Chen looked like he meant it, too.

"Shit, nigga, what's stopping you?" I asked. "Oh yeah, Jay Carter, 'cause I wish you would touch me, pussy-ass nigga."

"Bitch, I don't know why you think he don't bleed like the next nigga." He yelled.

I could tell I was making him feel like less of a man.

"Who gives a fuck! Call 'em." He shrugged, trying to contain his anger. "As a matter a fact, I'm'bout to call 'em and tell him that I'm gon' beat yo ass." He screamed on me. "Why you right here though, and then I'm gon' beat yo mu'fucka ass." He paused. "I wonder if he knows you up here drunk as fuck and looking real dumb."

"You know what? I got your bitch, nigga." I said, hitting his ass with another brick that was right beside my feet. I cracked him right in the eye, and rushed to my car as quick as I could make my drunk self go and dipped to the crib.

I fell all over the couch when I got home. The clown-ass shit I'd done earlier was getting to me. I felt really stupid, but then another part of me was laughing. Like hey, that's what both of them clowns get.

Hearing a bang on the door caused my heart to skip a beat. *Damn, I know this nigga ain't at my door. Shit, he probably about to beat my ass. What I'm gon' do?* I heard the sound of keys.

Trailing Donteice was Cheno and J.P., of course.

"What the fuck you be on, Jayah?" Cheno asked. His tone was more confused than ready to beat my ass.

"Man, beat it. The question is what you be on, pussy?" I wasn't gonna hold shit back from this nigga, especially not with all the Goose in me.

"Nah, you the one clowning. Do you see this gash by my eye?" This time, the anger exploded in his face.

"Yeah, whatever, you clown." I brushed it off.

"You the clown, talkin' about we ain't together, but you had a sucka when you seen me with another girl."

"And you right, my cat!" I said, pissed. "Because, she was salty that I took her nigga and then gon' hate on me, for what? Why she have to hate on me to get you?" I whined.

"Yo, all that's irrelevant. Man, it really is. Either we gon' fuck around, or not." He sighed. "I don't have time for the childish-ass games, Jayah, I really don't. What you gon' do?"

"What type of question is that, boy?"

"What the fuck you mean? Do you want to be together? Or do you want me to do me and you do you. And I do me very well."

"Oh, do you? Well then, I can do me very well too. It's butter baby."

"So, what you're saying is no, we ain't together?"

"Man, holla at me in the morning." I was too tired and fucked up to deal with this nigga now. All I wanted was to lie down in my cozy bed.

Sleep didn't come right away, my thoughts were too busy bouncing around in my damn head. *Fuck! Why? Why do I got to have feelings for him? I'm salty. Man, it don't suppose to be like this. Why? What is it about him? I just don't understand.* Tears slid down my cheeks and fell from my face onto my bed.

Donteice entered my room.

"Jayah, what's wrong?" She sat on the edge of my bed.

"I don't know. I just don't understand why I like him so much." I wiped my face.

"Maybe because he was the first nigga you fucked with tough, and y'all done the sex thing, you know?"

"But I don't like Maine as much, and I did the sex thing with him." I whimpered like a sad puppy.

"He didn't eat you out though, and you only messed with Maine once. Chen always eating you out"

"I know, but still."

"Still nothing, and Maine don't always be around, so that could be it too."

"Yeah, you right." I said, sniffing.

"So what you gon' do?" She asked.

"I'm gonna fuck with him tough." I wiped my face clear.

She nudged my side. "You get on my nerves. You could have let everyone know that, if you was gon' be on it anyways." Tee teased.

"Shut up, 'cause I'm still gon' do me regardless, on the low though." I said, laughingly.

"Right, that's all I'm saying." Tee was right with me. We both giggled.

"You silly. I ain't gon' do nothing that he know about though." I clarified.

"That's how we gotta do it." She smiled and stood up. "Now, I'm 'bout to have him come back here and y'all can solve y'all problems."

"Okay, thanks Tee."

Tee walked out, and a few seconds later, I heard Cheno heading up the stairs.

"Babe, I'm just gonna lie next to you, and we can act as if this never happened."

"Okay." I agreed. He placed his warm body next to me. I snuggled underneath him, before I knew it, we were snoring in a dead sleep.

Chapter Nine

I'ma do me!

The following day, we were back to our usual, attending an earlier morning breakfast and spending cash. After we'd picked up a few items from the Dophin Mall, Cheno needed a haircut for real bad, so we headed to the barbershop. While he was receiving his service, I got a 30-minute facial in the same spot. Honestly, it felt wonderful to be in his company. Once that was finished, we went to get his window repaired.

"Bay, why somebody broke my window last night, yo!" He laughed, playing entirely too much.

"Oh really, that's fucked up." I shook my head, playing along. "It ain't shit. I'm gonna cash you out for the clown that did that lame-ass shit." I went inside my Prada bag and retrieved three crispy Benjamins.

"Okay, I see ya, big banking it."

After we got the situation together, we followed each other to the beach park. On my drive to the beach, I cruised through the streets, thinking about the future: *Damn, ain't that something. I'm about to be 18 in less than two months, and I'm gon' graduate a few weeks after that. What am I gonna do with my life? Shit, I can be a player and just say fuck it, or just be with Cheno. Damn, shit just seems to be happening too damn fast. And, I still remember all the things people was telling me at school about Veronica and Tyiesha, sayin' they pregnant by him. But I know when I come back from Dayton, we gonna have that conversation for sure.* It was crazy because I was strategizing a totally different notion, but somehow, this nigga had me literally wondering how it'll be if we were in a genuine commitment.

Pulling up at the park was never disappointing. It was always jumping, filled with chicks, but with mostly niggas. Donteice and Na'daijah were already in attendance. Daijah had the Ashley bitch with her, so you know what that meant. I had to call and tell Tasha to come up there, so that we'd get shit straight immediately. 'Cause if she was talking shit about us, Na'daijah didn't have any choice but to beat the bitch up, flat-out.

Tasha arrived promptly. She had to be doing at least 100 mph. She popped out her whip real quick. Leaning against our cars changed in a swift second, and just the sight of Tasha brightened my day.

Tasha didn't hesitate, either. "What's up, you thieving-ass bitch?" She approached Ashley.

Ashley, thinking she too hardcore, replied. "Bitch, I could never be a thief hoe. I got money. Steal from you and all them bum-ass kids of yours, for what sweetie?"

Me being the gutta chick that I was, interjected. "Now what do them kids got to do with anything?"

She sucked her teeth. "Yo, Jayah, I don't know why you think you so hard. What the fuck do you got to do with anything?"

I laughed, finding her hilarious. "Oh, so you wanna try to play hard because we in front of all these niggas? Fo'real, though?"

She cocked her head back. "Bitch bye, this me all the time."

"You right." I agreed. "You do talk shit all the time. But one thing that these niggas out here know is I ain't gon' play with a bitch. I beat ass and take names, it's simple."

"Yeah, well not mine." She hopped down from the hood of the car.

I laughed, mad-like. "Bitch, I just slapped you the other day, and you didn't do shit."

"You could've NEVA, so girl stop making up shit."

I snickered. "Okay you are a pathological liar. Tee and

Daijah both know I slapped you." I turned towards Donteice. "Right Tee?"

"Yeah, she did though." Tee agreed.

"Fuck all this shit. Tasha, what she say about us?" I got straight to the point.

Tasha immediately spilled the beans. Ashley was fuming because Tasha was telling Daijah's business, and Daijah knew it had to be Ashley because she was the only one who knew her personal shit. Daijah wasted no time and stole on her with about five swift jabs. I could tell Daijah was hurting.

Yup, if one fights, we all fight. We jumped in and were beatin' the fuck out of her. Even Tasha joined in. Cheno and J.P. facial expressions read clear, these bitches ain't gon' play, they straight hood. Finally, after Ashley was receiving a serious beat down, some people came to break it up and Ashley sprung to her feet. I surmise she didn't get a good enough ass whipping because she was still bumping her gums, although, her face was fucked up.

"I got y'all bitches. Y'all gon' have the nerve to jump me? And Donteice, you need to worry about J.P. having herpes, hoe. Daijah I don't know why you so salty either, you is a hoe. A young whore at that. You know I can expose you right now." She yelled crying.

"What?" Tee replied to her mentioning her name. Tee wasn't the type that argued.

"Bitch what the – "

Ashley didn't even finish her sentence. Only so much talking was within limits. Tee ran back up. Daijah, Tasha and, of course, me, ran right back up behind her, too. Joining in and beating that ass once more. All the way until beach security came. Not wanting to get arrested we all popped in our cars and dipped out at crazy speeds.

For some reason, I couldn't get the bullshit out of my head. It just wasn't sitting right with me. When Ashley was saying J.P. had herpes and he really didn't defend himself, had me wondering. He'd supposedly fucked this girl around the way named Boony, and Boony was undoubtedly a nasty girl and giving the virus out like a wildfire. The entire city knew that Boony carried the herpes virus. It was a known fact. She wound up falling out with her best friend, and her friend printed her results paper out, and made copies. The girl actually planted them all over the neighborhood. That was crazy news to my ears though, because Tee wouldn't know what to do. Nah. I instantly erased the thought out of my head.

♛ ♛ ♛ ♛ ♛ ♛ ♛ ♛ ♛ ♛ ♛ ♛ ♛ ♛ ♛ ♛ ♛

When I was leaving to go to Dayton, Cheno was fuming hot.

"Damn, Jayah, why you got to go man?"

"I told you, it's my Auntie wedding and I gotta show my love."

He didn't have a choice but to fathom it. "Okay, baby. Just be good and be careful."

"I will." We kissed, and then I got out of the car.

Once I made it inside Miami International Airport, my daddy and Tee were inside eating cinnamon rolls, waiting on my arrival. We checked our luggage in and finally made our way through the standard procedure and security checks, taking unnecessary time, thanks to them clown-ass foreigners. I loved flying though. I could fly all day. We loved Delta Airlines, their first-class was superb, and that's the only way me and mine flew. We boarded our flight, and I rushed to my seat, placing my seatbelt around me. Before the plane made its takeoff, I was fast asleep. When I woke up, the airplane was landing on Dayton International Airport's runway at a fast, shaky speed. We were sitting in the best seats on the plane, which made it easier for us to exit before it was flooded by passengers that was trying to depart. *These people better have my car down here, I know that*.

The sky was all gloomy and dreary. The trees didn't have a leaf to save a life, it was freezing cold outside and our body temperatures wasn't used to the weather that city had to offer at all. Tee was furious, and she had the biggest attitude ever.

Jazzman was already outside, waiting on us, and so excited when she seen us trotting in her direction, carrying our Louis Vuitton Grimaud, Eole 60 and Pegase 65 luggage, swagging, like we owned the airport. But I knew Jazzy was more elated when she seen me and Tee rides arrive in Dayton two hours earlier, the ones she picked up for us.

"Damn, y'all living that damn good in the MIA, huh cuz?" She greeted me. "Hey Tee and Uncle Jay." She hugged them. "Unk, y'all living good, can I get some money?" She joked around, but this was how she usually asked for some cake from my daddy.

"You good for it. I'll hit you later." My daddy didn't hold back for family. We strolled to the car where some local d-boys who he knew picked him up. Of course, my daddy was supplying many of Dayton's trappers, and being honest, them Dayton niggas admired his ambitions in the game.

"You silly, girl. I told you to move down there with me."

"I know." She smiled. "But I can't get used to that big-ass city. You know everybody up here knows one another." She chuckled. "I be jumping in my lil city, girl." She said, proudly.

"Alrighty then cuz, I see you."

She giggled. "I'm gon' show y'all a good time down here. How long y'all staying?"

"Until next week." I replied.

"Okay, y'all staying at my house." She told me.

"Whud, you stay by yourself?" I asked, surprised.

She puckered her lips and nodded her head. "Girl, yup. I stay in the hood though." She shrugged. "But hey, that's all I can afford right now. You know I'm in school, but you better believe I got it plushed the fuck out." She pranced around in her imaginary circle.

"Okay then, where it's at?" I asked, familiar with the tiny city a lil bit.

"You remember where Aunt JoAnne used to live at, in them projects called the DeSoto Bass Courts? Where all them fine, money gettin' niggas be?"

I laughed. "Oh yeah, I do remember. It was a few cuties I seen when I came down here last time." I nodded in agreement. "That looked like they had potential and was on their way to becoming the man."

"Yeah, and what, that was about two years ago?"

"Yup, sure was." I answered.

"So most of them got their money all the way together now." She rubbed her thumb and index finger together, singing. "Money, money, moneeey."

"So, do y'all have a lot of niggas that's gon' trick on you?" I wanted to know how Dayton niggas really got down.

"Girl, yeah." She said, bragging on her Gem City niggas. "This one dude I fuck with just bought me two." She proudly threw up two fingers. "Dooney & Bourke bags and a Roca Wear outfit."

"Oh, word?" I said. *Oh, these niggas small time ballers, but it don't matter to me. I need it all.*

"Yeah, they ain't gon' play with 'em especially the ones that thinks they gettin' big money." She informed me.

"Okay, so what do y'all do daily?" From the looks of it, there wasn't shit to do.

She clarified my thoughts. "Shit, well, it really ain't shit to do, except to go eat at one of our chicken joints. Those jump on the weekdays." She paused. "Really that's it, but you know I jumps girl anyhow." She said, excitedly. "I be with somebody nigga or all the hood niggas be kickin' it at my house." Jazzman told me.

"Okay, I see you got the hood house." I joked.

"Yeah I do." She laughed, agreeing. "I also be going out almost every night wit them niggas too. Shid, the Kill-Nine be cranking, the Knife-and-Gun-Show and MJ's used to jump, fo' real. I'm mad they closed that place." She pouted, like she was truly mad. "Fo'real, it was the place t – "

I interrupted her hastily. "Y'all got a club called the Kill-Nine? And had a club called the Knife-and-Gun-Show?" My eyes wandered.

She laughed a little. "Nah, it's not literally called that it's called the K-9. Some niggas nicknamed it that. And the other club original name was Majestic's nightclub. It went down so much, they named it some deadly shit."

"Y'all folks crazy." I shook my head. Because I'd heard some dire stories for the city to be as small as it was. It literally went down in that little city, on the real.

"I want y'all to go out with us, too. But I know y'all can't get in because y'all young."

"What that mean? We both got fake IDs, girl."

"Okay, well, we gon' be jumping honey. You gonna see how we get down in the DYT, and tonight is Wednesday, so Club Rain gon' jump."

"You crazy, but damn, girl, why is it so cold?" I was shivering.

"Girl, you know this is way up at the top of the map. But our weather is stupid because today, it's 29 degrees, and tomorrow, it's gon' be hot, girl, like 56 degrees."

"Damn, that is dumb as hell, but 56 degrees ain't hot."

"Well, up here, it is honey. Bitches gon' be scantily. Tomorrow gon' be the first hot day of this year, so everyone is gonna be out." She said, happily. She was real excited about the temperatures rising.

At first, I was kind of skeptical about leaving my car outside of her apartment complex. Hell, when my Aunt used to live over there, some thirsty-ass niggas used to steal her car all the time. Just think, she only had a decent ride. Shit, me and Tee had a Benz and a Jag. They weren't used to them late model rides sitting in their hood. They were more with the norm, Chevys, Buicks and Pontiacs, but Jazzy said it was cool, so we just drove our rides over there anyway.

I was expecting her crib to be normal. Fooled me. Her shit was actually decked out for it to be in the hood. I had nice shit, I admit it. But she wasn't lying, her apartment was nice, too. From the outside of the mahogany bricks that held the projects together, you would have thought that her crib was filled with roaches and rats. I guess it wasn't the outside that counted, 'cause her inside made up for the poor environment outdoors. That's why the niggas like chillin' in her place.

We walked through the back door from the parking lot. To my surprise, it was immaculate. I knew this girl had to have somebody install her own appliances. My cousin had an all black kitchen in the center of the hood, with a black and gray checkered area rug to match with her gray and black marble counter top. That bitch remodeled her kitchen, I knew she just had to. It was just that nice. A large, black dinette piece was propped against the wall. The living room was funky fresh, too. Her suede gray and black 3-piece suite sat crammed, but pretty in the living room. A 42-inch flat screen mounted on the wall and a digital cable box rested on a floor entertainment system. She had a couple elegant paintings on the wall and a huge spider lamp sitting in the corner. And this was the roughest projects in Dayton. I had never seen nothing like it in my life. I couldn't do nothing but laugh as I toured her home.

She was right about her having the hood house, though. It was also a lot of niggas in attendance. They were gambling, and a few was playing the video games. As soon as we walked inside, we were attacked. It was obvious that they'd never saw any real stallions. These niggas was actually going crazy.

"Damn, Jazzy, who is these bitches?" Some disrespectful, ugly-ass nigga asked.

"Damn, Jazzman, where did you find them at?" One of the fine guys inquired.

"Damn, y'all niggas act like y'all ain't never seen bad bitches before." Donteice yelled, rudely.

"Girl, it ain't that serious. You ain't all that." The same disrespectful dude spoke up again.

"I gotta be. You surely want to know where I came from, you fuckin' bum." She spat.

"Bitch, I can never be a bum." He pulled out approximately three stacks.

Donteice laughed, angrily. "What is that, boy? Like nine hunnid? You real funny, my nigga, pulling out my nail money!" She exclaimed, snobbishly

Jazzy interrupted. "Tee, don't pay him any attention, and Meechie, leave her alone. Damn." She fussed.

"Nah, that's her. She think she the shit."

"How about I know I'm the shit. So quit the fucking hatin', y'all." She inhaled, taking a deep breath. "Dayton niggas is lame as the fuck." Tee yelled, storming up the stairs.

Nobody understood what was wrong with her but me. She really hated being there, and that boy didn't do nothing but make it worst. I didn't say anything because she would eventually get over it.

While Tee was upstairs, I was downstairs having fun with the hood niggas. I was starting to enjoy myself. They were cool once you got to know them. Dayton dudes were a lot different from niggas 'round my way, but a lot of them held authority and had major swagger, too. Jazzy was hissing to me who she had fucked, and there was about 15 niggas that was in the house. And she fucked like five of them, literally. Hell, the city was so small everybody seemed to be fucking everybody. Jazzy was a hoe, she had admitted it herself, and would let anyone know she was grown and she did what she wanted to. Fuck all the haters. I never judged either, to each his own.

It was one dude in the house that stood out amongst the group. I kept locking eyes with him, and Jazzy noticed it. So, she informed me with the necessary low down on dude. She was telling me that he had a girlfriend that was a little older than him, and he really loved her, but he had bitches also. Galore of hoes. Jazzy informed me that he was one of the popular fellas in the city that'd have a different bitch in his car every time you saw him in traffic. He was the type of nigga that'd have you fighting over him in the club and be with another hoe at the bar. Buying the broad a drink or taking a picture with some hoes while y'all engaging in a physical fight. He is a wild one, but sexy as hell. Jazzy continued running down his history.

Not really caring 'cause I was only gonna be in town for a week anyway, I talked to him. Hey, why not talk to him for the time being? Plus, he was something that you couldn't turn down anyway.

Bitches must really had him having the big head, because he didn't even beat around the bush when he approached me. "Ride with me for a minute, baby." It came from him more as a command than an invitation.

"Where we going? I don't even know you," I looked at him with one eyebrow up.

"You about to get to know me, that's why I want you to ride with me for a minute." He conveyed.

Honestly, I wasn't tryna stay in the house anyway. "A'ight, let me go grab my sister." I darted upstairs to see if Tee wanted to go. She didn't, she had some nigga up there all in her grill. I was certainly happy that somebody had gotten her to smile and told her I would be back later on.

Noticing what I was riding in, dude wanted to ride with me. I couldn't blame him so he got in and directed me to the mall. He needed to get him something to wear out for the night. I was wondering what they mall had. Quickly remembering that their malls were bullshit. I already knew that I would put on something that I brought from home.

The mall had a few people in it, but not how it is in Miami. I knew that we would be in and out. Forgetting all about what Jazzy had told me until we stepped inside that mall, I noticed bitches were pointing and staring every time I turned around. Even the hoes that were working in the stores were staring and glaring. The nigga was surely hot shit to them bitches because they flocked over him like birds traveling to their next destination. One even had the nerve to come up to him.

"You on that Lil C, fo'real?" She asked, scanning me up and down like I was an item.

"Man, don't come up to me with that shit, I don't fuck with you, damn bitch, gone."

She giggled, irate. "You wanna show out 'cause you with this bitch." Girl had to think I was a punk bitch, but had the game fucked up. Baby girl had me straight twisted.

"Hold on. Don't disrespect me, though. You clowning, 'cause you don't even know me, so you can kill all that noise coming my way, real talk." I said, placing my arms underneath my breasts with a mean mug.

I could tell she thought she was a tough bitch, but didn't know me though. "Fuck you, bitch." She screamed. "I don't give a fuck about you." She flared up her nose and pointed her fingers at me from a distance. "Bitch, do you know who I am? I know you ain't shit. Don't nobody know you, bitch. You a lame, I ain't never seen you, not around my parts."

I simply laughed. "Babe, you wish I was a lame. You might be known in Dayton, but I'm well known in Miami. Yeah that's right, Miami Florida. You don't know me, and I don't think you really want to." I glared. "So, my advice to you is to keep it moving, one some real G shit." I motioned my hand through the air brushing her off.

"Now, just gone Brenna, with your bum-ass, man, for real." Lil C told her, pulling me away.

"I see you "that" nigga in y'all lil city," I giggled. This shit was too hilarious.

"Man, nah, I ain't. This hoe just be clowning." He formed a slight grin across his face.

"You gotta fuck with her, she having sucka attacks and shit."

"Nah, I just fucked her and now she can't get enough of this nigga." Lil C explained as we continued looking to purchase something stylish.

On our way back to Jazzy's place, he asked me to swing past this store that they had in a shopping plaza. He wanted to go inside Deveroes and Step 'N Style, because their malls were straight up garbage and shitty. They hardly had anything that I liked. He didn't get anything and I just grabbed a Dooney bag that he bought, and a Roca Wear fit. He thought he was really doing something, buying me that stuff. Those niggas really loved buying Dooneys and Roc fits.

Cheno was so far from my mind when my phone rang. It was him, probally checking up on me since I'm away. I didn't know if I should answer or not. I decided to answer. "Hello?"

"Hey babe, why you didn't call me?" He asked, excitedly.

"I was sleeping, and now I'm out with my family." Lying seemed like the way to go.

"Oh, why don't I hear nobody?" He was curious, since we were usually making all kinds a noise when we get together.

"Because, I'm in the car by myself." I replied, looking at Lil

C with the "you better not say shit" look.

"Okay, you said you coming back next week?"

"Yeah, babe."

"When though?"

"Don't worry about it. I will be there." I sighed. "And I know why you wanna know, so you can be doing all kinda shit."

"Nah, I got a surprise for you that's why. Always thinking, you know, something."

"A'ight, well just know it's gon' be next week and you better do all you can while I'm gone 'cause it want be none of that when I get back home." I joked.

"Whatever baby, I love you."

"I love you too, bye." I said joyously. That was the first time we exchanged those vows.

Lil C looked at me. "Damn, you in love ain't you?"

"Nah, but you are." I reversed it on him before he could even get on me.

"And you're right." He smoothly nodded. "But I can man up and admit to it. I ain't a child."

"Okay, I can admit to it to, I'm not in love." I kept my eyes on the road.

"So, why would you say something that you don't mean?" I told that nigga I did love him, but in love was totally different and quickly deadened the conversation.

Something caught my attention. It was this raggedy-ass Chevy outside the store parked right beside my car. It was very weird, 'cause when I came out the store, it pulled off. I asked him if it seemed weird, but he wasn't worried, so I left it alone. Why did I do that? I should have listened to my first instincts. We were on some side street and the Chevy came from out of nowhere, two niggas popped out.

"Where the fuck is the money, bitch-ass nigga," the bum-ass jackboy demanded, pointing his gun directly in Lil C's face.

"So, you pussy-ass niggas go rob me, for real?" Oh my God. I was scared shitless, this fool was actually talking shit to the gunman.

"Yeah, we starving nigga. We gotta eat too."

"A'ight." He hissed tryna hurry up the process so it could be over with.

One nigga scared the hell out of me. He told the other, "Let's kill him and this bitch."

"Fuck that nigga. She ain't got shit to do with nothing." Lil C informed them.

"Shid, she with you and she in this Benz." He chuckled, menacingly. "I should take this mothafucka too." He pointed at my car. "But it might got an all-star, on-star whatever the shit called on it," the dumb-ass jackboy said.

"Man, just take this shit." Lil C said in between clenched teeth, handing him a handful of money. Why the thirsty-ass niggas made me take off my diamond set. Yes, the one I had received when I was 14 from my dad. He paid a good $300,000 for all five pieces. The dude told some dirty rat bitch to get out the car and obtain my jewelry. And the bitch really had the audacity to say thanks and began to laugh, as if the shit was funny. *Oh this bitch gon' get it for that shit. My daddy 'bout to bring a war down to this small city. He gon' be pissed.*

Zooming off at a remarkable speed, I was numb. I drove in shock. Lil C was talking, but I wasn't listening to him at all. I did manage to hear him say, "I'm gon' kill that nigga Tyrone."

"You knew him?" I yelled, enraged.

"Yeah, they some weak, bum-ass niggas that's been hustling forever and still ain't got no money. So they got to be the stick-up kids of the city."

"Oh, yeah, my daddy gon' wanna holla at you because they about to do some damage." I warned.

"Nah, baby girl, me and my goonz gon' handle this." He told me.

I shook my head. "I gotta call my daddy and tell him to meet me at Jazzy's place so you can give him details." I said retrieving my cell phone from my bag. Dialing his number, I explained everything that had unfolded as soon as he answered. He was pissed, and said he was on his way.

Everybody was already at Jazzy's house waiting for us to pull up. I hopped out quick, my daddy bolted in my direction without delay.

He was in hearing range and instantly probed. "Who is these niggas that did this shit? Where can I found them niggas who took my baby diamonds?" Then he shifted his attention on me. "And Jayah." He screamed. "Why in the hell you going places you don't know shit about?" He yelled, enraged. That was one of the few times he got angry with me.

Lil C already saw in my daddy's eyes that he was the epitome of a real goon and was serious about his shit.

He answered his questions. "They be over there off Gettysburg in a spot and one of the niggas baby momma that got the shit lives in Parkside Projects."

"Word, well lil nigga, I'ma need you to show me."

"Oh, sir, you ain't even gotta worry about it. Me and my niggas gon' handle this." He said.

"Nah, I'm gon' handle it too." His voice was stern and clear.

"That's fine." Lil C knew he wasn't gonna be takin' care of business alone, so he let it drop.

My daddy roared in pure angry. "I hate this thirsty-ass city. These broke-ass pussies wanna rob another nigga. But the thing is, they will rob a nigga for a few bans that ain't shit." He threw his hand down, like he wanted to punch something.

I felt so bad. My daddy was mad, and I didn't like seeing him like that. "I'm sorry, Daddy."

He kept quiet.

"My bad, fo'real, I didn't know it was gon' happen like this. I wouldn't even had her with me if I knew." Lil C told my father.

"I understand, but she shouldn't have gone without Jazzy. She don't know how grimy this city is." He looked at me. "Now what if you had gotten killed, Jayah, then what? I would have killed everybody in this fuckin' city, man." He bellowed. "Jayah, schedule your flight. You're leaving out on the next flight." He sighed and paused. "I mean that shit. Now." He shouted.

"Yes." I heard Tee mumble.

"Daddy, what about the wedding…" I whined, dragging my words out.

He looked at me like I was dumb. "What about it! Fuck that damn wedding girl, CALL NOW!" He yelled.

I'd called for the next available flight, but they were booked until tomorrow morning. Unless I wanted to catch a casual flight, and that was something I wasn't gonna do.

That was cool with my daddy, cause that's when his goonz was arriving. He said soon as his baby girls departed, him his team was gonna kill four people. The driver for driving, the niggas that robbed and the bitch that got out to get my diamonds. They didn't know who they were fucking with. And I felt sort of sorry for them, 'cause of their stupidity. My father was a true killa, a notorious killa. He wasn't to be fucked with and had a reputation of killing someone without questioning. If the niggas knew better, they would have killed us. But I guess since they robbed, them pussy-ass niggas in Dayton think they got away with it Trick no good, not fucking with my daddy's pride and joy.

I was thinking that maybe my dad was right. I shouldn't have left with Lil C because I didn't know him. Now four people were on their way to meet death over a Dooney and a Roca Wear outfit. If I didn't leave with him, four lives could have been spared, but hey, fuck those fuck niggas. They needed to take their thirsty asses and worked for their money. Thirsty, clown-ass, pussy-ass niggas, with that thirsty-ass bitch tagging along. If she chose some diamonds over her life, more power to her ass. 'Cause I knew she knew the life we live is always so real. So she had to know that we would retaliate.

Later on that night, Jazzy wanted to go out to Club Rain. Of course, Jazzy had to ask my daddy if me and Tee could attend the party with her. It really didn't bother him for us to go, 'cause he was gon' be outside in the parking lot lurking anyway. My daddy was a smart killer. He would watch you for a couple of days and make sure shit was right before he killed. And after the coast was clear of witnesses, he'd burst inside the enemy's crib and handle business.

We arrived at the nightclub close to midnight, which was indeed jumping to be an average hood club. Girls were in the club wondering who we were as we slithered our way through the crowd. We did step in fly, so I couldn't blame them. I rocked a pair of Juicy Couture denim skinny jeans, mustard-colored fitted T with Juicy Couture embossed across in navy blue, and mustard-hued, strappy, Giuseppe Zanotti, open-toe, 3-inch ankle booties. To set the outfit off, I had on my mustard and navy accessories, oversized mustard satchel bag and huge frames, thanks to Juicy. I felt as if I should have been Juicy's runway model. Donteice had on the same thing. Hers was just white-and-purple. Tee had allowed Jazzy to wear her Juicy tracksuit, so we all were the hottest thangs in the place, with our outfit game on a hunnid.

After a few minutes of browsing the crowd, I spotted the girl. She had the nerve to have on my jewelry. Man was I hot inside, I was like a bomb getting ready to explode. And what was even worse, the bitch wore a pair of beat up Reeboks with an

Aeropostale jogging outfit. Dirty bitch.

"OH, HELL NO! Do you see that girl over there Tee?" I inquired, grabbing Tee's head.

"Which one?" She asked.

I shifted her head towards the girl's direction. "The dirty one with the Aeropostale outfit."

"Oh, yea I see her."

"Do you see my diamonds, BITCH?" I roared pissed off.

She covered her mouth. "Aww, that's the bum-ass bitch?"

"Yea, that's the bum bitch. I'm 'bout to go over there and steal on her." I said as the nigga walked passed that robbed us. What the fuck, Dayton niggas are really bold. I had to admit myself.

I immediately darted to the restroom and called my dad. He told me to have fun. He was outside and informed me that I was gonna get my shit when the club was over, bottom line. So that's exactly what I did. I had a ball. Jazzy had us at the picture booth taking a million pictures with her Bass-Boyz. Those were some natural born hood niggas. Lil C had me in front of him holding about seven bans, not giving a fuck. He had his pistol with him so he weren't fretting about anything. You would've thought we were the new and upcoming, how many damn pictures we were taking and posing like superstars. I gotta give it to the lil city, it did jump and was straight hood. I could tell a few of their folks were cool, not many though.

The parking lot was jumping as if people knew what was about to happen. My daddy instantly popped out the car with an all black Gucci hoodie on that didn't have a Gucci logo or signature print indicating that it was Gucci at all. That's how playa my daddy was. He didn't need all the extras to display that he was that nigga. His swagger did all the talking.

"Point the BITCH OUT!" My daddy wasn't playin'. I quickly pointed her out, and we walked up on her.

"Bitch, you gon' either give me my daughter shit, or I'm gon' take it off of you." He said, sternly.

"Nigga, you ain't takin' shit off me!" The girl yelled. That was, until she saw him pull out that big, long-ass pistol.

She started unsnapping shit hurriedly. "Here, it ain't even that serious. I don't want this fake-ass shit anyway." She retorted, not knowing what she really had in her possession. That was one dumb bitch.

My daddy told me to steal on her. As instructed, I did just

that and then he followed up behind me and dropped her ass. We hopped in our whips and hauled ass.

Showing up at my Aunt JoAnne's was a surprise to her, and she knew something was terribly wrong because it was real late. We told her what had happened. She was upset, but she knew that my father had to do what he had to do.

Back to the beautiful Miami felt real good to us. Especially to Tee. I immediately phoned Cheno when I landed and told him what happened. He said. "Damn, them niggas thirsty." And he was surely right about that shit.

Chapter Ten

Jay's back!

Entering my condo a couple days later, my daddy sat down enthusiastically at a job well done. He began recounting the events that took place. He informed me on how they ran into the spot, and the same four dumb-ass people were still together. He said Lil C was indeed in an intense fury and went in there like a straight gangsta maniac. He was torturing them, beating them with pistols, bats, brooms and dustpans, anything that was in his vision and reach he was beating them with. I cracked up laughing at my daddy when he was telling me the story. That nigga Lil C was really mad, beating folk up with dustpans and shit!

My daddy said Lil C signaled for all them to go to the basement. And he didn't waste any time and killed the dudes without discussion. I surmise he had a soft spot with killin' chicks, so he had the girl pleading and beseeching for her life. Shit, Big Tommy on the other hand didn't give a shit if you pissed sitting on the toilet or standing up. He shot a hole through the girl's chest. They weren't sparing nobody's life and didn't even give them a chance to explain. Lil C was right, I had to admit, he could've handled it by himself. My daddy didn't have to do nothing. He sat there and observed like the boss he was. He didn't even need his men to come down, but being cautious and prepared kept us alive.

♛ ♛ ♛ ♛ ♛ ♛ ♛ ♛ ♛ ♛ ♛ ♛ ♛ ♛ ♛ ♛ ♛

A few months had passed, and Cheno and I grew closer than ever. He cut all his girls off and was trying to get used to being a one-woman man. He explained to me that Veronica was not pregnant at all, but Tyiesha was, and that he was almost sure that the baby wasn't his. I was upset, because I hate thirsty-ass bitches that try to trap a nigga with a baby. But I really couldn't be mad at Cheno because it was way before my time.

One day, the Candace girl texted his phone while he was asleep. The text read: I miss you baby. That pissed me off, so I threw the phone at his head, with intense force I might add.

The phone landed smacked dead upside his head. That had woke him up right quick. "Why the fuck you do that?" He jerked and shifted over, massaging his head.

"Why the fuck is this Candace bitch texting your phone?"

"Jayah, you done lost your rabbit-ass mind throwing phones." He yelled.

"Like the fuck I said, why the fuck is Candace calling you, bitch?" I bellowed.

"Damn, baby, you want me to call her? I ain't talked to her since that night."

"Yea, I want you to call her you fuckin' liar." I roared.

"A'ight!" Cheno said, retrieving his cell from the bed. He dialed the number back.

She answered on the first ring. "Hello?" She voiced, seductively.

"Yeah, Candace, this Chen. Can you please stop callin' my phone? My girl don't want you calling and texting my phone."

I threw my phone at him this time. "Nigga, you don't want her calling your phone neither!" I screamed.

"Damn, Jayah, you right. Candace, just stop calling my phone, she trippin'." He hung up.

"Cheno, have you been fuckin' with that girl, be honest?" I asked, folding my arms.

"Can I be honest?" He paused for a brief moment. "When you

were in Dayton, I did fuck her once."

"I knew you did." I sucked my teeth. "You a clown, but it's cool though." I turned over on his ass, 'cause I knew I wasn't gonna do the relationship thang for long. I had to get back to business, fuck my feelings. I knew I would get over it, and I was in my prime, so I had to act like it. *Fuck niggas, get money*. Yeah, I was on some straight Notorious B.I.G. shit, but more on some Lil Kim shit: just a lil somethin' to let these muthafucka's know.

I felt him surveying the back of my body. He scooted close and placed his dick on my butt, instantly he had an erection. Cheno whispered in my ear, "I wanna taste you so bad," he began tracing his lips down my spine, applying light pecks. He gently turned me over and started kissing every inch of my body. Starting at my forehead, ending in the middle of my legs, putting his hands in my panties to see if I was wet. I was, and I knew it was about to be on. Slowly taking my panties off, he climbed on top of me and slowly entered inside my tight honey pot of sweet creams.

Once he inserted his thickness deep inside my wetness, I softly moaned. I then moaned loudly, but it wasn't the pain, it was the pleasant feeling I was experiencing. I was in sheer pleasure. I was really enjoying that moment until I started bleeding from his deep hard strokes; It was blood everywhere. *Damn, this nigga popped my cherry*. I washed up and we got right back to it. After a while, he turned me over and started hitting me from the back. I was throwing it back at him like a pro. I was feeling at my all time high. Cloud nine was my current residence. Screaming at my highest tone, I came, and I came about three times.

That's when I decided to finally return the favor. I started sucking his big black dick. I knew I'd never indulged in this sort of activity before, but I also remembered how people would say it's just like sucking on a popsicle, with more jaw gestures. I certainly knew how to do that, so I just put the head of his shaft inside my mouth. He grabbed my head and had me boppin' at a steady pace. As he was about to reach his peak his body jolted and he came. Lying down sleepy, he conveyed. "Yo, baby, I love you so much. You gon' do what gotta be done to keep your nigga."

"Boy, you crazy. I wanted to try it, so hey." I giggled.

"Man, you a beast you had me cum in like five point two seconds," Cheno said, exaggerating a bit.

"I ain't gon' play," I said in my serious grown woman tone.

School was almost over, the senior dinner dance had come and gone. It was prom season, and I didn't know who I was attending senior prom with. Of course, many people were asking at school, but I turned them all down. I really didn't want Cheno to join me, but then again I did, because hoes would be certain to be hatin'. I loved when people hated on me, so that's what I did. I invited him to carry me to my senior prom. He was pleased that I'd asked him because he didn't want to have to fuck nobody up for going with me. At least that's what he'd told me. He knew it was bound that he was and would always be psycho over me.

We attended the prom raw. I wore a long peach sparkling Versace dress that cut off of my shoulders, with an O-shape cut around my navel that revealed my beautiful tattoo pattern on my lower abdomen. Diamond-cuts rested on the front of the dress while my back was completely out. Versace peach stilettos encrusted in diamonds sat on my freshly pedicurde feet. Cheno wore an all white Versace suit with a peach vest, tie and a handkerchief that peeked from the breast pocket. Versace gators completed his look. Of course, we were the best dressed there. Tee didn't attend because she and J.P. were running into a lot of problems. I was happy that I won senior Prom Queen, and angry that Dajuan won King. Cheno was livid when we had to dance together, but he quickly got over it though.

All that senior shit was over for me. Graduation was around the corner and my birthday was here. I didn't know what I was wearing or what I was doing for the day. Since the prom, I really wasn't conversing with Cheno everyday like we used to, so he was out of my birthday plans, except where my night would end with him for some birthday sex. I felt like our relationship was probably getting old, and we just needed time apart to do us.

Sometimes, when I called him, he didn't answer, and it was vice versa with me. That was definitely a sign that we were getting tired of each other. Cheno would still bring me money and gifts though, but he wouldn't be there long at all. I already knew how dudes operated. He knew he wasn't really for the one-woman thing. Plus, we were still young, and he probably didn't know why he even tried committing. But he would avoid telling me that he wasn't ready for a serious relationship. I figured maybe he thought it'd hurt my feelings. But what he didn't know was that I was on the exact same thing. I really just wanted to be his friend and didn't understand why I started having sucka attacks anyway. That wasn't nearly my MO at all.

Time passed and my daddy still failed to tell Amelia about the baby. I knew she was gonna be pissed, but more emotionally hurt. Especially once she learned the news that he'd moved her out of the hood, purchased her all new furniture and bought her a brand new truck. Jaylah was my daddy's baby, and he loved that lil girl so much it almost scared me. Turns out her mother, Tasha, was actually really cool. I fucked with her hard and we partied hard at the clubs and everything. Donteice was going through a dilemma at this time, and I had no idea of what it was, but I knew that was the reasons I didn't want to have a man.

Everything was going great, and I was back jumpin'. I wound up hooking back up with my Cuban friend Rico, and added some new members to the team. They were cashing me out on a regular, too.

Snapped out of my thoughts by the phone, I answered. "What up wit' it?"

"Sup babe, what's good?"

It was Tasha. "Shit, when you coming?" I asked.

"I'm around the corner."

"Oh." I paused. "What cha got on, ma?"

"This Miskeen outfit."

"Okay I see you… I got on my Ed Hardy True Love shirt with the matching jeans and the Ed Hardy hat and some all white Air Max."

"Yeah, you like that Ed Hardy shit, don't you?" She laughed. "You stay off that Ed Hardy," she continued, laughing.

"You right, plus, I rarely will be caught in the club with some heels on. Girl, I got too many haters for that." I admitted. "Bitches a fuck 'round and sneak me in my stilettos."

"You silly, girl. I'm outside though."

Tasha popped out of her ride and hopped in with me. We were headed towards the hood so I could see my granny before I went out later that night. I pulled up to the hood and everybody was outside. That's just how it was in the hood, especially when the sun came out. Before I even got to get out the car, Donteice called.

"Man, where you at? These bitches following," Tee spoke quickly.

"What?" I screamed.

She took off faster than a rocket. "When I was at the mall grabbing something to wear so I could go out with you, some bitches was yapping off at the mouth and said they gon' beat my ass and all type of shit." She stopped to catch her breath and continued on. "It was about eight or nine bitches. So I just told 'em meet me tonight at the club. Some hoe was like, nah, we gon' get that ass when we leave the mall. So, when I was leaving they all rushed to their car and started following me."

"Bitch, I'm in the hood. Let them bitches follow you here and it can go down. My daddy out here with Big Tommy, so hey, if they gonna keep following you, let them." I suggested.

"Okay, I'm on my way in like 10 minutes, sis. These hatin' bitches got me fucked up. I don't even know these hoes." She huffed and puffed.

Hopping out of the car quickly, I told my peoples what was going on. Tommy simply stated. "Let them follow her here on everything. I'm shooting up the entire car." He pulled out his gun that was tucked in his waistline. "I don't give a fuck who in it man." Daddy agreed by a simple nod of the head.

"Okay. that's that. They shouldn't be following people," I said, not giving a fuck what was about to unfold.

Seeing Donteice's Dodge Magnum pull up with a Suburban tailing inches behind her. My daddy quickly pulled out his shit. Tee parked and jumped out. The girls parked directly behind her, and as they were about to step outside the car, my peoples started lighting that entire truck up with rounds. All you heard were gunshots and all you saw was firing flying through air. They already knew what it was and sped off with the quickness. We didn't know if somebody was shot or not, but truthfully, nobody cared if someone had been. From then on, my daddy knew it was time for him to give us our own protection. He gave us both 9 mm pistols. The guns were custom, a purple one that belonged to me, and a hot pink one that was Tee's. My daddy was loud and clear. "Use this on any hater that you have to. Fuck it."

"Damn, daddy. If somebody hatin', you just want us to kill 'em?" I said, jokingly.

"No, girl, but I do want y'all to protect y'all self."

"I don't even know who they were, I really don't." Tee said, recounting the entire story.

Later on that night, we hit up Level. It was a little after midnight when we arrived. That was the best way. The grand entrance was a mothafucka, especially after everyone had been there for a while. I was flooded with attention when I stepped on the scene. Folks was showing me so much love, and all night, all I heard was "Happy Birthday." All kinda people was pinning money on my shirt. Even unfamiliar niggas was pinning crispy hunnet's on me.

I danced for the first hour, then I begin perspiring and I felt my hair sweating out. That was my cue, so I went over to the bar and we all sat on the barstools, surveying the crowd. After five straight shots of Moët, I was drunk as hell. But I was truly happy that I was finally grown and ready for the real world. I knew the world had something to offer me, I just didn't know what it was.

As we continued posting at the bar laughing, cracking on folk and joking, we were approached by a brown-skinned, pretty girl, resembling me a little. She wasn't shy at all and walked straight up to us.

"Excuse me, do y'all go with J.P. and Cheno?" She asked nicely in thick New Orleans accent.

"Why, who are you?" I asked, snottily.

"Nah, it ain't nothing like that." She clarified. "I just wanted to let y'all know what was going on, because word is y'all don't even know why the girls were following you today." She stated, pointing at Donteice.

I waved my hand through the air. "So what you know? Speak on it!"

"Oh, well two of the girls fuck with Cheno and J.P." As I continued looking at her, she even acted like me a lot, talking with her hands and shit. "And the rest of them is the girls' people. One of the girls been messing with J.P. for like three years, and she heard about you and wanted to fight you."

"Really, so how do you know this?" Donteice inquired really hurting. I could tell because everything was all starting to make sense. It was finally all coming together, J.P. had started playing her because his chick found out.

"Like, five months ago, they did the same thing to me for messing with J.P., only thing that was different was that the hoes jumped the hell out of me." She giggled. "'Cause I don't

really have family down here like that, so I just let it go." She shrugged.

"Oh really," Tee chimed.

"Yeah, I just thought y'all should know." She paused, gazing over us with a slight smile and continued on. "But fo'real, them bitches is weak that's all they do is jump people. They got a lot of fat-ass bitches in their family, and they think that they can go around getting that shit off. This like their fifth time doing some hatin' shit like this. They got they issue this time though. One of the girls got shot in the arm."

"Well good, that's what they get, tryna fight over them hot, dick-ass niggas." I said. "What the fuck, their nigga's the one that tricks their money off on us." I sipped on my drink. "It ain't our fault that the lames ain't doin' something right at home."

"Girl, that's all I'm saying. I told the bitch to check her nigga, what the hell."

"Right, my cat. What do bitches be on?" I chuckled. "By the way, what's your name?"

"La'Rai."

"Oh, who you come here with?" Tee asked.

"Girl, myself." She responded. "Shit, I don't fuck with bitches. They ain't good for shit but hatin' and getting their counterfeit friendship on."

"You right. That's why we fuck with each other and now we fucks with her." Donteice said, nudging Tasha as Tasha just laughed. "Yeah, we certainly understand though. You can fuck with us, it ain't shit," Donteice said, because the girl Rai was real down to earth, and she had style.

"That's cool."

La'Rai was a cool person. She went through hurricane Katrina, so that made us have mad respect for her as an individual, 'cause she'd been through it. She was telling us how she had lost everything, and when she came down here, J.P. was the first person she met. It really wasn't nothing like that, though. He just helped her out from time to time, and after that incident, she was cool on him because she wasn't with all the drama. She didn't have anybody to help her either, so she was good on dude most certainly.

Rai told us that she was happy that she had finally met some real bitches that she could tell wasn't on no fake-ass shit. And she was glad that she came up to us, because she met some real friends and we treated her like family, too. Usually, we didn't take people in at all. But it was something in her that we adored. Maybe it was because she was the splitting image of me, just two years older. Ever since that night, she'd been rolling with us super hard.

The club was almost over; and in comes a rat pack of hatin'-ass bitches. Veronica, Tyiesha and Tamera had came out together. The hoes knew it was my birthday, so they knew I would be on some drunken shit. Drunk and all, I could hold mines; believe that. They wanted to keep walking pass, low key, tryna bump and brush up against me and shit.

"Man, this ugly bitch tryna be funny. I swear to God, she better act like she know what it is my way, 'cause I'll drop this bitch." I leaned over to whisper into Tee's ear.

"Girl, you know she just be hatin'. Let that shit go, don't let her fuck up your birthday. You know that's all she wanna do. We ain't on the bull. Not tonight." I knew Tee was right. But why fuck with me? I had never done anything to this girl, never. I had no understanding of why she didn't like me, only concluding that she had to be a certified hater. I was cute, and that bitch in my city while she was black with a face decorated in acne. Hell, they had proactive. I told her to go get her some. See, I don't have a drop of hate flowing through my blood, and I knew if she fixed that problem, maybe she'd be cute. She already had the body, all she needed was to upgrade her attire and see a dermatologist. Maybe she'd be half as bad as I was.

Listening to Tee, I let it go because it really wasn't shit. That was, until Tamera tried to play hard. Like I was soft because I didn't do nothing when she pushed up against me softly. Truth be told, it wasn't that heavy at first, but she definitely was pushing my buttons. "Tamera, one the real, while you tryna dance and shit, you bumping into me. You need to move over because next time you brush against me, we gon' have problems."

"Jig bitch, please, you ain't no fuckin' body. This bitch thinks she the shit and ain't nothing but a li'l hoe." Tamera hissed, to her friends who laughed unnecessarily loud. Entertaining her cats, she continued to dance by me and this time she threw her elbows crazily and then had the audacity to threw her shoulders into mines with force. Oh, and when she threw her shoulder in with that shove. All I knew was I had a bottle in my hand and I had cracked the bitch with the bottle dead in her skull. Instantly, she was leaking. I didn't care, cousin or not, bitch shouldn't have been trying to play me. Next thing I knew, Tee grabbed me because she knew I was gonna attack her again. We all were up and out of there with the quickness.

On my drive home, I wound up phoning my daddy, recounting the entire story. He had some words on the matter. "Fuck her, she shouldn't have been tryna show her funny looking ass off." I felt the same way. Hell, she tried to entertain her friends, but she really couldn't. So I just showed them how a real entertainer got down. I put on a great show for them hoes, too. That was one dumb broad though, because she was still hanging out tough with the bitches after that day, and they hadn't even helped her simple ass. *Dumb ass bitch*, I thought, pulling up to my place, ready to call Cheno for some late night sex.

Chapter Eleven

Graduation!

The day of my graduation was finally here. It seemed like it took an eternity. I told y'all I was a smart chick and wasn't gon' play when it came to school. I graduated with a 4.0 GPA and I was valedictorian. When they called my name to speak, I cried and was choking over my words. The audience cheered me on. It was so beautiful, they were encouraging me to keep on speaking, 'cause I was whimpering like a little two year old child. I searched the audience and saw my daddy with a huge I love you smile plastered on his face. After I thanked God, I thanked my daddy. "I would love to thank my father, Jay Carter." He rose, we exchanged smiles, I saw Amelia along the side of him taking pictures and my mother recording the ceremony. I continued showing my father my appreciation. "Without my father, I don't know where I would be now. He has been so supporting all my life, and I just wanna thank him for being the best dad ever." I blew a kiss with teary eyes. I was so emotional that day, it was crazy. Honestly, I was just happy that my dad was in the audience and actually got the chance to see me receive that important document. "I love you, Daddy."

I said to close my speech. The crowd clapped and applauded my job well done.

The greatest feeling ever was when they called my name to get that diploma, Jayah Donteea Carter. I shook the principal's hand and received my honors diploma. An arrogant feeling rushed down my spine. That was just so tight to me. Man, I was overexcited.

The graduation was over and we were ready to celebrate. I hugged and kissed cheeks what seemed like forever. Finally, everybody went outside. Me and Tee both spotted these bad-ass Range Rovers that were parked right in the front, wrapped in red ribbons. My first thought was, *damn! Whose Ranges are these? Man, shit, they are so so major. I'm kinda jealous*. My daddy laughed at the expressions that sat on our faces and he finally handed me and Tee the keys. We were feeling good, to say the least.

He had gotten me the purple one. The truck had white leather guts, the trimming was in purple with my name written in the headrest in purple suede. Purple, soft, low cut mink carpet sat comfortably on the floor. TVs was equipped in the front and in the back of my headrest. Tee had the same one. Hers was hot pink though. I knew he'd gotten the vehicles custom like that. It had to be an estimate close to 100 G's. Our cars was banging, daddy even gotten the trucks lifted and had some 26-inch chrome rims supporting the frames. We already thought we were the shit, but after that day, we really knew we were shittin'. Range Rovering on bitches, at the mere age of 18, though. Hence, from that day forth, we weren't gonna play.

My mom and her husband had purchased Tee and I both roundtrip tickets to visit a few places across the globe, for whenever we felt the need just to get away. She suggested Tahiti, Africa and Paris. We were excited especially when my mom had given us both a $100,00 shopping spree on Rodeo Drive. Unable to hold off, we went to all the places a week later and enjoyed ourselves. Tasha and Rai joined us, like they did most of the time.

Other people had gotten us lil gifts, like outfits and shoes. We appreciated everything, even if it was just a card.

Cheno attended my Graduation and sat with my family like we was a couple. It was cute, and I could tell he had mad love for me, but neither of us was ready for that ultimate commitment. We had came to a conclusion and decided that we was gon' be friends for life, no matter what. He bought me a lot of shit, tailored shit by

Coco Chanel, ranging from glasses to handbags. Also purchasing me Gucci everything, Prada, Christian Dior, Dolce & Gabbana and Marc Jacobs, too. He was like a shopping maniac, just for me. Adding at least three bra and panty sets in each designer name. He also bought me a matching Rolex, like his. See, he was still doing the matching his and her shopping, like we were together. Truth be told, I really liked it that way.

Donteice was mad because her and J.P. were really beefing and for some reason she was started to believe that she was pregnant. She had missed her period and it had just dawned on her that she hadn't had it. She was scared to tell me at first and ended up telling La'Rai. La'Rai always kept pregnancy test lingering around with her, and she gave one to Tee. Rai told her not to take it until the next day, 'cause she didn't want her to be upset on the greatest time in her life. So Tee waited.

Downtown Miami had some banging food. My mom made us reservations at a seafood restaurant. We all ate and drank to Tee and my achievement. My daddy still had to give us our last presents. He told us that he had to go get the gifts from his house, but for some reason as we were cruising down the street he bypassed his house, and went up a couple of blocks and around the corner. He came to a halt amid the street, climbed out the car and stepped on to the black pavement. He signaled for us to get out, motioning his hands. I huffed and puffed. I was furious because I was really ready to have fun and he was taking us way out of the way.

I slowly exited my new truck, and dragged my body up to him with a slight frown and I stated angrily with my arms folded tightly underneath my breasts. "Dang, Daddy, what you be on? We could have got our last gift tomorrow we is tryna stunt tonight." I pouted even harder.

"This couldn't wait, sweetie." He smiled, handing us both a small black box, one that a ring could fit in.

I whined. "Daddy… " I held the box high in the air, with one hand on my hip. "All this for a freakin' ring, or whatever is in this lil-ass box." I sucked my teeth.

"Girl, shut up, and just open up the box." He ordered.

We spoke simultaneously, noticeably mad. "Man, what. You got us another car or something?"

"Nah, y'all dumb, do them look like car keys?"

"Oh. Ohhh. OMG Daddy, this is our house? You got us a house!" I screamed, running around in circles.

"Yeah this one yours, and that one on this side of the street is yours Tee." He stood with both his arms straight out, pointing to our houses.

"Uncle Jay, you got us different houses." Tee eyes were bucked. "Dang, I thought that one was both of ours."

"Me too." I added.

"Nah, y'all my babies and y'all did good. I'm so proud of y'all." He hugged us for the hundredth time that night.

"Thanks, this is so nice Daddy, what is we gon' do with these big-ass houses?"

"Live in 'em, silly." My daddy laughed at our excitement.

"Aw, that is so nice what he did for y'all." La'Rai chimed.

"Well thank you, sweetie." My dad slightly smiled. "These are my babies. I gotta have them on some polish shit." We giggled.

"Man, I wish I had people that care about me like y'all do them."

"Oh, well, it's just a blessing from God, that's all."

"Well La'Rai, you can move in one of our condos if you want to." Tee suggested.

"Nah, that's okay. I'm really not use to people just giving me shit."

"Well, you can get use to it, because that's all people do is give to us. And now you're one of us." I scuffled through my bag, retrieving the keys to my Charger. "So, girl, take that condo, and you can have my Charger." I handed her my keys.

"Really, Jayah? Are y'all serious?" She cooed, her thick accent coming out high pitched. Scanning between the two of us, she asked again. "Fo'real though, y'all serious?"

"Girl, yeah." I smiled. "Now take that shit, and believe that this is just the beginning honey. We amazingly get it in, we're in money-making Miami girl, we don't have no other choice but to shine until the sun stop shining."

Her eyes already were filled with tears. "Well, I'ma repay y'all when I get my cake up."

"We said don't worry about it. It's a blessing from the Lord, girl." I playfully shoved her.

"I can feel that, man. I love y'all like family, man." She hugged us.

"We love you, too." Me and Tee replied in unison.

"Anything you need, just holla at me, you gotta." My daddy assured her.

"Okay." She wiped her face, even though I already knew how she operator. She would never ask my daddy for a thing.

We partied real hard that night. We wounded up taking so many drinks to the head, celebrating to the extreme. We were clownin', especially me and Rai, dancing and taking so many pictures at the booth. Donteice wasn't really up for partying that night; she was feeling sleepy and sick. Some fine ass dude approached her that night in particular. He was dark brown with a laidback swagger, but a demeanor that screamed "I'm that nigga." He was fitted simply in a light gray Roca Wear collared shirt, a pair of light gray jogging shorts and a pair of all gray Jordans retro elevens. A small, glistening chain laid flat on his chest. Dude wasn't a flamboyant kinda nigga; I could just tell. But was getting his simple attire off.

Donteice didn't really wanna holla at him because she was sick of niggas and the lies they told. I had a different mentality than Donteice. She really wasn't up for the heartbreaking thing, which her heart was equipped to love and trust, the complete opposite of mine. If she got attached to a nigga emotionally, it was always hard for her to get over them. Tee said it was something about that dude that she couldn't resist, so she just took the chance.

"What's up? What's your name, shorty?" The dude asked, taking a sit beside Tee.

"Donteice." She told him.

"So, how is it that a girl cute as you, ma, are sitting here all alone?" He asked out of curiosity.

"Being honest, I don't know, I should be at home sleep." Tee flashed a fake smile.

"So why aren't you?" He inquired.

"Because I graduated from high school today and my sister wanted to kick it." Tee replied, referring to me wanting to hang that night in particular.

"Congratulations."

"Thank you."

"So you're a youngin', huh?" The mysterious guy questioned.

"I mean, if that's what you wanna call it." Tee said. "But I'm living in a grown woman's shoes."

"Really, are you?"

"Yes, I am. I live by myself, got three whips and no kids. Well…"

"That's good." He nodded. "That's a real good look ma." The guy paused on his words. "One thing though. Why when you said you don't have any kids you said well?" He asked, not missing a beat.

"Being the honest person that I am, I think I might be pregnant." Tee stared, waiting to see his facial reaction.

His facial expression remained the same. "What makes you think that?" He asked, like they had been the best of friends.

"I missed my menstrual cycle and I been feeling sick." Tee, the dummy, answered, like they were the best of friends.

"Oh, okay, so that means you got a man?"

Tee shook her head profusely. "Nah, that don't mean that,"

"So, you don't mess with the nigga anymore that you might be pregnant by?"

"I sure don't. Is that a problem?" Tee asked with a slight attitude.

"Nah, baby, that's not a problem." He smiled, licking his lips. "I'ma grown-ass man. I don't be on that childish shit." He said, sternly.

"Really." Tee twisted her mouth up.

"Yeah, really. That nigga was before my time." He showed his pretty whites.

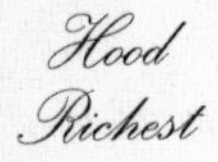

Tee blushed. "So how do you know you gon' get any time?"

"I'ma real-ass nigga, that's how I know." He voiced with confidence.

"Okay, I like that in you. What's your name?"

"Adrian, but folk call me Driano."

"Okay, Adrian." They both laughed.

"Well baby, can I call you sometimes or you call me?" Adrian asked.

"Yeah," Tee fumbled through her bag and grabbed her cell phone out. "Oh, do you have a girlfriend or anything regarding that?"

"Nah, shorty, why you ask that?"

"I just don't want to have to go through another situation like my last one." Tee sighed.

"Baby, you don't have to worry about that. I will treat you like the Queen that you are." He said, assuring her.

"Aw, that is so nice." Tee's yellow tone was flushing. "What's your number?" She stored it in her phone, along with locking her number inside his phone. "Call me once this is over." Tee told him.

"I will." Adrian said. He tapped the rose man, and he bought her all the roses that were left.

"Thanks, I appreciated it." Tee cooed, grateful for his generosity.

Adrian waved her off, implying it was nothing. "You cool. I'll holla at you later on though ma."

Donteice was overjoyed. I'd read it from across the room. She hadn't been that happy since she and J.P. were together. Tee had told me if anything escalated between the two of them, that she would most likely take it slow.

After I'd noticed Tee chitchatting with the guy, I wanted to know who this mystery man was. I slithered through the crowd as fast as I could. It was like me and Rai was in a relay race against each other, we was both hastily rushing to Tee, trying to see who her chatting buddy was.

"Girl, who was that nigga you was talking to?" Rai asked.

"Some cool nigga that just came up to me tryna holla."

I asked, being the person I am, "Do he have any money?"

Tee got mad at my question because she said she really didn't care at that moment. All she knew was he was a cool dude and she was feeling him. Not I, I didn't need a nigga in my perimeter that was broke. I even had Rai on some fuck niggas, get money type shit.

The club had let out, but me and Rai still had partying in our blood and wasn't tryna call it a night that early. We had met some niggas in the club. They wanted us to meet them at the Pancake House. That was a plus because a bitch was famished.

We requested for Tee to come along. She passed, unenthusiastically, and I could see she was depressed. She decided that she would chill in her new home instead. It was a good thing that Daddy had the whole house already furnished, decorated extravagantly and beautifully. Of course, we knew Amelia chose the style, or he hired an interior designer.

Once Tee reached her home, all she wanted to do was shower. After she was finished, she stepped out, wrapped herself in her fluffy towel and took a deep breath. She removed the pregnancy test from the package and sat on the commode. It took her a minute to pee, so she ended up turning on the faucet to help her relax. Her results confirmed that she was indeed pregnant. She was so upset. Donteice burst into tears gazing at the two lines. She didn't know what she was gonna do. Her immediate family didn't believe in abortions. She knew that J.P. would try to clown her if she told him. Her body froze up and she panicked as her brain battled a whirlwind of thoughts. The first thing that came to mind was what Jay Carter was gonna say. He told me and Tee that we had plenty of time for kids. That was a speech that he'd preached often. A billion more thoughts ran into her head as she walked to her room and put on some pajamas. She was snapped out of her trance by the shrill sound of her cell phone ringing. She answered with a shaky voice.

"Hello?"

"What's up? You made it home, huh?" Adrian asked.

Hearing his voice comforted Tee a little. "Yeah I did." Tee said, still saddened at the whole situation.

"What's wrong?" He asked, hearing the pain in her voice.

"Man, nothing." Tee's voice cracked.

"Yes it is. I know it ain't that bad though."

"Yea, it is that bad." She replied, struggling to keep her tone steady.

"Tell me. You can tell me anything," he told Tee in a sincere tone.

Tee's brain cells bounced around and decided it wasn't any need to keep it a secret. "Okay, you remember what I told you tonight in the club?" She didn't wait on him to respond. "Well, it's true."

"What, about you being pregnant?" He asked, nonchalantly.

"Yeah," Tee answered.

"Oh, okay, baby. I kinda figured that anyway 'cause you was having the symptoms," Adrian told her. "That shit don't matter to me though. I told you, I'ma real nigga, so that ain't stopping shit over here."

Tee sighed. "Man, I just can't believe this. I don't want any kids right now, especially by that loser," she exclaimed.

"Who is the dude? If you don't mind me asking."

"Some lame name Jason Patterson."

"J.P. that be with Cheno?" he asked, very concerned.

"Yeah, why you ask like that? You know him?"

"Yeah, I know that nigga. He's a sucka. Dude a straight up hater."

"Why you say that?" Tee asked, nosily.

"I'm the nigga that got his punk ass rolling. When I went to jail, he made up all this shit to my girl SaNara to fuck her." Talking about this brought back memories for Adrian. "He didn't look out for a nigga when 5-0 confiscated all my shit, nothing. But it was cool, 'cause when I got out, I got right back, so fuck 'em."

"Yeah, that sounds like something he would do. And that girl was following me from the mall one day over him."

"Yeah, that's her. I know she regret messing with him because I never gave her any problems. That was my bitch, too, but she fucked up."

"For real."

"Yeah. Every time she sees me, she is tryna get at a nigga. Tryna explain, talkin' about she was young and now she grown so can we make it work. She miss how it used to be and shit. Needless to say, she be talking bullshit. I be telling that broad I'm cool."

"Dang, that's crazy." Tee giggled at SaNara's stupidity.

"It is though." He switched back to the main subject at hand. "So, what you gon' do?"

"I don't know. I really don't."

"Well, just know that I will be here for you no matter what decision you make."

"Well, that's sweet." Tee said, blushing.

"Yeah, baby, I'ma real cool nigga, which that shit is just an honest mistake. We all make mistakes."

"You right, and I really appreciate you."

"You cool, ma."

"Well, enough about me. How old are you? Do you have any kids? What do you do in your spare time?" Tee threw the questions at him.

"I'm 27. No, I don't have any kids," his words took a halt briefly. "But I have one on the way, and I really don't do shit in my spare time." He answered.

Damn, Tee thought. *He got a baby on the way. I really ain't on that shit. I'm already pregnant.*

"So, what happened to you and your baby momma?" She inquired genuinely, only fair for her to know why they weren't together..

"Nothing." He replied, flatly.

"Boy, what you mean?" Tee asked, not happy with his answer.

"I mean what I said. Nothing, we cool." He answered very

coolly.

"How cool are y'all?" Tee asked, growing irritated.

He chuckled, "You tell me. How cool are we?"

"Umm, huh? What?" She stumbled over her words.

"Yeah, how cool are me and you?"

"Oh, boy, you so silly." Tee was relieved.

"Nah, I'm serious. You don't have to tell that nigga you pregnant or nothing. I'ma step up if you decide to have the baby."

"I wouldn't do that. I'm not that kinda of person. I would at least want him to know, and if he do take care of the baby, that's cool. If he don't, that's cool too."

"I feel that, ma. So, when you gon' tell him?"

"Soon." Tee wasn't about to wait for her to start showing and word to get around.

"Okay, just let me know what's going on, and if you don't mind, I will step up if that nigga don't."

"All that's so nice, Adrian, but you really don't have to do that."

"I want to, I really do." He sounded sure. "It is something about you that's meant, because I was just about to leave out the club, then I spotted you, and I don't even be on females, for real. I just be on getting this money and figuring out what I'm gon' do with my life."

"You're such a sweetheart, but I'm really glad you came up to me, but I really want to take everything slow." She was pleased with him, but informing him on their status.

"I truly understand, and we can take it as slow as you want, ma. I will never pressure you into anything."

"Okay, but I'm getting sleepy." Tee yawned. "So, you gonna call me in the morning?"

"Yeah, and have sweet dreams. I'ma holla at you."

"Okay, and thanks. Bye." Tee said hanging up the phone. She was happy about Adrian's reactions. He made her heart feel whole, and she knew that he would be around for a long while.

♛ ♛ ♛ ♛ ♛ ♛ ♛ ♛ ♛ ♛ ♛ ♛ ♛ ♛ ♛ ♛ ♛

Me and Rai was devouring when Tee called Rai's phone.

Rai scarf down her pancakes as she answered her phone on speaker. "Sup, babe."

"Hey. When y'all leave there, come to my house, okay?"

"Okay, I'ma tell Jayah." Rai said, closing her phone.

"Who was that? Tee?" I lifted my face from my food. "She wants us to come over there?" I asked, making sure I'd heard correctly.

"Yeah," Rai replied.

"I'm ready now," I said, gulping down my apple juice.

"Me too."

I turned towards D-Nice, who was higher than a kite. "I will certainly call you in the morning." I assured. He was a cool nigga.

"Make sure you do that." D-Nice smiled with his weed-slanted eyes.

Donteice was sleep when me and Rai arrived. Once we entered the foyer, we kicked off our shoes and dipped up the staircase. Rai slowly walked to her bed, sat on the edge and gently rubbed Tee's back. Tee's eyes opened. Rai asked. "What's wrong?"

She massaged her puffy eyes, turning over. "Hey y'all." She rose and propped her back against the headboard. "I don't know, I just can't believe this shit here, man." She whined.

I flicked on the room light switch. "Believe what Tee? What are you talking about man?" I asked, not knowing what was wrong.

Bursting out into tears, Tee started yellin. "I'm pregnant." The words took a few seconds to register in my brain. When it was clear, I started tripping.

"So, how you know this? Who you pregnant by? How far along are you? Man, what the fuck!" I exclaimed.

"I took this test." She reached over and grabbed the test that sat on the nightstand. Swaying it slightly through the air, I could see it had two clear lines. "I'm pregnant by J.P., girl, ain't that some bullshit." She huffed. "I don't know how far I am, but I know I haven't came on in two months."

"So what you gon' do?" I asked plopping down on the bed, folding my legs together.

"I don't know. What should I do?"

"I mean, that's up to you. I know I ain't having kids until I'm ready though." I said.

"Well, the baby is in there now, so just have it and fuck J.P., girl." La'Rai suggested.

"Y'all, I really don't know. However, I do know J.P. gon' try to shit on me, and I don't have time for that."

"Man, he better step up, he knows that y'all was fuckin' without a condom," Rai said.

"But still, you know ever since his bitch found out, he be on some other shit." Tee added.

"Fuck that bitch and that nigga. You know the baby wouldn't have to want for shit." I gazed into her eyes. "We got all type of niggas on deck, plus daddy and all the money we got…so fuck that nigga, Tee. Fuck the both of them muthafuckas," I said.

"I still think he should at least know," Tee wasn't about hidin' shit, even if her baby daddy was a clown-ass nigga like J.P.

"Okay, I'm 'bout to call him." I said, retrieving my phone from my Zac Posen bag.

Tee huffed and puffed, about to blow the house down as I was dialing his number. "I already know what he 'bout to say," Tee whined while I waited for J.P. to pick up.

"What up, Jayah?" J.P. asked when he answered.

I lay down on my belly, positioned my elbow in the soft thick upholstery of the bed, propped my palm on my face, and placed J.P. on speakerphone, sitting the phone by my mouth. "What up, Jason. I need to holla at you."

"About what?"

"Some important shit."

"Okay, what is it?"

"Donteice pregnant."

"Oh. fo'real?"

I couldn't tell how he was feelin'. I was pissed that this nigga could just play off news like that. "Yeah, fo'real."

"Who she pregnant by?" J.P. asked, sternly.

"J.P. Please don't get brand new. Nigga, don't play fresh."

"Nah, Jayah. That ain't me." He laughed, actin' like something about this shit funny. "Man, I fucked her like two, three months ago."

"And what the fuck that supposed to mean, nigga? She about two or three months, boy," I yelled.

"Nah, tell her I'm no fool. I know for a fact she was fucking other niggas."

"So that's how you gon' play it?"

"Shid, what you want me to say, Jayah? That its mine if it's not?"

"You can least say when the baby get here, y'all can take a mothafuckin' test." My voice grew louder. "You pussy-ass nigga.

You weak as they fuckin' come." I screamed through the phone as Tee leaned in and snatched the phone.

"Man, listen to this, it don't mean shit to me." She cleared her cracking throat. "I got this shit one hunnet and ten percent! I got niggas that's already ready to take your spot. Fuck it, I tried to give you the benefit of the doubt, but how you tryna play me is so cool. Believe me, this other nigga willing and ready to replace your spot anyhow, so don't even trip, my nigga."

"So, why y'all calling me?" He laughed, tryna shit on her.

Tee was fuming and roared through the phone. "Nigga, Jayah called you. Like I said, it ain't shit. You be careful, I'll holla." She tossed my phone to me.

Donteice tried to hide the pain. She couldn't. I knew her to well. She was really hurt. Tee sat back in sheer agony. J.P. was dead wrong. This was his second time playing Tee like she was a nothing bitch. He knew that Tee wouldn't lie on him. It was cool though, 'cause she was sure to bounce back.

A couple days had passed, and Tee and Adrian was hanging with each other hard. He told her she didn't have to worry about J.P., that he had her covered. He was gon' be the daddy, and assured his word from the bottom of his heart.

Tee dreaded having to tell my daddy, because she knew he would be hurting. After Driano decided to go with her, she finally built up the courage to tell him. I told her he was understanding and it wouldn't be nearly as bad as she thought it would be. Once she got the words out, he was slightly upset, but quickly got over it because she was grown. But, my daddy was certainly pissed at J.P. actions. He kept it cool though, because he knew exactly how youngsters could be, but he guaranteed that they would get a DNA test once the baby was born.

Chapter Twelve

Hatin'-ass people!

Time flew by quickly. Donteice was eight months pregnant with a little girl. She thanked God that she didn't run into any pregnancy complications. Her pregnancy turned out to be great and flew by. Tee shape remained the same, only gaining a few extra poinds. Tee still knew she would have to hit the gym though. She said she didn't want any extra baggage hanging from her once flat stomach.

Adrian and Tee had started dating tough, very much in love. Although he was a street nigga, he made time to spend with her. He spent the night at her house, every night. He didn't live there because they said they were still taking things slowly. Please, he just should've stayed there. Most of his things were there. I could tell they really dug each other, inside and out. To me, they were more like best friends than lovers. They were definitely that too. Their bond was invincible.

He was the main man in her life, and she was the only chick in his life. He loved her and the baby unconditionally, showing her his appreciation by purchasing all the baby's needed items, such as, the bedroom suite, including an oversized crib, basinet, car seat, stroller, swing, playpen, walker, and decorations for her entire room. It was all made by Ralph Lauren, even the pink teddy bear print all over the rooom. That left everybody else to get her material things. I wound up getting the baby about 40 to 50 designer labeled outfits, 10 pair of shoes, and diamond earrings. Daddy put $50,000 on a CD for the baby. Tee's mom and sisters bought toys, sleepwear and pampers that'd last her at least five months. Rai and Tasha added to her clothing collection. The only thing Tee had to buy was milk. She was pleased with her life, and I was happy that she was in love. Tee had stopped stressing over J.P. not being there and just appreciated what she had at that moment. It was certainly funny how the tables turned.

One day, Tee and Adrian was out enjoying dinner at Red Lobster. They happened to run into J.P. Tee recounted the entire story. J.P. had walked up to them, furious.

♛ ♛ ♛ ♛ ♛ ♛ ♛ ♛ ♛ ♛ ♛ ♛ ♛ ♛ ♛ ♛ ♛

"Man, what the fuck is this, Donteice?" J.P. approached their table, pointing in between the two.

"Excuse me?"

"Man, bitch you heard me."

Adrian, being the calm, cool and collective nigga he was, simply stated, "Bra, get away from our table 'fore it be a lot of problems."

"Pussy-ass nigga. I don't give a fuck about problems, nigga," J.P. pulled his shirt up, showcasing his gun.

"Okay, that's the game we playing, Jason?" Driano challenged.

"Yeah man, this my baby momma. I gotta holla at her. Get up, Donteice," J.P. nodded his head directing her to get up.

"So, I'm your baby momma now? really?" She rolled her eyes in the back of her head.

"Man, get your ass up," J.P. demanded.

"Dog, she ain't getting up. You done lost your mind." Driano wasn't backing down.

"Fuck you, nigga. This my bitch." He looked at Tee. "Get yo' ass up now, Tee!" J.P.'s yelling caused a commotion. "Get the fuck up." He repeated. By this time, he was going up into flames. Tee ignored him. "Get yo' ass up, Tee, and stop playing with me." He demanded, laying hands on her and grabbing her up by her shirt.

Adrian was heated now. Tee grabbed onto her stomach, like she was in pain. Driano instantly jumped up and stole J.P. in the jaw, causing him to drop instantly. Driano stood over J.P. "Nigga, this ain't your bitch. This my bitch, nigga, and I stepped up to the plate. You had your chance."

Adrian threw the money for their meal on the table, heading for the door as quickly as possible. He wasn't taking any chances of J.P. being a coward and shooting him, so they bounced.

♛ ♛ ♛ ♛ ♛ ♛ ♛ ♛ ♛ ♛ ♛ ♛ ♛ ♛ ♛ ♛ ♛

Tee sat on her sofa, pondering on the performance J.P. had put on. She couldn't believe what had happened. She was really tryna understand why he did that. *All this time had passed, and now he wanna claim my daughter? He can beat it*. Her phone interrupted her thoughts.

"Where that soft-ass nigga at?" J.P. hadn't calmed down at all.

"J.P., stop calling my fuckin' phone!" Tee yelled.

"Bitch, you ain't shit. How you gon' fuck with a nigga while you carrying my baby?" He sounded enraged.

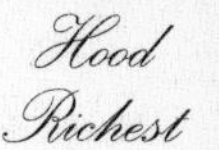

"Dig this. Fuck you, nigga. This ain't yo' baby, remember? So you can continue fuckin' with that lame bitch of yours. Bottom line," Tee finished by slamming her phone shut.

It rang right back.

"'I'm gon' kill that bitch-ass nigga, and I hope you know he only fucks with you to make me mad because I took his bitch," J.P. threatened.

Tee laughed. "So, the jealousy comes out now that I got a nigga that's higher in rankings, huh?" She laughed even harder. "Well, if that's the case, so be it, 'cause shit still moving my way my, nigga." She laughed an Eddie Murphy laugh, knowing that unstoppable laugh would make him stop calling. He hung up and didn't call back. Tee knew J.P. was on some hatin' shit and didn't bother to mention it to Adrian. She didn't want to start up any form of beef that was preventable.

♛ ♛ ♛ ♛ ♛ ♛ ♛ ♛ ♛ ♛ ♛ ♛ ♛ ♛ ♛ ♛ ♛

While Donteice was playing housewife and Tasha was being

a mother, me and Rai was taking in the pleasures life offer divas. We were out everywhere on the daily. We couldn't keep still, not missing a beat. I was still fucking with D-Nice. He was a cool cat, somebody to have fun with. Rai messed around with his cousin, T-man. Every day we were living a glamorous life. We partied like fuckin' rock stars. Bitches couldn't stand the fact that I started hanging with Rai tough. Hoes envied that. They had already knew what it was when we came through. We walked in, shutting down parties and putting bitches to shame. Niggas would show us all the attention and word was starting to float around that we were hoes and all kinda fictitious hatin' accusations. Niggas even was starting to stoop low and hate on us if we didn't give them no play, just crazy shit.

This one day, me and Rai were at the beach chilling, just lounging around in our Chanel two-piece swim gear. The one chick SaNara, the one my daddy shot at, had the audacity to approach us, questioning like we were supposed to explain or carry on a conversation with her, as if she was tight and we were lames.

"I heard Tee saying that my baby daddy is her baby daddy," SaNara said.

I giggled and threw my head back. "Nah, she ain't told nobody no shit like that, but it's true though." I glared into this bitch eyes. "But he might be spreading it because she don't even talk to him at all. She's wifed up by a real nigga that already stepped up to the plate, so she don't need 'em."

"Well, he said she be callin' him and he be hanging up on her."

"He is a mothafuckin' liar. He the one that stay calling my sister." I sighed, growing irritated by her presence. "Now that he knows another nigga 'bout to take care of his baby, he wanna call. Bottom line, yo boy salty."

"Aw, well if it's true, me and that nigga is over." She declared, like I was supposed to care.

"That's on y'all. But one thing, sis ain't gon' lie, man. That's J.P., baby, but Driano got it covered, so tell 'em don't even trip."

"What? Who? Not Adrian?" Her eyes bucked.

"Yeah man, it's the A nigga." Rai added, laughing 'cause she knew about the situation between them.

"What? Nah, he don't fuck like that." She talked while shaking her head. "I know him. He don't even be on bitches like that."

"You right." Rai scrunched up her face. "But believe me, he

don't be on bitches at all, he just be on the fam', that's it. Donteice is the only one that gets attention, so thanks. We really appreciate your fuck up." Rai clapped her hands together, ready for SaNara to jump stupid. Rai owed her an ass whooping anyway.

"Well, I'm about to call and ask him that." SaNara whipped out her phone.

"SaNara, girl, you need to find you something to do. Ain't J.P. yo' man?" I asked, rolling my eyes.

"Yeah, but A is my first love, and I'm his. So I can ask him what I feel." She retorted very fly as she dialed his number, placing him on speakerphone. I was 'bout to slap the fuck out of that bitch, but I held my composure.

"Hello?" He answered, already sounding agitated.

"Adrian, you fucks with some chick name Tee?" Already knowing her voice, he flipped out.

"Man, bitch, don't call my phone with that shit. Yeah I fuck with her. That's my bitch."

"Aw, so that's what we on. I thought you weren't going into another relationship for a while?" She spoke sadly.

"Girl, you crazy. I done meet the love of my life. Donteice. Shit happens."

"That's cool, too." SaNara said, salty as fuck.

"Bitch, I know it is cool. You lame-ass hoe, don't call my nigga phone no mo', bitch." Tee yelled, seemingly snatching the phone from his ear.

"Girl, I still owe you one anyway." SaNara said. *This bitch must have forgotten we are standing right in front of her*, I thought to myself.

I already had it in my head to steal on this bitch but Rai beat me to the punch and commenced to beatin' SaNara's ass. I was feeling so sorry for the girl. Rai was slinging her like she was a rag doll, constantly kneeing her in the face. She was doing her so dirty, I couldn't even force myself to jump in. When girl got up, she had a busted lip and two shiners. You know what that is, two big-ass black eyes. She literally dogged her, obviously taking every bit of anger that she had inside her, letting it all out on SaNara.

Rai was geeked up that she finally got to get SaNara back from when they jumped her before. Rai was jumping around as if she had just won the heavyweight champion boxing belt.

"Jayah, bra, you don't understand how happy I am I got that bitch." She jumped up and down, obviously delighted.

"Girl, you beat the fuck out of her, for real. That's crazy. I knew you could fight, but I didn't know you could bang like that." I laughed, mimicking her previous moves. "Bra, you a beast. I gotta give you your props. Let me call Tee."

Calling Tee up, she answered on the first ring, amped. "Bitch, the SaNara bitch just called Adrian phone and shit."

"I know. We were right there when she called y'all."

Tee was furious. She didn't understand why the girl was all in her business. I told her everything that SaNara was saying. Tee put her words in. "I can't wait to drop my load, 'cause I'm at that bitch pussy." Tee spoke in her determined voice.

"You ain't even got to worry babe. Rai handled that shit better than Tyson."

"What?" Tee shouted.

"Yeah. Girl, when she said she owe you one, Rai just stole on her with a hot one before I could."

"Fo' real, bitch?"

"Yes. She beat breaks off that hoe. SaNara got a busted lip and two black eyes. She was so embarrassed, 'cause everyone was out today. I know she sick wit' it." We all exploded into laughter, 'cause she had that shit comin'.

Chapter Thirteen

The baby here!

The day Tee was admitted into the hospital, she was going in for her weekly appointment. The doctor told Tee that she had dilated to six centimeters and it was definitely time to take the baby. After a million pushes and the sickening scene of blood gushing out of Tee's coochie, twelve hours and 15 minutes later, Tee's beautiful princess was born on December 23rd.

Adrian fell in love with the baby when he held her in his arms for the first time. She opened her eyes and started smiling at him, like she already knew that he was her father. He was the one who cut the umbilical cord, feeling as if she was his daughter. He was gonna certainly treat her like his very own.

Donteice was holding her daughter. She knew from that day forth, she would be the best mother ever. Now that she had her beautiful daughter, she knew what life was all about. The baby looked just like Tee, light-skinned, pretty eyes, medium, rounded nose, firm cheekbones, dimples and jet black, straight silky hair.

Tee finally decided to name her Adrianna Jaycia Dontee Williams.

Adrian was happy with his family. As the months passed,

Adrian was still there being daddy. J.P. was burnt. He found out that Tee named the baby after Adrian. J.P. tried calling on several occasions, but she never would answer and ended up getting a number switch.

J.P even went as low as calling my daddy, asking him to get him in touch with Tee. Daddy was a cool-ass nigga, but he told him it was too late. She already had a family, and she wasn't gon' mess that up for anybody. Better to leave it alone until Tee was ready for him to be in the baby's life. J.P acted as if he didn't know why she was acting like that. He was having every excuse to see his daughter, his first daughter. He had a son already by SaNara, but he wanted his little girl to protect her against the cruel world. I just laughed. Karma was a bitch, and now his ass was getting' it good.

♛ ♛ ♛ ♛ ♛ ♛ ♛ ♛ ♛ ♛ ♛ ♛ ♛ ♛ ♛ ♛ ♛

Things in my life was going well. My family was happy, I was great and we were all living life to the fullest. It was too good to keep at the same pace. I got the shock of my life when this call came through my phone.

"Hello, Jayah?"

"Yeah, who this?" I asked.

"Dis Rico. Baby, I need you to meet me. I got something to give you."

"Okay, where?"

"My shop on 96th ."

"Okay. I will be there in about 20 minutes."

After the meeting, getting home was my number-one priority. I had $750,000 in the trunk. Rico told me it was a gift for being so true. I didn't quite understand what he really meant, but I just went along with it. I had never had that much money in my possession at once. I mean, I had more than that in the bank, but it took plenty of time to accumulate that amount. I didn't know what to do. I had no idea how I was gonna put it all in my account at once. I was confused. *Damn. Think Jayah, think. Let me call my daddy.*

"What's up, baby girl?" He answered.

"Hey dad." I took a deep breath. "I got to holla at you about something. Meet me at my house."

"Okay. I'm at home. Be there in a sec," he said.

It wasn't even one minute later that my daddy walked in the

door.

"What's up, princess?"

"Man, Daddy, why the one Cuban dude gave me a huge bag of money?" I pointed down at the bag.

"Okay, Jayah. You always get money." He didn't understand what I was sayin'.

"No," I shook my head, pacing back and forth. "But no one has ever gave me seven hundred and fifty bans in my hand at once."

"That's seven hunnid and fifty stacks," his voice rose a couple levels.

"Yeah," I answered, slyly.

"You done hit a lick. Call and tell the nigga thanks," my daddy just laughed.

"Nah, fo' real, Daddy. I don't know. Something ain't right."

"Well, why did you take it?"

"I don't know."

"Girl, shut up. He must really like you. Shid, something. I done tricked off plenty of cash, but nothing in that range. Hell nah, he feeling you Jayah."

"Daddy, real talk. I haven't even been around him for more than an hour," I chimed, whining.

"Really?" My daddy asked, stunned.

"Yeah, Dad, really."

"Just call and say thanks at least." He rubbed his chin. "He don't know nothing about you, so you straight. I'll fuck that nigga up, Cuban or not, if he fuck with my baby." He smiled, making me feel secure.

As I was dialing his number, I was thinking what I would say.

"Hello?"

"Thanks Rico." I said.

"Thanks for what?"

"Don't play dumb."

"Who is this?" The voice spoke.

"So you don't know who this is?" I inquired.

A deep voice came through my phone. "This ain't even Rico I just blew his head off. He owes me $1.5 million, you might know something about that?" The deep accent asked.

I had to be quick on my feet, 'cause I knew to never fuck with them crazy Cubans. Never get on their bad side. Those folks are

psyched out for real.

"Nah, I just met him at the club a couple nights ago. He got me a dozen roses and I thought it was nice, so I decided to call and say thanks," I said, catching my breath quietly.

"All that's nice, and I'm sure he knows you appreciate it," the man said, laughing crazily.

"Well, bye." I was tryna sound not scared.

"Hey wait, you sure you don't know where my money could be?"

"Nah, I don't know what you talkin' about." I hung up feeling bad about what happened to Rico, but I knew that he should have played the game right.

My dad was looking at me the whole time. He was looking so confused. I let him know I was scared about the whole thing, but he told me it was cool. I ran into some money that no one knew about, meaning nobody would ever find out that I had it. He said Rico must have gotten caught up into some shit and didn't have anyone to give the money to, so he gave it to me. He must have knew he was gonna die. I guess, the game is crazy and I didn't want no parts in the heavy roles. That day was one of the scariest days, but after that for some reason it made me stronger. How could I be scared of something that's gon' happen regardless. Hell, we all live to die.

Still not knowing where to place the money, I just stashed some in my basement, stored some in the attic, and I put most in the safe in my bedroom. I decided to put the money in the back of my mind.

I felt like being on the scene with my girls that night. So I picked up my phone to dial Rai's number. On the hundredth ring, she finally answered out of breath.

"Hel…hello?" She answered, heavily.

"Damn, hoe, what were you doing?"

"Just got finish fuckin'."

"Okay, I didn't need to know all that."

"You asked," Rai giggled.

"Shut up, man. I'm bored. You tryna hit the club?" I asked.

"Hell yeah, why wouldn't I?"

We both laughed.

"Girl, I'm tryna be in there. Plus we ain't been out in a while." I was really feelin' hangin' with Rai.

"I know. Call and ask Tee do she wanna go, and I'ma call and ask Tash." Rai said.

"I'm just gon' call on three way." Within seconds, I had us all on the phone discussing if Tee was going or not.

"Tee, why? Pleease. You ain't been out in centuries." Rai implored.

"You right, but I don't think Adrian want me all in the club."

I sucked my teeth. "I'm 'bout to ask him for you," I said, hanging up to call him on my cell.

"Whud up?" Driano answered.

"Sup babe, you good?" I asked.

"Yeah, I'm cool. And you?"

"I'm like Tony the tiger, grrrreat!" I giggled.

He chuckled. "You silly, girl. What up though?"

"I was just wondering if Tee could go to Club Paradise grand opening with us tonight."

"Shid, if she wants to. Why you asking me, ask Tee!" Driano was laughing.

"That's her. She acting like you don't want her to go out." I put him on speakerphone.

"Nah, shit, she can go. I didn't think she was waiting on my approval. She could've been went. That's on her. I can't tell her where to go and she's a grown-ass woman, like I'm a grown-ass man." He sounded very amused with the idea of giving Tee permission to do anything.

"Okay, thanks. She going with us." I told him.

"A'ight. I might slide through there."

After hanging up the phone with Adrian, we all exploded into laughter, said our goodbyes and rushed off the phone to get ready for an incredible ladies night out.

Tee definitely felt it was time for a special club appearance, so people could know that ain't shit changed after the baby. She still had it going on. Tee had got a fresh haircut, the sloped bob, short on one side, long on the other. Her new looked allowed her facial features to show, and she looked even better than before. Tee was determined to get sexy that night. She rocked this mean, colorful, satin, Dior, short plunging dress that barely reached the middle of her thighs. That was one bad dress. It was royal blue, hot pink, yellow and a pretty bright green with big purple specks decorating the dress. Tee stepped in a pair of YSL purple thigh-high boots to set it off. Silver dangly earrings set in her ears, two wooden, purple bangles hung from her wrist and a silver and purple necklace rested on her chest.

Rai was lookin' cute, too. She wore a pair of Akademik skimpy red denim shorts, a fitted white baby T-shirt that drove the designer name across the front in red and gold glittery lettering. She decorated herself in gold accessories and her gold pumps. Her hair laid in a curly body wrap. Tasha had on something similar to Rai, except hers was Miskeen, and she had on yellow instead of red. Her hair was cut in a cute short bob, which fitted her perfectly. She was a dark brown color, with sex appeal, but she still had the hood, hardcore look to her, that wasn't going anywhere.

I wore a pair of Rock & Republic, light, faded skinny jeans, a white and grape-colored Rock & Republic fitted T-shirt, patent leather, Prada, open-toe ankle stilettos, and a huge patent leather Prada bag. Diamond hoops dangled from my ears, while a diamond bracelet adorned my wrist. My beautician straightened my hair. I looked too cute that night.

Club Paradise was packed and had the Island theme going. For once, it was more niggas than chicks. It seemed like everywhere I turned it was a slew of them. I guess the bitches was waiting for next weekend, 'cause the first was next Saturday. When we walked in the club, it was late, just how we liked it. All eyes were on us. We were only the hottest bitches in the club. Bitches was staring so hard their fucking heads was about to pop off. It was funny to me, though. I loved when bitches stared. It's letting me know I'm doing something right.

Spotting Cheno at the bar, I acted as if I didn't see a thang. Me and my comrades walked to the bar and ordered a drink. As we sauntered over in his direction, he was bobbin' his head to the hip hop beats, receiving his bottle of Dom P from the bartender. He gently turned his head and spotted me.

"Hey, babe. You looking good," he greeted me with a hug.

"Well thanks. You know I don't do too much."

"So, who you come here with?"

"You know, nigga. My goonz, who else?" I said, pointing to my friends.

"You crazy, girl." He shook his head at me.

"Am I really?" I voiced, sexily.

"Yeah. What y'all drinking on? I got y'all." He paused. "I know what you want, Jayah. A Long Island."

"Shid. Get me a double of that Goose." Tasha said.

"Me too!" Rai added.

"So, what you drinking on Miss Tee?"

"Nothing. I'm good." She turned, slowly bobbing her head.

Cheno cocked his head back. "Damn. That's how you gon' play a nigga? You looking nice. Damn, you cool?"

"Yeah, I'm straight." She sounded, nonchalantly.

"Damn. You don't fuck with me, huh?"

"It ain't nothing like that. You still my nigga. You good?" She asked, not tryna be rude. She knew he hadn't did anything to her.

"Yeah. I'm just getting this money." He nodded, agreeing with himself. "That's all I'm tryna do."

"That's what's up," Tee answered, bein' polite.

"How that baby doing? And how old is she?"

"Like Tony man, she's grrrreat. She three months."

He laughed. "Girl, you and Jayah are silly for that shit."

"Nah, I'm for real." Tee flashed a half-smile.

"Oh, okay then. I'm glad to hear that. I saw a picture of her and she pretty as fuck, with that pretty hair and them deep dimples."

Tee patted her face smugly. "Yeah, you know she get her beauty from her momma."

"Yeah, she do look like you. But I can't stunt, she look like J.P., too," Chen stated.

"Who!?"

"Stop playing, Tee." Cheno put his serious on.

"For real, who? J.P.? Ummm, never heard of the dude." Tee turned around, disappearing into the crowd, finding her way to the dance floor.

Cheno turned to me. "Damn. She ain't on that shit for real, huh?"

"Nigga, I told you. The A nigga got her, she straight she don't need him at all." I informed him flat out. "You should just say that that's Driano daughter."

"I guess their crazy," Cheno said as some project bitch approached him.

"Damn, baby. Why you haven't called me? I been tryna fuck with you." She sounded off trying to be seductive. I laughed, finding the girl amusing.

I knew he was a bit embarrassed for me to see her, 'cause I'ma diva and that bitch was simply not. "Man, girl. I will get with you later. I'm talking," he said, cockily.

"Okay baby," she said, walking away, tryna stick her butt out. It was so funny, we were rolling.

I doubled over into laughter. I could barely get the words off my tongue. "Hell nah." I was dying. "You need to get yo bitch on, 'cause that bitch down bad." I continued laughing, gasping for air.

"Fuck you, Jayah," he shot playfully.

That was a funny nigga. We had gotten cool over the course of a few months. We were still fucking, but knew our limits. It wasn't any sucka attack performances occurring, none of that extra, lame bitches acts.

I was propped up on the barstool, sipping on my Long Island Ice Tea, just observing the crowd. I wasn't really on any niggas for real. I was tryna have a good time and chill for a change. Rai had started chatting to some dude. I was profiling her flirtatious movements when my eyes shifted and got my attention of J.P. slipping his way through the crowd. OMG. This 'bout to be some crazy shit.

J.P. didn't hesitate and walked straight up to Donteice as soon as he caught a glimpse of her. I was relieved and surprised. He didn't act a fool like I thought he would. Tee was looking at him like he was a fool, she wasn't tryna hear any bullshit. I could hear what she was sayin', that she would think about him seeing his daughter before she strutted off. He didn't bother her anymore after that. I guess he was respecting her mind and couldn't do nothing but feel where she was coming from.

As the night moved into time, I talked to folk that passed me and continued sipping on my drink. Rai wound up approaching me and asked if I wanna holla the friend of her dude, 'cause he was feeling me. I really wasn't up to it. I was tryna have a good time with my girls, especially Tee, because she really didn't get out much. But Rai kept imploring and pleading. "Okay." I had her tell him I would holla at him after the club, 'cause at that very moment, I was chillin'. Tired of posting up at the bar, I took my last sip and moseyed my way to the picture booth, and there Cheno was. I knew he was gonna want me to take a picture with him. Of course, I was right. He had me take at the least, 20 flicks with him. Everybody was looking, tryna see who Cheno was taking pictures with, or who I was taking one with. It was crazy. Bitches started to look at me funny and everything. I wasn't on it, though, long as everybody stayed in their place, we were greatly good. I wasn't on fighting no bitch that night.

Around two, Driano came strolling through, looking a'ight on some real shit. He was a handsome nigga, but I didn't look at him in that way, so he was just alright and cool. He had crazy-ass P with him. P was a cocky-ass nigga and wasn't to be fucked with. That nigga was psyched the fuck out. Adrian was his right-hand man, so if anybody fucked with A or tried to play him, P would surely make a nigga feel somethin'. That's the main reason why I thought J.P. didn't step too far out of line, because he knew P was notorious, just as crazy as Big Tommy.

"Sup Jayah?" Driano greeted me and bent down to give me a hug.

"Hey Driano, you a'ight?" I said, returning the hug.

"Yeah," he nodded. "Where my baby? I wanna take some pictures with her?"

"Shid, she on the dance floor with Rai and Tash." I pointed in their direction.

"Okay." I watched him move through the crowd and grab Tee so they could take some photos.

While they were at the booth, I seen was SaNara glaring at him hard, arms folded. That broad was burnt. You could read it in her eyes. She was salty because she knew she'd fucked up a good thing. He was really every hood girl's dream. He was caked all the way up. He possessed a mean swagger, he was respectful and not a sucka,insecure nigga who always accused his bitch of shit. He took his woman places, and he did it often. He made sure Tee and him had fun together. What else could a bitch want in a nigga? Shid, dude was a'ight, and SaNara didn't like that another bitch was getting what she used to get.

"Baby, you looking and smelling good," a familiar voice hissed in my ear.

I turned around. It was D-Nice. I smiled.

"What up?" D-Nice asked, greeting me with a hug.

"Shit. Just chillin' with my girls."

"I haven't heard from you in a few days," he said, playfully.

"I been chillin'. That's it."

"Well, I was wondering if you and Rai wanted to go have fun somewhere this weekend."

"I'ma ask her to see if she do, and I will just call yo' phone tomorrow."

"That's cool, just holla at me, babe."

"Fo'sho." We hugged again and went our separate ways.

As we were walking out the club, all we saw was a nigga and

a bitch fighting. We was wondering what lame-ass clowns it was. Not a big surprise, it was J.P. and SaNara. If only they knew how dumb they looked. They were going hard though. He was fighting her like she was a nigga, but she wasn't giving up on that shit. She continued running back up, swinging and screaming how J.P. had her fucked up, that he wasn't about to keep playing her. She was dumb as hell, embarrassing herself like that. If that was me he would have been history a long-ass time ago. Fuck that. He had so many bitches, it was ridiculous. Word that was floating around was she mad because he was in the club all up on some chick. SaNara walked up and stole on her. I couldn't help what I was thinking about the whole thing. *Why have a sucka attack and the shit gonna still happen? Just get what you can get out of the nigga and bounce*.

That nonsense wasn't appealing to me, I hopped in my Range Rover, Out of nowhere, Cheno popped up at my window.

"Damn, babe. I'm going home with you?" he inquired, grabbing all on me from outside the car.

"Nah, we ain't gon' do nothing like that, my nigga." I pushed his hands playfully off me.

"Why not, babe?" He asked, I could tell he was a bit drunk.

"I'm going somewhere with Rai." I said, putting my head down in my chest as if I was being sneaky.

"Okay. Don't be giving my pussy away." Cheno said. We both started laughing.

"Boy, you crazy." I chuckled.

Bitches were salty. Me and Tee started stuntin' in our whips and the niggas was really on us super tough, tryna see who the bad bitches were in the candy Rovers. I was crackin' up. My music was blastin' all the way up, allowing a funky fresh mix to blare out of my alpine system. I saw the sideline hoes hatin' as they were climbing into their mink mink rides.

While we were exiting the parking lot, Rai's cell phone rang. It was an out of town area code.

Rai answered. "Who is this?" Placing dude on speaker so I could hear.

"This Loyal."

"Oh, what up with it?" She mouthed to me that it was the Ed Hardy dude from earlier.

He laughed. "Damn, baby. What up tonight with you and me and yo' cat and my nigga?" He tried sliding that in.

"What you mean?" Rai asked.

"Shid, me and my nigga tryna kick it with y'all while down here."

"Oh, that's cool, but we ain't yo' average type bitch. We just don't kick it with any kind of nigga and fuck them." Raid was pretty blunt, especially with niggas.

"Shid, I didn't say that. But that would be nice," he chuckled.

"Nah, dude, we don't get down like that." Rai spat.

"I already know. Just from y'all swagger, I know it take a lil time and money spent." He spewed out my favorite words.

"And you right my nigga." Rai replied, now laughing.

"I know, but that ain't nothing. Money ain't a problem this way."

"That's what's up, 'cause we don't fuck with broke or stingy niggas." She told him how it was.

"Okay, so shid. I got a stack for you," he replied, showing his excitement.

"A stack. A stack of what, nigga?" Rai inquired, concerned.

He laughed, as if he was throwing around big money. "Yeah, man. That's how we do it, yo. I'm that nigga." Rai and I were both laughing at his dumb ass.

"I hope you not talking about a G, nigga." Rai giggled, insulted. "'Cause we got that in our pocket right now. That ain't shit. What? You thought I was playing? We not the average bitch, boy."

Feeling dumb, he tried again. "Shid, I know that ain't shit. I was just seeing where y'all minds was at. So what up? We ain't tryna fuck y'all, we just wanna kick it." He sounded sincere.

"That's cool, too."

"So, what y'all doing tonight?" Loyal asked.

"Shit, the bed, nigga. That's about it."

"Aw, okay. So what, y'all gon' kick it with us tomorrow?"

"Yeah. Just call my phone in the morning."

"I will." He assured.

Chapter Fourteen

Dumb and Dumb-ass!

These were some dumb-ass niggas, literally. Clown-ass niggas been watching too many damn gangsta movies, not realizing that the ending of gangster movies usually ends in death. Dumb fucks.

The next day, Loyal and his friend Dre had met us at the Aventura Mall. That was right timing because I was going to light shop anyway. They ended up purchasing us a few outfits and a pair of tennis shoes. I wasn't tripping over the little shit they got us though, my whole intentions were to grab a couple Bebe and Juicy tracksuits, and that's what I got, keeping my few hundreds in my pocket.

The one nigga had gotten on some reckless shit after awhile. He got to yapping off at the mouth, too damn much. Talking about if we set some niggas up around our way, they would give us 20 percent of their earnings. He had to be dumber than a box of bricks, because he did really think I would do such thing for his ass. And plus, that's that thirsty-ass shit. I hate jackboys with sheer passion. It goes to show that their hustle hand was feeble.

These are some dumb-ass niggas. If they're some jackboys,

they should be wondering where I get my shit from. 'Cause last night I was in the Range, and today I'm in the Benz. Most robbery niggas was so dumb. If they had an ounce of common sense they would have came at us on some G shit, and got to finding out important facts. I was glad they were dumb and couldn't wait to dip on their asses. Then I heard them sing the wrong tune. This muthafucka mentioned the wrong name.

"For real y'all, I'm down here to get this baller name Jay Carter. Word is he got Miami on lock, and everything that's rolling around the city is his." Me and Rai just looked at him and began laughing. We knew what it was, dude was certainly clowning. He didn't even know he was right in front of Jay Carter's pride and joy.

"What's funny? Y'all know of the nigga?" He asked, seriously.

"Yeah, we know him. He do got Miami on lock, and I'ma do you a big favor." I smiled and nodded.

"What's that?"

"Shid. I'ma let you get to know the nigga very well."

Loyal had on this dumb-ass grin. "Okay, you know him like that?"

"Yeah, real good." I began. "I'ma tell you where his spot at and you can just go in. I'ma make sure nobody is in there." I spoke trying my hardest not to burst out in laughter.

Happy as fuck, the nigga started makin' plans. "Damn. Thanks, I knew y'all was just the people that'd get me to that nigga's money."

"Yeah man, but we gon need our money up front," I said, tryna make some extra cash. Shit, you can never have too much dough. Right!

"We gon' give y'all money for telling us the shit, after we get the money though."

"Nah," I shook my head profusely. "Last time, we got played on something a lil similar to this." I had no problem lying my ass off to these clown-ass niggas.

"Oh, okay. Shid, I'ma give y'all about 15 bans a piece first. Then, after we get what's in there, we gon' give y'all a nice piece of change." Loyal smiled.

"That's cool. So, when y'all gon give us the money?" Rai added, knowing that this was the quickest money that we ever ran into.

"Shid." He voiced in excitement. "Today, we got it at our hotel. We just hit some niggas last night," dude burbled, hyped.

"Okay, get that. And we will handle business. Nobody will never know." I winked and kissed his forehead. It was the kiss of death, 'cause I already knew it was coming. Them fools brought that on themselves. Fuck 'em.

"Nah, thank y'all. 'Cause I know we gon' make at least a half million." This jackboy was so fuckin' eager.

Soon as we parted from them niggas I rushed to the car and got my daddy on the line.

"Sup Jayah cakes?" My daddy answered on the first ring.

I laughed. "Man, Daddy. You ain't gon' believe this unbelievable shit here, real talk."

"Speak on it."

"Me and Rai met these clowns last night at the new club, right?"

"Right. I'm with you."

"And they took us to the mall. We got a couple outfits and a pair of shoes." I couldn't help but laugh again. "So, they just got straight to the point. Like, I'ma need y'all to set some niggas up for me."

"What?" My daddy yelled.

"Daddy, let me finish, 'cause that ain't even the funny part. He gon' say I wanna get this big time Miami baller name Jay Carter."

He laughed. "Hell nah! I know he didn't, baby girl."

"Yes, he did. And I told him I could set that up right now, once he go get me some cash for doing it."

Cracking up, he said. "They 'bout to go get you some money to kill themselves?"

"Right! Daddy, these niggas dumb as hell." I shook my head at their stupidity.

"Yeah, they are some dumb young niggas. Send the niggas to the spot where Big Tommy at on 65th street."

"And you know it. I'm coming." I wanted them to see me in the flesh.

"Nah you don't need to. That shit gon' be unhealthy for you." He was joking and serious at the same time.

"Okay, I'ma call when they on their way."

"Okay cakes, love you."

"Love you more."

"Nope, I love you more." He said hanging up 'cause he knew we would go all day on that.

Later on that night, dude told me and Rai to meet him at his hotel. We went up there. As planned, he gave Rai and I the money as promised, and we gave him the directions then we all departed. I called my daddy up and told him that they were on their merry little way. It was on from that point. My daddy and insane-ass Tommy were awaiting their arrival. They even called Driano to come up there just to make sure they had enough people just in case they brought somebody else with them. Crazy P went along also. I felt so sorry for the lames. It was surely going to be a closed casket. That's if they found the remains.

♛ ♛ ♛ ♛ ♛ ♛ ♛ ♛ ♛ ♛ ♛ ♛ ♛ ♛ ♛ ♛ ♛

Dre and Loyal walked in through the back door. I told them it would be unlocked. He went straight into the back room, like I instructed, and my daddy and them were so silly. They had about 50 bricks on the bed with a bag full of money. My daddy did that to get them hyped up so they could think shit was gliding smoothly. When they were walking out the room, it was a AK pointed at their skulls. I know at that moment, their hearts jumped out of their chests. It was Crazy P and Big Tommy that was aiming the guns. Driano and my daddy came from the living room.

"Where you think you going with my shit?" My daddy questioned, menacingly.

"Damn, man. We caught, we caught. It was his idea." Dre said, literally pissing on himself.

"Yeaahhh niggas." My daddy slowly nodded. "Y'all caught red handed. You know y'all should have been thinking about it before y'all thought about robbing me. I'm that fuckin' nigga," Daddy said, hitting Loyal with the butt of the gun in his face.

"C'mon man, I'm sorry. I didn't know this was yo' shit, Jay Carter." Loyal screamed in pain.

"Aw, you didn't." Daddy paused. "I could have sworn my daughter said you was looking for me." He pointed his finger into his chest.

Looking confused, Loyal spoke up. "What are you talking about?"

"You know, nigga." Daddy said, striking him again with the gun. "It's dumb-ass niggas like you that make me the way I am now. You fuckin' fool, that was my daughter who you was tryna get to set me up."

Looking dumbfounded, Dre chimed in. "I knew this was too good to be true. I knew them bitches weren't shit." He shook his head.

"Nah, my baby is better than the shit, pussy. She owns a five-bedroom home, four bathrooms and a swimming pool in the backyard, nigga." He sighed in frustration. "And she got a Benz, a Range Rover and money in the bank at 18, lil nigga. Name one hood chick doing better than her." He didn't let him answer. "Not one bitch. My baby AIN'T LACKING IN SHIT!" Daddy screamed, bragging.

"Man, fuck all you pussy-ass niggas. And just for the record, yo' daughters give some good head." Loyal tried playing hard his last minutes of life.

My daddy laughed. "And for the record, we gon' take a vacation with that lil change you gave my peeps."

P huffed, 'cause he was smelling blood. "Man, cut all the small talking. Let me kill these niggas." Crazy P insisted.

My daddy laughed. "Kill 'em P."

Chapter Fifteen

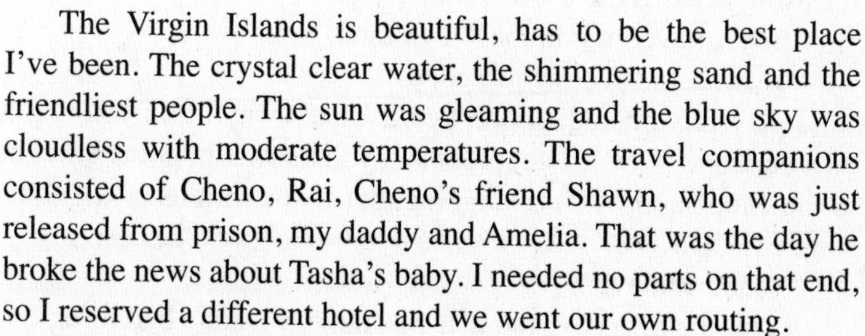

Week vacation!

The Virgin Islands is beautiful, has to be the best place I've been. The crystal clear water, the shimmering sand and the friendliest people. The sun was gleaming and the blue sky was cloudless with moderate temperatures. The travel companions consisted of Cheno, Rai, Cheno's friend Shawn, who was just released from prison, my daddy and Amelia. That was the day he broke the news about Tasha's baby. I needed no parts on that end, so I reserved a different hotel and we went our own routing.

Cheno and Shawn were some straight hood niggas. They were acting so goofy, I already knew they were gonna make it fun, even if we were in the most boring place in the universe. They were certain to get it jumping. They were non-stop grillin', being that Shawn acted as he could have been a paid comedian. He had us laughing the entire duration, and we did everything. Scuba diving the first day, and we was acting a fool while performing the sport. The second day was even better. We went jet skiing and sky diving. That was a great experience, even though me and Rai were scared shitless. That third day was when we did our shopping thang, me and Rai dug in their pockets deep.

"Damn, Rai. You too damn expensive," Shawn said, jokingly.

"You right, nigga." She giggled. "I don't even think Bill Gates can afford me." We burst out laughing, 'cause Shawn threw out 50 jokes following her statement.

I had a blast, especially the fourth day. Me and Cheno made love on the beach. That was the best sex that we ever had. We were doing some crazy-ass shit. That nigga had me in all sorts of positions. All the while we were making love, he kept saying, "Jayah, I love you man."

"I love you too Chen," I replied with a moan.

"Nah, I love you, real talk, more than anything, though." He would stop and gaze into my eyes.

"I love you too baby. I really do." We both knew that we shouldn't have been exchanging those love words. As friends only, our feelings should have not been that deep. He was reaching his peak. "This my pussy, man, who pussy is this, Jayah?"

I replied, screaming. "Yours Chen, yours baby."

He bit down on his bottom lip, pounding my shit. "I know it's mine, and its gon' be mine forever." He stroked harder and faster. "I looovvee you Jayah."He groaned, and collapsed on top of me, releasing his kids off. I was fuming.

"Boy, did you nut in me?" I chimed.

"Yeah, it was feeling too good."

I playfully pouted. "I don't care. That's why I told you to put on a condom. Now if I get pregnant, you know I'm going straight to the chop shop." I said laughing, but I was serious as the third stage of AIDS.

"Yeah, whatever."

It was the fifth day, and that was the day Daddy had informed his wife on his secret. I heard the whole story. Now Amelia, I love her to death, but she is one crazy and foolish lady. I understood where my mother was coming from now.

In the hotel suite, he walked over to her and asked her to seat up.

"Baby, what I'm about to tell you is serious." He began. "But I apologize for it deeply, and if you wanna divorce me, I completely understand, but I hope you can just find it in your heart to forgive me," he lowered his head as he spoke.

"What now, Jay, what?" She huffed, already expecting the

worst.

He let out a long sigh. "A few years ago, I was in the hood and it was some chick name Tasha that I was fuckin' with. She told me she was pregnant with my baby."

"Okay."

"And I gave her the money for an abortion." He paused. "But she didn't get it."

"So, what are you tryna tell me Jay?" She exclaimed.

"I'm saying I got a daughter that's one years old."

"What, Jay, what!?" Amelia screamed, tears falling from her face.

Gently grabbing on her, he reiterated. "I'm sorry, baby. I didn't mean for this to happen, I really didn't."

"I want you to know that you are a clown Jay." She shook her head in disappointment. "You are a true clown, having me in the dark for a year Jay. What type of shit is this, man?" She rose and walked to stare outside the window.

"I know. I just didn't know how you would react."

"Jay, you know if you would have told me, that would have been it," she mumbled. "But now, since it took a year to let me know," she paused, sniffling. "Now I'm pissed. I'm very hurt from this ordeal, I really am." Tears streamed down both sides of her cheeks.

"I understand, baby, but I can't take it back now. So, can you forgive me?"

"Jay, did you get a test?" She asked.

"Nah, but look." He pulled out a picture of me and the baby.

She grabbed the picture with a mug, then her facial expression switched. "Damn, she looks just like Jayah," she sounded stunned.

"I know, that's why I couldn't deny her."

She gaped at my dad. "She looks like y'all twin." She nodded. "But I still want a test, just because looks are deceiving." She spoke slowly.

"I know, and we can get a test." He exhaled. "Amelia, do you forgive me? Baby, that's all I want you to do is forgive me, and it won't happen again. Baby, I promise." My daddy wasn't shit. Love sure has the weakness come out of a nigga.

"Of course I do. Do you still mess with the girl?" She gazed into his eyes.

"Not at all." He shook his head. "But!"

"But what?" She voiced, sadly.

"Nah, I don't fuck with her like that. But I do give her money and I moved her out the hood and bought her a new truck because my lil girl can't live like that if I got anything to do with it," he spoke, truthfully.

"Oh, well I guess I understand. But you got a lot more making up to do." Amelia said and walked out the door.

I told y'all, she love that nigga dirty boxers. Couldn't be Jayah Carter allowing a nigga to have a baby on me, and just forgive so easily.

♛ ♛ ♛ ♛ ♛ ♛ ♛ ♛ ♛ ♛ ♛ ♛ ♛ ♛ ♛ ♛ ♛

When we returned back home, shit was chaotic. There was eight indictments out on the local big time drug dealers, including Adrian, Big Tommy, Crazy P and my daddy, of course. We didn't know what the fuck happened that fast in a week. Soon as we touched down, Tee was at the airport with Booboo Kiddie, the baby, waiting for us to exit our flight. We knew something was wrong. Her eyes were puffy, like she had been crying the whole time we were gone. We were staring at her, asking what was wrong. She couldn't even let the words escape her mouth. After five minutes, we finally calmed her down and she carried out the happening. "They got Big Tommy, Crazy and Adrian." She cried, frantically. "And they lookin' for you, Unk."

"What the fuck you mean, Tee? What happen, what happened?" My daddy calmly inquired.

"I don't know. All I know is when me and A was coming out the mall a car surrounded us and they grabbed Driano, and started reading him his rights, talking 'bout they got him on some shit, and they looking for you and Big Tommy." She cried, recklessly. "They had gotten Crazy P already." Tee cried hysterically, irking my last nerve. She was taking too long to explain the occurrences, all the weeping she was doing. I was scared to death, hoping that they didn't find out about Loyal and Dre.

"Daddy, you think they know?" I asked, nervously.

"Nah, I think this something 'bout some dope shit, but they ain't got shit on me. I'm careful. You know I ain't even worried about it." My dad said quite frankly.

"Oh, okay so what you 'bout to do?" I asked.

"Shid, go down there turn myself in, 'cause they can't book

me on shit. They ain't caught me slipping." He nodded, agreeing with himself. "Believe that, and if they keep me, just bail me out." He shrugged like he didn't have a care in the world. "And see if the three of them got bonds. If so, have Amelia go down there to bail 'em out."

"Okay," I responded. He called his lawyer to meet him downtown at the city jail.

That didn't go how we thought. They booked my daddy in on four charges. When I found that out I couldn't do nothing, tears instantly fell from my face and I started to panic. *It's all over. Just to make me have a good life, my daddy risk his life to make shit better for his family.* I was snapped out of my deep thoughts by the piercing sound of Amelia's phone. She quickly answered and placed my father's lawyer on speakerphone.

"Hello Mrs. Carter. It's not looking good. They are trying to figure out where all the cars and houses come from." My heart dropped to my toes. I knew it was over from that point. "The clothing business that you own can't account for all of your expenses. One agent was talking about bringing you and Jayah in for questioning."

I interjected. "What the fuck you mean,? They ain't never seen me with shit. What the fuck! One thing about it, they can't get me on shit."

"Miss, calm down. I'm gonna try my hardest to have the charges dropped. You will need to come down for questioning tomorrow."

"Man, they ain't got to talk to me about shit." I screamed. "If they want me, they better come get me. I know for a fact that I ain't going down there." I said, rudely.

"Listen, it will be better if you cooperate. If you choose not to appear voluntarily, they will arrest you as well."

"Fuck them. They ain't got shit on me, like I said."

"Even so, you will be much beter off if you cooperate early," the lawyer said, polite but firm.

Amelia stated, angrily. "They don't have shit on us, but yes, we will be there in the morning." She slammed her phone shut, enraged.

"What the fuck we gon' do?" I spoke, worriedly. "Ain't none of our things counted for, fuck." I whined, tears streaming down my cheeks. "I knew this shit was gon' happen. I need to go get that money out the house before they try to go search my house."

"What money?" Amelia asked, anxiously.

"This one Cuban I was messing with gave me almost eight hunnid bans and it's in my house." I replied, uneasily.

"Jayah, he just gave it to you in cash?"

"Yeah, he did. To make a long story short, some shit was about to hit the fan. Before the money went sour, he just gave it to me. I didn't know where to put it, so I stored it in my house."

Amelia sighed, rubbing her temple. "You should have put it in the business account, girl." She spoke, irritated." What the hell, your daddy never told you about putting large sums of money in one of the business accounts? You could have put it in the nursing homes account. You know, the ones my mom owned before she passed away and left it to me. That brings in about that much every month once everything is paid. And some people pay in cash money, that's why we make large cash deposits from the drug money unworriedly." I was starting to breathe regularly. "So, believe me everything we own is counted for," she assured me.

I had forgotten all about their family business. Amelia never lied, that place did bring in a nice amount of cash. It wasn't an average nursing home, either. It was one for the rich and famous. It was about three in the Florida area that she owned herself, and she had other people running them. I should have placed the money in the account, but I wasn't even thinking at all. That's why they didn't say anything about the $20,000 that went into my account each month. She was legit, and I had forgotten all about that.

"Let's run to my house and put it in the account now."

"Yeah, because they would try to say it's your daddy's drug money or something, they sheisty. They'd try to find any reason to put him underneath the jail."

"I know." I agreed.

Rai was looking the whole time in utter silence, not knowing what to do. She had never been in a situation alike. She was involved with a few dopeboys, none as large as my daddy though.

We pulled into my driveway and darted for the house. I told Amelia where all the stashes were and we split up. It seemed like everything was moving in slow motion as I traveled up the staircase. In a matter of seconds, we returned to the downstairs living room with the bags of money. I walked over to the window, retracted the blinds, only to find a black Taskforce van outside. We panicked. Not knowing what to do or where to go, I almost fainted.

"Jayah, it's a hiding place on the third floor. It's a wall that you can't even tell that can open from three knocks. It is the wall right next to the small bathroom on the right. When it open, make sure y'all set it to be knocked on 10 times, just in case they bump into the wall You and Rai run up there and take it now, before they burst inside." I immediately took off up the stairs. I knocked on the wall three times it swiftly opened. I was relieved, stashed the cash inside and set it for 15 knocks. Fuck that shit.

We ran down the stairs and the FBI, fuck all that, all the uniformed involvements with the law were at the door with these papers.

"We came to remove all residents from this home to conduct a search," a Federal Agent stated firmly. "Are you Miss Jayah Carter? We have an arrest warrant for you, ma'am. We also have notice of seizure of property for any cars under the ownership of Jay Carter or Jayah Carter on these premises."

"What? Y'all got me fucked up!" I exclaimed. "Y'all can't take my shit. All this was a present, especially that Benz. That don't have anything to do with Jay Carter."

"I'm just following standard procedures, ma'am. We have a judge's order to remove everything that's on this list.

I'm very sorry for the troubles ma'am."

"Okay, you can think that." Amelia said, already phoning her high paid attorney.

"We're just doing our jobs." The Agent smiled, as if that phrase justified what they were doing in my house.

"Y'all some haters and I feel so sorry for you fuckin', broke-ass crackers. Harassing people for a living, how much you make? About $20 an hour?" I popped, angrily. "I would be mad as hell too after harassing people for a living and still ain't making shit." I was beyond irate.

His faced flushed, and his forehead furrowed. "Young lady, this is a federal investigation, and I can understand your feelings, but interfering and not complying with authorities can only lead to more difficulties for all parties involved."

"I'm glad you think that, pussy." I snickered.

"That's it! Handcuff her! Get her up out of here, now!"

"Fuck y'all, I got bond money." I spat, just like the cocky and arrogant bitch that I was.

♛ ♛ ♛ ♛ ♛ ♛ ♛ ♛ ♛ ♛ ♛ ♛ ♛ ♛ ♛ ♛ ♛

I was salty as fuck that I got booked in on disorderly conduct, but I got right back out a couple hours later. Rai and Amelia were right there waiting on me, talking shit, too.

"Damn, Jayah. Can you keep your mouth closed sometimes?" I already knew Amelia was pissed because she rarely fussed me. "Damn. We already in a weird position, and you making shit extra." She flared her nose, rolling her eyes.

"Yeah I know, but that hatin'-ass agent was talking shit."

"I know, but still." She looked at me with her lips puckered. "And I talked to your daddy, he said you better stop acting like a fuckin' fool."

I smacked me lips. "Okay. Y'all didn't have to tell him." I was growing irritated.

"We did, girl,. He would have went loco if he would have found out another way," Rai chimed. I had to agree.

While my daddy and his comrades were in jail, we were trying to find a way to speak to a judge in the morning. They were clowning, tryna take our belongings like that, especially my fucking Benz and Range. I didn't play like that, hell-nah.

♛ ♛ ♛ ♛ ♛ ♛ ♛ ♛ ♛ ♛ ♛ ♛ ♛ ♛ ♛ ♛ ♛

Adrian sat in the interrogation room.

"Well, well, well. I see you still don't want to talk Mr. Wells. I know who supplies your criminal enterprise, and I know that you think you are big time around here." The federal agent paced back and forth. "If you let me know, I will be happy to let you go and your access will be granted," the agent said.

"I don't know what y'all talkin' about. Tell on what?" He played dumb. "I said I don't know what y'all talking about for the umpteenth time." Adrian already knew the game. They don't know shit. If they did, they wouldn't be tryna spare you by telling you to rat your team out. They wouldn't be wasting their time if they already knew everything about the drug empire.

Crazy P was in the interrogation room across the hall, and Agent Thomas slammed the steel door as he left Adrian in the other the room.

"We have a deal for you," Agent Thomas began, placing the file on the table.

"Well, whatever it is, does it involve me leaving this

mothafucka tonight?" P asked.

Thomas smiled. "It depends. Are you willing to tell us what you know?" He raised his brow at the end of the question.

"Oh, that's no problem, 'cause I gotta go now. I need some pussy. Shit."

"Okay, I like you." The Agent nodded. "You're going to cooperate with us. Here's a pen. Write everything you know, the drug houses, the drug distributors, everything."

"That's it?" P retrieved the pen from the table. "All I gotta tell you is where we get shit from?" P asked the agent, excitedly.

"It's that simple," Thomas agreed.

P wrote on the paper a short story.

To whom it may concern:

I'ma money go-getta, and me and my niggas Jay, Tommy and Adrian gets our shit from all type of places. It depend on what we getting. If we getting clothes for the needy, we will get it from Xclusive Swagg. If we getting stuff for sick kids, we get the money from Jay's businesses. We get shit from everywhere, and we getting this money by blessing our community. So, if you know any people that need help, you can just call on us. Yeah, and by the way, I'm no fuckin' clown, you fuckin' losers. I'm laughing at you pigs. Thought y'all was about to have me on that way. Nah. It's like Burger King, have it my way. Fuck y'all, pigs.

P handed the agent the letter. Assuming that P had made his confession on paper, Thomas anxiously read over the pad with a sly smirk spread across his face. That smirk slowly contorted into a frown. Thomas became infuriated. His veins bulged out of his forehead. Balling up the paper, Thomas stormed out of the interrogation room. From lack of evidence, they had to let Crazy P go, but they still had the other three on some intense allegations.

♛ ♛ ♛ ♛ ♛ ♛ ♛ ♛ ♛ ♛ ♛ ♛ ♛ ♛ ♛ ♛ ♛

I cracked up when P recapped that scene to us.

The fool still had two other people to try and convince them to rat out their entire operation. But they could've never thought my daddy or Tommy was gon' snitch. That was a waste of time.

The Agent's that was working on my daddy's investigation

wasn't very intelligent after all. They'd jumped to a conclusion and didn't once stop and think where the money could have came from.They just wanted him, trying some bogus tale. Although most of it was drug money, still, they couldn't prove it.

Like the smart person she was Amelia, went straight to the federal building that very next morning. She filed a lawsuit against the Federal Bureau of Investigation. She raised hell because a lot of the seized paperwork they used was fraudulent. They couldn't confiscate anything from us. Everything was accounted for from the businesses that Amelia had. Every cent added up, and they would never be able to get my dad unless they caught my daddy in the act. That would never happen. My daddy was here to show all these wannabe drug dealers how to be a real American gangster. His shrewd hustle was the best. No snakes on the team is the first scoring, and the second is like the first, nobody snitches on the squad. Can't get any better than that. Never get caught and still spend money like we're the owners of the Federal Reserve.

Chapter Sixteen

Back to the usual!

A year had passed by since me and Cheno had been messing around. We had been through our ups and downs, but we managed to overcome the worst and remain close friends.

It was a beautiful, moderate Saturday, and I surely wasn't staying in the house. Plus, it was time for me to get my wig split and some special spa treatment. I dressed myself soon as I woke up that morning. My black and silver baby T-shirt read, "Obviously Hood Richest". After breakfast and a few sitcoms, it was noon. I decided to call Rai up to see what her plans were.

She answered on the third ring. "Girl, you tryna go to the salon, and after that go to the spa? Honey, I'm bored. Girl, I need to get out this house."

"Girl, yeah. But let me tell you this sucka shit. I'm over here with Shawn, and he was telling me how J.P. was hatin' on me, him, Tee and Driano."

"Really, what was he saying?"

"Talking about Tee dumb for fuckin' with Driano because he really don't like her. He a broke-ass nigga, and Tee a dumb-ass hoe for being my friend because he used to fuck with me. Shawn a silly nigga 'cause he had me first and they niggas. So, he didn't know why he was tryna wife up a hoe."

"Bitch, shut up lying, he wasn't hatin' like that, what the fuck?" I asked, hoping that a nigga wasn't hatin' hard like that.

"Yes, he was."

"That nigga a straight pussy, hatin' on another nigga like that, and Adrian got that cake. I mean, he got that throwback cake." I spoke, truthfully. "Who cares that he used to fuck with you? What that mean to us? You still our right hand. So what? And he hatin' on Shawn, too, that's crazy!" I shook my head. "He just salty that he ain't got neither one of y'all. That's it, fo' real."

"That's what I said." She giggled. "Girl, come get me though, I'm riding with you."

"Alrighty," I said, hanging up the phone. I slipped into my silver Emilio Pucci cropped jacket and set the alarm. Grabbing my Miu Miu hobo handbag by the door, I headed out.

We arrived at the salon around two and it was packed. When we entered, I instantly spotted SaNara, and she had the Candace girl with her. I laughed at the sighting.

"Damn, Rai. Bitches always tryna hang and shit, when that happen?" I said, confused. It seemed like they'd gotten cool off of our beef towards them.

"Right. That's all I'm saying. When that happen?" Rai added, skimming over them with a mug. They ignored our presence, which was their best bet. Talkative Anne was in the shop, and she was about to spill the beans on everybody. That's one chick that knew everything that went down in Miami, from South Beach to Carol City, to Liberty City, to anywhere else that mattered. Her and her sister was like the Miami news, but with 85 percent accurate information.

"What's up, Rai and Jayah baby?" She greeted us.

"What's good, babe."I replied, with my ears tuned in like a RADAR. I already knew what time it was, when she appeared on the scene.

"Girl, let me tell you what's been jumping. You know Cheno beat the shit out of Tyiesha in the club last night?"

"Really? For what?" Rai asked.

"Let me tell y'all." She sucked her teeth. "Girl, she kept coming in his face, talking about he a dead beat dad and why he tricking on mothafuckas all in the Virgin Islands and he ain't bought his son shit."

"Damn, Jayah. Why the bitch gotta put you all in it?" Rai laughed.

"Right. That bitch is a clown. She need not get me involved at all. I know for a fact that she don't want these problems my way at all." I had no problem handlin' a bitch, but damn, it seem like they don't ever stop hatin'.

"Girl, right, and word around town is that you and Donteice got Herpes."

"Who and Donteice?" I said because I knew I only fucked two niggas and only one without a condom. I needed to know because I would hate to have to murk Cheno's ass.

"Not you, Jayah. You." She pointed at Rai.

Rai jerked her head back. "Man listen, tell all them hatin'-ass niggas and hatin'-ass bitches to keep my name out their mouth, because they don't know what I got. The mothafuckin' haters act like I gave it to them or something, what the hell."

"That's just word. And Rai, they was saying how you got beat up by SaNara."

"Beat up! Man listen, I got these man hands, real fucking talk, and you can ask that bitch who got that ass beat. It surely wasn't me."

"Damn, Rai. You shouldn't take this lil shit to heart like that, you know it ain't nothing but a bunch of haters out here. We ain't got any kids, so we the shit. So, that's all they gon' do," Anne said.

"Fuck that shit. I'm mad as fuck. Herpes and I got beat up," she laughed, angry. "That bitch already knows what it is," Rai said, pointing at SaNara.

"Yup, and you know it. It's nothing. Any bitch that want it can get it." I giggled. "Bitches know shit real on this end." I finished.

"Oh, and girl, let me tell you somethin' else. They said that Driano still be fucking with SaNara and everything. They said that came out of her own mouth."

"Man, dig this," I said, shrugging. "If so, she the fool. And I mean a fuckin' serious fool, because when she called and asked him about Tee, he played her. So that's on her man."

"And girl, they said that Candace was gon' beat yo' ass when she see you on the street. I guess from the incident that went on the night she was driving Cheno Benz."

Laughing my ass off, I got my words out. "Man, I ain't hard to find. I stay in the hood and stay in the clubs, so it ain't hard for her to find me. I threw the brick right at the driver side and the glass cut her all in her face." I giggled. "Don't you know I would have been at a bitch pussy the next day, you know?"

We laughed. "That's all I'm saying," Rai said, high-fiving me..

"Girl, it's so much shit going on."Annie paused, locating more information in her brain. "Oh, I forgot to tell you girl They was saying why y'all be biting on Tasha pussy, the baby ain't even your daddy's."

"Word. Well, if it ain't, it's his now and I sure DNA don't lie." I informed, knowing she'd spread the word on the results confirming my dad was the father. "And biting on her pussy! Not neva! That's our cat. Bitches just mad 'cause we fucks with her. That's all that is." I shook my head. Bitches are indeed some true haters.

Don't you know, Anne was gossiping until we left the salon. She started telling us other people business. Rai was pissed off at all the shit she heard. But me, I'ma boss. I didn't let that shit burn me up. Hoes just be hatin' for no apparent reason. Something I learned in my earlier stages.

"This mud bath is the shit," Rai squealed as we relaxed at a lavish spa resort off Ocean Drive.

"Tell me about it, honey. I know I been needing some spa treatment in my life. So, did you and Shawn fuck yet?"

"Girl, yeah. He got that work, too. Oh my God, that nigga got that gotdamnit man."

"Okay, then I see you." I laughed at Rai's response.

Rai closed her eyes and took a deep breath. "Isn't this just great? Girl, we living like superstars."

"Yeah, we the hood superstars," I spoke quite frankly.

"Man, we got everything that we could dream of." Rai was right. We were still young and sitting on racks. "Girl, I'm so happy that y'all showed me the way. Honey, I probably would be out here on some weak-ass shit."

I giggled. "You so silly."

"Naw, I'm serious girl. Y'all put me on game and made it better for me down here, because bitches down here didn't like me at all."

"Shid, they don't like you still," I joked.

"I know, but shit, now I don't give a fuck, 'cause I got three best friends."

"Yeah, I know."

After our relaxing hours at the spa, we enjoyed dinner with Cheno and Shawn on my daddy's yacht. Later, the four of us joined one of Diddy's all white parties. Upon our arrival, I couldn't believe it. I thought my eyes was playing tricks on me. That place was filled with all kind of celebrities. We all definitely fit in the crowd. The party was held at a beautiful glass beach house. We exited the limo and watched all type of celebrities getting out of their exotic vehicles.

We saw Russell Simmons climbing out of a Rolls-Royce. Then, I turned around and seen Keyshia Cole looking marvelous. Me and Rai were tripping when she told us to come over there and take some pictures with her. We took a few pictures with her and her entourage. She chopped it up with us for a minute, just an average casual convo, nothing major. I knew we had to be at a major event, and I couldn't wrap my head around how Cheno got invited to something so extravagant. As we mingled, we bumped into the host.

"What up, Chen? I'm glad you could make it," Diddy greeted him with a brotherly hug.

Me and Rai exchanged what the hell glimpses.

"This is my gorgeous date, Jayah, and my nigga Shawn that I was telling you about. This his beautiful date, La'Rai," Chen said, introducing us.

He nodded his head gently. "I'm gon' get with you on yo' mans Cheno, but who is these beauties? Where did you find them at?"

Rai and I stayed cool. We kept our composures, though my flesh was ready to explode. We were geeked that Diddy complimented us on our beauty.

"Oh, this my girl and her friend. They stay right here in Miami."

"Oh, really? Y'all don't model or nothing?" Diddy questioned.

"Nah, we just be chillin'," I said, shaking my head.

"Well, I think y'all should model for Sean Jean."

Shit, that will be something fun to do, just to get away.

"So, are you asking us that?" I asked.

Diddy half-smiled. "Yeah, I guess I am. Are y'all interested?"

"Of course we are," Rai said, eagerly.

"Okay, well give me y'all number and I'm gonna get with you beautiful ladies later." He directed his attention back towards Cheno. "And tomorrow, bring ya mans to the studio so I can hear his skills."

"That's what's up. I will be there 'round noon."

"Yeah, Y'all have fun. I got to entertain my party." Diddy winked and strolled off.

"Damn. Y'all 'bout to be runway models. And shit, I see y'all," Shawn said, playfully covering his mouth.

"And what, you gon' be a singer?" I retorted.

Shawn frowned. "Fuck you, Jayah. You got jokes, huh?"

"Nah, but you do though,"I told him, smirking. "I just wanted to know what you gon' be doing at the studio."

"Rapping, fool. Do I look like a fuckin' singer?"

Rai burst into laughter at Shawn's response.

As the night moved in time, we mingled and got to meet a few stars. The 5-inch stilettos I wore had my feet burning. We ended up sitting in a room and rolled up a blunt, talked, had a few drinks. I can't lie, it was one of the most fun nights of my life thus far.

Chapter Seventeen

Bitches gon' learn to respect me!

Amelia's lawyer had us looking at a good $6.5 million because the FBI wanted to take justice into their own hands.

As I was sitting comfortably in my Range Rover, droplets of rain hit my windshield. Dazed, I was thinking about that day that changed my life. That day got me to where I am at now. Here I was with $2.7 million that I had saved in one year. And the thing is, I had did nothing really to get it. What was I gonna do with my life? I had the greatest feeling, until my phone rang. And remember, when it rain it pours, which that's some straight bullshit.

"Jayah, it's Tee. I'm here at Uncle Jay's house and I just so happened to go to the bathroom. Now I hear three niggas downstairs saying show me the safe or I'm killing you and this bitch. I don't think I recognize the voice, or I can't match it with a face. Sis, I'm so scared. I can't lose another daddy, man. Fuck, what am I supposed to do? Damn. Why didn't I have the pistol he told us to carry," Tee hissed, panicking.

My body became numb as her words registered in my brain. *Not my daddy. This shit ain't happening. Seconds ago I felt unstoppable, but now, shit is hectic. Oh my Lord, what would I do without my daddy and Tee? Shit, fuckin' shit.*

Everything just started looking clear to me. Life is great until shit happens. I just started looking back on the good life. I had 30 seconds to come up with a plan.

"Look, Tee, I got a plan. I'm 'bout to call daddy and tell him to meet me. I got his money. So I'm gon' call you right back. Make sure yo' phone on silent, okay?"

"Okay. Hurry up, and call Adrian, too."

Calling the phone, my daddy answered like normal. I knew something was wrong though, 'cause he never calls me by my name unless it was serious or he was mad.

"What's up, Jayah Carter?"

Knowing that I was on speakerphone, I got straight to the point.

"Ay, Daddy. Driano just met me with yo' $5 million. He said he sold them thangs quick."

"Word." He said hold on. I knew my plan was working.

My daddy told me to meet him at the house alone. He seemed to catch on that I knew what was happening, going along with the plan.

I had to call Adrian, Big Tommy and Crazy P real quick. First, I dialed Big Tommy.

"What up, Lil Jay?" Tommy's deep voice came through crystal clear.

"Hey, Big Tommy, somebody at the house robbing my daddy, right now. Tee over there hiding and she just called and told me."

He yelled. "What? How the fuck anybody know where he stay at?"

"I don't know, but we can't worry about that now. Just work on getting my peoples."

"Calm down. I'm 'bout to kill these niggas. You said Tee in there, right? So she can direct us?"

"Yeah," I confirmed. "I'm 'bout to tell Driano and P to meet me over there."

"Nah. I'm gon' pick 'em up and you just stay there."

"Hell naw. I'm going too," I shouted.

"Okay, but make sure you don't pull up in the front of the house. We going through the back door."

"Okay, I'll call yo' phone when me and Rai get there."

I hung up, quickly calling Tee's phone.

"Hello?" Tee whispered.

"What's up, what's going on?"

"Man, bitch." I could tell Tee was irate. "I heard one of the dudes on the phone. He must've been at the top of the stairs. He was yelling at some chick talking 'bout why she say it was money in the house." Her whisper was fading, so I had to smash my ear to the phone. "I guess the girl said whatever she had to say, and he was like 'Fuck that, Ashley. Y'all said it was in here. Now we waiting on his daughter to bring it, but that's cool too. We can pop her for the shit they did to you."

My eyes bucked and I was fuming. "Word! That bitch got me fucked up!" I roared in pure anger. "I'm killin' that bitch and that's personal. I'm doing it myself." I was wondering how in the hell she knew about my daddy's house.

"That's what I said. She is a fuckin' hater. I can't wait. I'm beating her fuckin' ass."

"Beating her ass?" I paused. "Fuck nah, I'm killing her ass, fuck that."

"Well, let me beat her ass first," Tee suggested.

"Fuck that shit. You better catch her before I do. It's gonna be no talking. I'm blasting."

"I feel you, she did put us in a bad situation."

"I know, I'm straight killing that bitch." A tear ran down the side of my cheek. "'Cause if you weren't there, my daddy could be dead." More tears streamed down my face. My feelings was hurt, even thinking about losing my daddy. "Since she wants to be a silly-ass hoe." I said. "If I don't do shit else, I'ma get that bitch, and that's a fuckin' promise to my daddy."

"Jayah, I'm scared, man. Ya'll need to hurry up. My baby." She lightly sighed through the phone. "I can't stop thinking about her. Mecia got her and I was supposed to been picked her up at five."

"Tee I'm on my way in like five minutes. We waiting on Tommy dem." We exchanged I love yous and we hung up.

A few minutes passed and Tommy pulled up, we jumped out and made our way to the backyard cautiously.

We crept in through the back door sneakily. These lame-ass niggas was on some clown-ass shit. The trio was chillin' like it was their house, sitting comfortable. What the fuck. They thought that I was on my way with the money, so them clowns had their guards down waiting on me. *How dumb*. While we was making our way through the kitchen, fat-ass Tommy made the floor squeak. We all came to a halt. Nobody in the living room heard it though, 'cause the niggas was not paying any attention. How ironic.

One fool was on the phone, sitting on the stairs. The second fool was sitting on the arm of the couch next to Amelia. I guess the boss of the whole heist was sitting on my daddy's couch with his foot propped up, watching 106 & Park. His gun sat on the table, which was too far for him to do anything. I could see impatience in my daddy's eyes, and he was pissed off.

Crazy P was directing everybody. He told Big Tommy to shoot the nigga in the back that was sitting on the arm of the couch. He was pointing at the dude on the stairs saying he was gon' shoot him being that he was a sharp shooter. Lastly, he whispered to Driano to run up to the dude that was on the couch. They decided to shoot him last, 'cause they needed answers first. P began counting backwards with a hand signal starting at five. Before we knew it, he was at one. All we heard was a slight pop, then Tommy shot the other dude in his back. He fell backwards. Driano ran up on the guy that was resting on the couch hastily, aiming the gun at him while he yelled for Donteice to come down the stairs. She kicked the dead body as she flew passed and started talking shit, as if he could hear her. The dude that was on the couch was looking shocked as hell.

"Yeah, man. It ain't my daddy's time to go yet, but it surely is yours, bitch-ass nigga." I chimed, smugly.

He just sat there still watching TV. My daddy kicked his legs off his table and started yelling at him, letting him know that he fucked with the wrong people. My dad even asked him if he had any manners..

"Man, who in the fuck sent y'all here?" P asked, coolly.

Dude ignored P and continued watching TV.

I sounded off, enraged. "Nigga, look. We will make shit simple for you." I shrugged. "You already know you 'bout to die. If you tell us what we need to know, we won't kill yo' family. I know you don't want yo' people to die with you."

At that moment, we knew he cared. "Y'all don't know my fuckin' family."

My daddy giggled. "Dumb fuck, you are really a dumb lil nigga." He shook his head. "Uhhhh." He placed his hand on his chin. "When they have yo' fuckin' funeral, asshole, we'll know who they are then."

That nigga didn't hesitate and got to singing like a bird. "Okay, man, it went like this. Shid, the bitch Ashley and her friend was talkin' about how they beef with your daughters, and that they wanted to hurt them in a bad way. They figured if somebody hurt you, it would be over for them and they wouldn't be shit."

"Ashley said this?" Tee interjected.

Me and Tee sat there flabbergasted. We couldn't believe she was hatin' that hard.

I walked over slowly to the dude. "So, Ashley wanted to have y'all kill my daddy, 'cause she thought I would be broke." I furrowed my face. "Listen, I got stacks on top of stacks, on top of them stacks, so that hoe could've never thought that shit."

"Well, it's true, but I don't got time to keep talkin'. Just kill me." He sat there like a warrior.

"Pop, Pop, Paw!" Was the sounds we heard. P's crazy ass hit him twice in the head, and my daddy hit him directly in his heart with his own gun.

"Man, we got to get these bodyies out of here," my daddy demanded.

"Yeah, you right." Big Tommy agreed. Him and Crazy P went to go get the robbers' truck and pulled it inside the garage. Big Tommy was the strong person of the clique. That nigga wrapped the bodies up quick and promptly threw all in the backseat. They rolled down into the river still inside the truck.

Amelia cleaned the mess up, and I was definitely on a mission to kill. I was out looking for Ashley and the other bitch that plotted against us. Donteice had called her sister up to let her know that she wouldn't be there to get her daughter until the morning. It was cool with Mecia, so we went searching for the bitch.

"Damn, y'all. Who else do y'all thing had something to do with it?" Tee asked.

"I don't know, but she gonna tell us." I said calmly, driving with my eyes on the road.

"Is y'all gon' kill her for real?" Rai inquired.

I turned and gazed in her eyes. "Girl, that ain't even a question. I'm gonna fuckin' murder that bitch."

For some reason, we couldn't find her anywhere. We looked everywhere to. That's when we decided to check the hood and post up. We were lurking like we were some seasoned killers. Me and Tee was ready, with our guns tucked underneath our shirt. We were quietly discussing the terms of the situation when my phone had rung.

"Hello?"

"Damn, baby, you was just gon' do me like that?"

"Who is this?" I asked, frustrated.

"Cheno."

"Do you like what?" I asked, nonchalantly,

"Not callin' or nothin'. I haven't talked to you all damn day." He joked around.

I half-giggled. "Boy please. Come 'round by my granny's. I'm in the front."

"I'm in yo' Granny's right now. I just got done putting some money up."

"Come outside. I need to holla at you." I told him.

He came strolling out the house. I let him in on everything that had occurred. We was just that cool and knew everything about each other. It was based more like best friends than lovers, even though we loved each other dearly and fucked often, we still were good friends. He was pissed at the whole scenario. He couldn't stand for my life to be in harm's way.

He wanted me to let him handle it. I laughed when he said that shit.

"Boy, this is personal, and I'm gon' get that bitch myself. Do you know where she might be right now?" I asked since he'd wanted to be helpful.

"As a matter of fact I do. She was just riding with J.P. lil brother, R.P."

I shook my head furiously. "What? That's crazy. She riding around like shit cool."

"Right, that's all I'm saying. Shit wild, man." Tee added.

We didn't have any time to waste, so Cheno called R.P. up, placing him on speakerphone.

"What's good, bra? You busy?"

"Naw, I just dropped the Ashley hoe off at the house and shit."

"Whud? You didn't stay to fuck? Somebody must've been there with her?" Chen quizzed.

"Nah, the bitch is a clown. All she do is lie about what she got and shit."

"Do she?"

R.P. sighed. "Yeah man, talking about tomorrow she'll have over a hunnid bans." He smacked his lips. "I looked at this bitch with an evil-ass look and told her I was about to drop her lying ass off." He paused, slightly laughing. "She got to saying, it's cool I'm 'bout to be caked up and all kind of shit. Bra, that rat bitch wack."

"Aw, so you just took her home, huh?"

"Yeah, she was salty too, 'cause everybody was gone. She wanted me to stay and fuck her." That nigga hit the nail right on the head. Cheno told him he was just hollering at him and hung up.

Chen nodded at us. "Yeah man, y'all can get that hoe right now. Y'all got this fool."

With that said, we popped in Tee's Magnum. Tee cranked that ignition and we flew over to Ashley's house.

We had Rai knock on the door, 'cause she hardly knew Rai's face. She opened the door right up. Me and Tee came from the side and directed her to come with us, with our pistols drawn.

"What? For what? What did I do?" She asked, jittery with bucked eyes.

"Man, bitch, quit fucking playing with me." I gritted me teeth. "You know exactly what you did."

"No I don't." Ashley instantly started crying.

"Matter a fact, go in the house," Rai said, pushing her inside the house onto the floor.

Tee and I walked up on her while she was on the ground. I simply asked. "Who else was involved?"

She cried, frantically. "I don't know what you talking about."

"Fuck it, y'all kill the bitch. Shid, we'll find out anyway from the streets," Rai blurted, growing peeved.

"You right," Tee said. With that, we exchanged killer glances and started blasting the bitch. We went in quick and vanished even quicker. I didn't have any remorse for the bitch. Now her mother would be burying her teen daughter over some hatin' shit she was on. I left the mothafuckin' grimy bitch laying there dead. Bet that bitch casket was closed. Shid, life goes on.

I keep it gangsta and they love that shit. I keep gangsta and they love that shit. If you a gangsta, you gon' love this shit. The sounds that we were listening to blasted from the car as we went to the house and changed our gear. That was crazy though. Me and Tee had out first dead body together. Because, for real, we didn't know which bullet killed her.We acted as if nothing never happened and went right back to the hood. Cheno walked up to me, pulling me into his chest.

"What up, man. You good?"

"Better than before." I let out a slight chuckle.

"You silly, man. So, did y'all find her?" He asked.

"No comment."

He sighed. "Did y'all get her?"

"I plead the fifth." I laughed, surrendering my hands.

"A'ight Miss Gutta Chick."

"You better know I ain't gon' play with these bitches, try dat." I playfully moved my waist in a slow rhythm.

He laughed, shaking his head. "Alright, so what y'all doing tonight?"

"Shit, I don't know. You got something planned?"

"Not for real. I was just wondering," Cheno said.

"Oh, so have y'all been to the studio? I want to hear Shawn rap."

"That's cool. Y'all can go down there with us tomorrow."

"That's what's up."

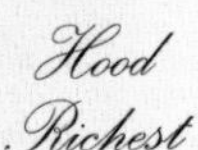

Chapter Eighteen

That's fucked up!

"Good afternoon, everyone," I said as I walked into Xclusive Swagg.

Like always, my dad's workers greeted me friendly. I placed myself in the chair behind the counter. I pulled out my Philly Cheese Steak dinner and got to bashing. I took one bite of the sub and was interrupted by a phone call.

"Bitch, what are you doin?" Rai voiced, nervously.

"Nothing, what's up?" I chimed, worriedly.

"Yo, bitch, meet me now at the house. Now!" She demanded.

"What, what's wrong?"

"Girl just meet me at my crib."

I didn't ask any more questions and dipped out.

I walked inside to find Rai on the sofa crying hysterically. She looked like she had lost her best friend. I didn't know what was wrong. I just hoped it wasn't nothing involving the murder. It wasn't, my ass was being paranoid. It was some other crazy-ass shit.

"Man, look," Rai hissed, and threw some papers on the table. It was test results saying she was positive of genital herpes.

I couldn't even open my mouth to speak. I wasn't able to find the right words to say anything. I couldn't say nothing. I knew that had to be a painful feeling. She finally broke the silence and blurted out.

"Man, Jayah, I can't believe this crazy-ass shit. It was really true, that nasty dick-ass nigga got that shit. What the hell!" She yelled with tear filled eyes.

"I know. Man, what you gonna do? Is you gon' tell Tee?"

"Yeah, I'm gon' tell her." Rai looked up. "I would want her to tell me, but I just hope that ain't nothing wrong with the baby."

"They did all the test on her when she was first born, so I doubt it."

"Okay, that's good. But what about her telling A? And what about me telling Shawn?" Her voiced cracked.

"I know." My words were hard to get out around the lump in my throat. "They will be salty." I slowly shook my head.

"I just wish I never fucked that clown," Rai screamed, crying. "Man, Jayah. I want to kill that nigga."

"That's cool, you know I don't give a fuck no more about another mothafucka." I nodded. "Why should I? Fuck it."

"So what? What we gon' do first? Tell Tee, then off that nigga?" Rai looked at me with her red and puffy eyes. I could barely take her staring at me like that without running out to blast a nigga right then.

"Yeah, I guess," I said. as

We called Tee, informing her of the news. Tee told us that it must have passed over her because she had just gotten check for everything the month before. She was disappointed that Rai had to be the one who got infected with the virus.

Rai was devastated. That was really some fucked up shit, but we knew she wouldn't die from it. We just kept it a secret, and she made sure she took her meds daily. Rai still got it in with any nigga she wanted to. I know that may sound fucked up, but many people does it.

After thinking it over, we just realized that we would leave it alone. J.P. wasn't even worth the trouble. His day would surface. It was just a matter of time. But we did not need to drink on that bullshit note.

♛ ♛ ♛ ♛ ♛ ♛ ♛ ♛ ♛ ♛ ♛ ♛ ♛ ♛ ♛ ♛ ♛

The night was live. Everyone came out that night. It wasn't anything in particular going on. I guess everyone just felt like bringing the next day in at Club Paradise. Of course, me and my girls were showing our special appearance. We even brought Daijah, and D'vena along. The Lord knew they were too young, but we was boppin' in the club at their age, so it was only fair.

That night, I dressed more grown. I rocked a pink, white and bright green Coogi track jacket, and a pair of light, faded, cuffed jean shorts with Coogi lettering across the butt. White Marc Jacobs pumps decorated my feet, a white, oversized Marc Jacobs bag draped over my shoulder and matching Louie shades shielded my vision. I was the baddest that night, even my hair was pinned up into an up-do. My star quality glitter consisted of pink diamond studs in my ears, a pink diamond David Yurman watch and a pink Gucci tennis bracelet glistened on my other wrist.

"Man, this shit jumpin', real talk," Daijah said, laughing.

"I know. It stay jumpin'," I said as I was blowing purple haze and peering off into the crowd of people.

I spotted this dude from all the way on the other side of the club. He was fine as fuck. Chocolate brown, muscular build and a low-cut-fade. Dude donned a pair of Miskeen shorts, matching shirt and some exclusive J-moneys rested on his feet. I was tripping there for a second. I partied so much, I knew damn near everyone, and my daddy was the best-known person in Miami.. That was my first time ever seeing that cat. I knew I had to get on him and soon, 'cause I knew bitches too well, and I knew they was also plotting.

"What up Jayah girl?" Anne said, walking up with her drink in hand.

"Hey man. What's good?"

"Shit. Just decided to come out and see what everybody up to."

"Oh, that's what's up, but I got a question?"

"What anything, you my girl."

"Who is dude over there in the Miskeen outfit?" I slyly pointed.

"Which one, Money?"

"What? He got money?" I asked, excitedly.

"Nah, I mean, yeah, he got money, but that's his name, too."

"Really," I smiled. "But is dude from here? Where did he come from?" I wanted all the details Anne could give me.

"Yeah, he from here, honey, but he is always out of town handling business, I guess." She sipped on her drink. "They say he got Omaha on lock. That's why he never be intown, but they say he crazy, too," Anne finished in a fit of giggles.

"So, he never be here?" I asked, not paying the crazy part any attention.

"Not really, but now he be here more than usual," Anne continued sipping her drink. "Shid, ole boy didn't come back home for a whole year one time. I guess he was getting that money all the way together. He must be down here for some serious business though."

Anne knew she talked too damn much. She kept going on and on until I told her I would be right back, lying like a mothafucka.

I wasn't the only one feeling the swagger, Money was checking me also.

"Whud up, baby girl? What's yo' name?" I turned around with an attitude.

"What's good?" I said dryly, never acting pressed.

"I was just wondering if you wanted me to get you a drink."

"Boy, beat it." I said playfully. "Tell me what you really wanted, and don't be childish about the situation."

"Okay, I see you a rude one, but you want me to get you a bottle of something?"

"If I wanted one, I would have got me one, don't you think?" I said, annoyed at his approach.

"Damn, ma. Calm down." He held his hands up. "I understand. I'ma get straight to the point. I was feeling you, and I was wondering if I could get yo' number."

"Shid, can you?" I said, testing dude's patience.

"Listen, if you tryna holla at me, I will be right over there. A'ight?" Money left it at that and walked off.

As the night progressed, Money couldn't resist. HE came over again and we exchanged numbers. I wasn't lying when I said everybody was in the club. Jay Jay's ass ended up approaching me when I was sitting at the bar.

"Damn, Jayah. I see you looking good and shit." He licked his lips.

"You too, and you look like you eatin' good." I told him. He was fresh to def. The nigga was dipped in ice. I ain't gon' stunt, he was blinding me. *Dude really got upgraded. He must be pushing some real weight now.*

"Yeah, I am," Jay Jay said, candidly.

"That's what's up. I'm glad you good."

"Yeah, when you played me, I knew I had to get my money right." He chimed with a grin.

"Oh, so that's how you feel," I giggled.

"Nah, that's what it is."

"Shid, being honest, you right." I began. "I gotta get to this money, man. Why not?"

He chuckled, lightly. "But the thing is, I was cashing you out all the time."

"You was, I can't even lie, but I got on my grown woman and I needed more than some clothes and shoes. For real, I had all the clothes and all the shoes. It was time for better things. You know what I mean?"

"Yeah, I feel you sweetie, but I'm salty you played me for Cheno."

"That's what this is about, that?" I asked. "Man, Cheno ain't my nigga, but then again, he is in some ways," I spoke, truthfully. "He done did so much for me just by being a friend, and me and him got an understanding that we will always respect each other. That's what we do, so call it how you call it."

"So, that mean you can fuck back with me?" Jay Jay quizzed.

"I'm grown as fuck, and I'm not committed to no one. So yeah, if that's what I decide that I wanna do, then that's what it is." I told him.

"Okay, so give me yo' number so I can get with you later." We exchanged numbers.

The Dj was doing his thang and my song came on. I jumped up, walking through the crowd on my way to shake my rump, abruptly someone tapped me on my shoulder. It wasn't a friendly tap either. I turned around quickly. It was Chassidy Brown. Ain't that some shit.

"Man, what up?" I said, mugging.

"Was you just in my baby daddy's face?" She questioned, snobbishly.

"Here we go again, hatin' on me as usual man. Look, I don't explain shit to bitches. Ask that nigga," I shot, glaring her up and down.

"Man, Jayah, I been wanting to beat yo' ass for the longest, hoe – " She didn't even finish her statement and tried to steal on me. The bitch must not have heard about me though. I leaned back before her punch could land on me and got to stealing her in the face. Security came and broke it up. Tee and everyone ran over to the fight, it was over by the time they'd reached me.

"Man, what the fuck just happened?" Tee yelled.

"That hatin'-ass bitch Chassidy came up talking reckless and just stole on me – "

"What?" Rai interrupted.

"Man, let me finish. The bitch ain't shit. She can't even fight, man..I tore her ass up." I laughed at her weak attempt. "But they broke it up too quick for me. I gotta get at the hoe one more time."

"Yeah, let's get that bitch after the club," Tee suggested.

"Oh, and you know it. Soon as this over wit'." We laughed and started back partying.

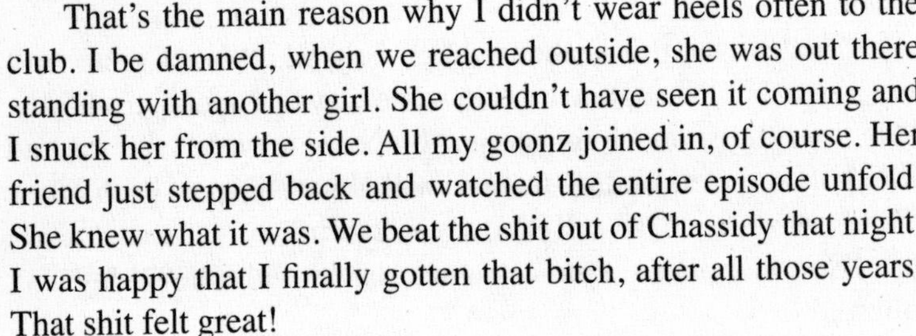

That's the main reason why I didn't wear heels often to the club. I be damned, when we reached outside, she was out there standing with another girl. She couldn't have seen it coming and I snuck her from the side. All my goonz joined in, of course. Her friend just stepped back and watched the entire episode unfold. She knew what it was. We beat the shit out of Chassidy that night. I was happy that I finally gotten that bitch, after all those years. That shit felt great!

Chapter Nineteen

That's why I don't trust hoes!

I fell asleep as I was watching my favorite movie. I sleepily grabbed at my phone when it rang.

"What's up baby?"

"What up, Cheno? I'm sleep," I whispered.

"I just wanna know if you could come lay with me. I miss you and I got to tell you something."

"Boy, it is five in the morning. I'm not 'bout to get up." My words dragged out in a yawn.

"Well, you don't have to. Just open yo' door up."

I know this nigga ain't at my house just sitting out there looking like some fucking psychopath. Let me find out he a stalker. I dragged myself out of bed and opened the door. He was looking sexy as fuck. My pussy was starting to get wet. There's nothing like that early morning sex, and I was on one, but I could tell that something bothering him. I could just feel through his vibe that he had something on his brain.

"What up? You didn't have a hoe to go with tonight?" I said, smiling, walking to sit in the living room.

"Man, Jayah, shut up. I got something to tell you."

"What man, what is it?" I asked, tugging my legs underneath me.

"Promise you won't be mad at me," he said.

"Man, mad at you for what?" I asked, puzzled. I didn't like how this was starting.

"You got to promise me first, okay?" He said, taking a deep breath.

I threw a pillow at him. "Man. Boy, quit playing and just tell me." I just wished that he would hurry up.

"Man listen! All I want to say before I say it is I'm sorry." He sighed heavily. "But like a week ago, I was drunk as fuck at the club, and I seen Daijah and Vena." He held his head down. "I was with J.P., and he was with Daijah. They had us go to their house and they both did it to us."

I sat there, understanding and collecting every word he was saying. The shock woke me up completely, allowing the information to register clearly in my mind. If looks could've killed, that nigga would had been dead and buried. I went off. "You mean you fucked my lil cousin D'vena?"

"Man, yeah. I'm sorry. I'm really sorry for that shit." He talked, keeping his head down.

"Man, get the fuck out my shit, nigga. I'll holla at you." I exclaimed.

"Jayah, I'm sorry, man. I was drunk, that's why I tellin' you," he tried to reason his way out.

"Man, I don't give a fuck about none of that shit." I jumped up. "I don't give a fuck if you was high off coke, nigga, that's not an excuse. Fuck you and that bitch." I stormed out the living room. He grabbed my arms. I snatched them back so hastily. "Man, get yo' hands off of me, bitch-ass nigga." I tried yanking away from his tight and firm grip.

"Jayah, just forgive me. Please, I love you more than you would ever know." He gazed into my eyes.

"Believe me, if you loved me, you would've never fucked my lil cousin. But it's cool, 'cause I'm gon' fuck yo' cousin, brother, daddy, somebody you close to, bitch, and you better believe that."

"I understand baby, but please, I'm begging, I really didn't know what I was doing." He implored.

I stopped, and something worse swam through my brain.

"Man, did you say that Daijah fucked J.P. nasty ass?" My entire face scrunched up.

"Huh, what you say?" He played dumb.

I slapped him in his face. "You heard me, bitch!"

"Damn, Jayah. Don't be hitting me all in my face. I done told you about that shit," Chen said in a high-pitched tone.

"Fuck you, bitch. You said that J.P. fucked my lil sister. That's some fucked up shit." I shook my head holding back my tears. "Man, bitches and niggas ain't shit!" I roared.

"Jayah, listen, I just want you to know I'm sorry and I was drunk and it just happened one time. I'll never let that happen again."

"A'ight," I said. "Bye. Leave up out of my shit, like now." I accompanied him to the door.

"I'm 'bout to lay down on the couch. I'm not leaving until you forgive me or forget it ever happen, because I did." He said, like he was quite sure I would listen.

"Okay, bitch." I said, knowing that he really wasn't gon' leave until he felt like it. I slipped on my Fendi slippers and walked across the street to Tee's house.

I rang the doorbell and knocked hard on Tee's wooden French double doors. *Damn I should have grabbed the key.* I could hear the sounds of someone darting down the steps. She peeked and then opened the door frantically. "What up, Jayah, what happened?" Tee said, thinking something tragic had happened.

"Man, your lil sister out here being a HOE." I said, walking into the foyer.

"What she do?" She asked, wiping the sleep from her eyes.

"Man, Cheno just told me that him and J.P. fuck Daijah and D'vena."

"Are you serious?"

"As a fucking heart attack."

"Man, them lil girls is too damn hot."

"Right! But all I'm saying is Daijah knows that that's yo' baby daddy."

"Yeah, but she young, so she don't know better," Tee said.

"Shid, bullshit!" I squealed. "She knows exactly what she doing, but the thing is, the nigga got that shit." My skin crawled.

"Damn, I hope she didn't get it," Tee said, concerned.

I furrowed my right brow. "Tee, you ain't mad?"

She cocked her head back. "Mad for what? I'm doing a whole

nother nigga. Fuck J.P., I honestly don't care." She shrugged.

"Well, I care. She dead-ass wrong, and Vena really wrong 'cause she know what me and Cheno got, what the fuck!"

"I can't even lie about that," Tee agreed.

"Man, both of the lil hoe bitches is wrong, I can't wait to holla at them in the morning." I tapped my feet on the floor, annoyed.

"I know that's right." Tee said. "I'm gon' clown Daijah, 'cause I do so much for her ass. She didn't need to fuck him. She know he ain't for the right."

"Man, it's cool. She just better pray that she ain't infected wit' that virus." We talked for a minute and I went home to get some rest.

♛ ♛ ♛ ♛ ♛ ♛ ♛ ♛ ♛ ♛ ♛ ♛ ♛ ♛ ♛ ♛ ♛

It was nine in the morning when I woke up. Cheno was gone, and I was happy about that. I showered and was in the direction of Daijah's house speedily. I walked straight in. She was on the couch asleep. I snatched that bitch up so quick.

"Man, bitch, what the fuck y'all be on?" I yelled, placing her back up to the couch.

"Girl, what are you talking about?" Daijah inquired, wiping her eyes.

"I'ma get straight to the point." I glared. "Y'all bitches dead wrong. Then you fucking J.P., and he got Herpes, dumb-ass," I said.

"Girl, I haven't been fucking no J.P. Who said that?" She questioned.

"Nah, mothafuckin' Daijah, don't play with me. Cheno told me and he ain't gon' lie about that shit."

Her surprised facial expression turned sad. "It was only one time, and I fucked him with a condom."

"You a clown-ass bitch! You know that's Booboo Kiddie daddy."

"Okay. It was a fuckin' accident," she rolled her eyes.

"Man, lil girl, you better lower yo' fuckin' voice, like now, bitch."

"Jayah, ain't no need for all of that," Daijah said as tears formed her eyes.

"Bitches kill me, supposed to be family and wanting to fuck after each other, what part of the game is that, man?" I said, angrily.

"It's cool though, Na'daijah. The nigga just laughing at y'all lame asses. I swear, you bitches are dumb." I slammed the door as hard as I could, calling Vena as I climbed in my car.

"What up with it, cousin?" She answered, enthusiastically.

"Aw, so we cousins now?" I said, slightly laughing.

"Shut up, cousin, but what's good?"

"Quit calling me that cousin shit," I yelled through the phone. "'Cause you wasn't screaming that cousin shit when you was fucking Cheno".

"What you talking 'bout? Who told you that?" She asked.

I laughed. "Bitches tryna play the not knowing role. It's mighty funny how that nigga was at my door at five in the morning telling me how he was so sorry for fucking you."

She flipped the game quickly. "Okay, that ain't yo' man."

"Aw. Okay." I giggled. "That's funny. I ain't his girl. But I'm the only one that stays getting cashed out. I'm the one with the Benz, ya dig? Cars, clothes, trips and jewelry! Don't get that shit fucked up babe! I can be wifey if I want to. But that's another story, you be careful, my cat!" I said hanging up.

I just couldn't believe J.P. and Cheno fucked family. I wound up going to the mall to clear my mind. That was the only thing that could make me happy.

The mall was filled with wealthy shoppers as always, but I was in my own little world. I moseyed along the walkways of the Bal Harbour Mall, going in and out of my favorite designer stores when something in the Gucci store caught my attention. I strolled inside to get a closer look at a pair of white Gucci loafers with the handbag and the hat to match. I was certain to get that, and browsed around for an outfit to compliment it well. *Fuck bitches. I'm gon' do this shit regardless*.

"Hello?" I answered my phone.

"What up, baby?" D-Nice sounded real good.

"Aw, hey. I haven't talked to you in a while."

"I been havin' to handle a lot of business. But that's what I was calling you for today. I want to kick it with you this evening."

"So, where we going?" I asked.

"I want to take you to this Italian Restaurant called Las Culebrinas."

♛ ♛ ♛ ♛ ♛ ♛ ♛ ♛ ♛ ♛ ♛ ♛ ♛ ♛ ♛ ♛ ♛

It was a beautiful evening. The temperature was modest, the air was clear and the sun was setting just right. We had a wonderful night on the town. I dressed in my newly purchased Gucci and wore my hair in loose curls with a part down the middle. I was looking very sophisticated. I parked right in front of the restaurant and found D-Nice waiting.

"How many?" The hostess asked.

"Two," I voiced, politely.

"Follow me. Right this way."

She led us to a secluded booth in the back to and seated us. Las Culebrinas was a very nice, classy and formal restaurant. Everyone in attendance looked like they were of wealth.

"Hi, my name is Toni and I'm going to be your waiter for tonight. Can I start you off tonight with any beverages?"

"I'll have a Dr. Pepper," I said, browsing through the menu.

"And I'll have a bottle of water and a shot of Moët."

"Damn D- Nice not some Mo!" I giggled.

The waiter scanned our orders into a machine roller and walked off.

He smiled. "Baby you looking real bad tonight." D- Nice said, gazing me in the eyes.

"You don't look to bad yourself brotha." I said, grinning.

Minutes later, Toni returned, setting our drinks in front of us. "Are you guys ready to order?" Toni inquired.

Waisting no time, D-Nice placed our order. We both were eating like we were from Africa, like we never ate before. We were so stuffed, it felt like my stomach was about to burst open. Neither of us had enough room for dessert.

"Thanks. I really enjoyed the meal. I needed that," I said, rubbing my stomach as he walked me to my car.

He hopped in the car with me and we were on our way to the pool hall. I parked in front of the pool hall, but before we could exit the vehicle, shots rang out. BOOM! BOOM! BOOM! The sound rang out over and over again. My body was burning and my heart dropped to the floor.

"D, get up." There was no response.

"Nice. Get up. Please," I reiterated again. Still no response.

I went crazy when I lifted him up and I seen blood oozing out of his eyes, chest, nose and mouth. I didn't know what to do. My hands was soaked in D-Nice's blood. I was traumatized, and I started panicking. I wasn't moving; I'd fell unconscious.

♛ ♛ ♛ ♛ ♛ ♛ ♛ ♛ ♛ ♛ ♛ ♛ ♛ ♛ ♛ ♛ ♛

Opening my eyes, I realized I was at the hospital. The lighting was bright, causing me to adjust my vision. First face I saw when my vision became clear was my daddy's.

"What happened, Jayah? Who did this?" My daddy asked, with eyes red as a cherry, like he had been crying for days.

"Daddy, I don't know. I really don't," I began. "All I know is they was shooting on my side. Once they started shooting, Nice lay on top of me. After they stopped, he just laid on his side and slumped straight down," I cried, remembering the horrific moment. "I tried to lift him up, but when I did, he was full of blood with holes in his body. That's all I remember. Daddy, is Nice okay?" I sniffled.

"I'm sorry, sweetie. He's gone. But I promise you, we'll find who did this." He assured me.

I continued crying as my eyes landed on the door. Cheno was staring in. He walked inside the room.

"Daddy, don't let him come in here!" I yelled, crying even harder. I don't know if it was from the pain he caused me or from what had just happened, but the tears were falling like a dire storm.

"Why, sweetie?"

"The nigga ain't shit." I cried. "He fucked Vena and that ain't even the rest. Na'daijah fucked J.P." I told it all. I didn't care.

"What?" My daddy said, quietly.

"Yeah. I'm so cool on him Daddy, it ain't even funny." I sniffled again. "But I can't even think about that today, worse shit done happened now! I seen this nigga with bullets through his body." I slobbered, with tears, snot and everything coming out my nose. "So don't even let him come in this room, AT ALL!"

"Damn, Jayah. I can't come in to check on you?" Cheno chimed, ambling towards me anyhow.

"Hell nah. You don't care about me, for real! All you care about is yourself. But Cheno, that's cool, too. I'm straight. Daddy, get him out my room!" I screamed.

"Jayah, I'm sorry. I will make it up to you, I promise baby. I know it's meant to be and I love you more than life itself, Jayah. I know you going through a tragedy now, so I'm gonna let you cool down, but I'll certainly be getting back to you." He blew a kiss at me.

Looking at the nigga with disgust, I knew I was already ready to forgive him. I just couldn't. He cut me deep. *We were supposed to have had an understanding*. I couldn't believe him, drunk or not. The shit was fucked up.

After the police questioned me, they felt it wasn't no need to try to find out shit since I was Jay Carter's daughter. They were certain that it had something to do with his drug operation. That was really discriminating. Even if it was pertaining to my Dad's drug enterprise, they were the law. We was the victims, and they should have tried to handle it. My daddy was surely going get down to the bottom of it himself.

Chapter Twenty

Life has good and bad days!

Several weeks passed after the incident with D-Nice. All I could do was sleep. X-pills, drinking and weed became my best friend. I have never in all my years just got fucked up to the point of losing control my body. My dad, knowing me so well, noticed the changes in my daily activities. I was infuriating him with my actions. That was the only way to clear my mind though, so I continued doing it. Truthfully, I didn't think that it was the murder that I was suffering from. I honestly knew that I was so fucked up because his death was my fault. *If only he had driven his own car.* We weren't even labeled as a couple, so why him? *Why all the good niggas got to die?* I questioned myself repeatedly. It was something to contemplate about, 'cause I really didn't know who could have wanted me dead. I was thinking it probably was somebody that knew Ashley. Then again, shortly after she died, word started floating around that she was setting up quite a few ballers. I just didn't know. I was clueless to the fact.

I started kicking it super hard with Money and Jay Jay. If I wasn't with one, I was with the other. I would always ride with them, though. Because I couldn't have lived with myself if the same shit happened again.

My daddy had gotten my Range fixed and sold it, just to get me another one. That one was was orange, sitting up on Asanti rims, and the interior was exclusively mean.

The sounds of a car horn caused me to jump up from the couch and sprint to the window. It was my daddy outside, yelling. "Happy birthday baby!" He sang, as I ran for the front door and darted to the truck.

I hadn't even realized that time passed so quickly. It was May already, and I had failed to notice the month I was born in. I was getting my lame on for real.

"Hey Daddy! This mine?" I asked with excitement.

"Yeah. You know you got to be upgraded yearly," he spoke with a loving smile.

"Dang, Daddy. That's what's up! I love you. Thanks!" I jumped up and kissed him on the cheek.

"All this ain't shit! We kickin' it today, okay baby girl? Put this on and me and you are having a ball." He handed me a bag filled with outfits inside. I darted up the staircase and hurried to get fly in the hot items my daddy purchased me. I decided on the purple leather D&G jacket, a pair of Akris cotton skinny pants and dark purple Bottega Veneta stilettos that matched the bra I rocked underneath my jacket. I smoothed my hair up into a donut that sat towards the side, then added dark purple eyeshadow to my eyes and Dior lip gloss to my lips. The look gave me a diva glamour appeal.

After getting dressed and refreshed, I felt as I was back to the regular Jayah Carter. I looked back on all the pills and alcohol that I consumed. It seemed like such a wasted of time and totally unpolished. It was cool though, because it gave me time to clear my mind.

My daddy took me to this banging restaurant on the South Beach strip. We ate, and once that was done, we conversed while walking along the beach.

"This is beautiful, princess. My baby, 19 years old." He shook his head. "That's crazy I remember when your mother first had you, and we was just the perfect family."

"I guess all good things comes to an end."

"Yeah, I guess so." My daddy stopped and turned towards me. "Baby, I'm leaving the game. Totally." He let out his confession.

"Are you really? What made you think about giving it all up?" I gazed into his eyes, tryna read him.

"Truthfully, Jayah." He sighed, a heavy breath. "You and Jaylah did. I mean, I been in the game since I was 12 years old. I'm now 35 and I got everything that a person could ever ask God for. I done got away with it for this long. I don't need to stretch my luck out at all."

I agreed. "I feel you, Daddy. So, who you passing the game down to?"

"Truthfully, sweetie, I think all my people good. We living tight, like we celebrities already, so I'm just gon' let it go. Even if my niggas ain't feeling it, I'm gone."

"That's tight, Daddy. What else after this though? We just will stop and still live in the city?"

"For real baby, me and Amelia was talking about leaving, going to Africa."

"Africa?" I squealed.

"Yeah, sweetie, moving to Africa." He nodded. "It's beautiful parts of Africa that people don't see. It's better than what you think baby, believe me."

"But Daddy, I love America." My face flushed. "I don't think we should move there. Maybe Texas, Cali, even the Big Apple," I let the words run out of my mouth quickly.

"I mean, sweetie, it's more to the world than those places. Africa, it's tight. No haters or nothing. That's all I wanna do anyway, is move away from all the haters." He let his true wish out. All his life, he had been surrounded by hatin'-ass folks, people that didn't even know my daddy who still hated on him. You know you gotta be the shit if you getting hated on by strangers.

"You right, but Africa is a place where I can't go. I love it here." I whined. "But I truly understand if you wanna move, and when you move, it's gonna be hard. But I'm grown, so I been learning to take care of myself. The money won't be a problem."

"I'm gonna make sure you have money regardless, even if you got a couple millions," he joked.

"Being honest Daddy, I got that. And it was easy, but it is time for me to holla at the Miami and holla at the Big Apple," I voiced my opinion firmly.

"I feel you, baby, but who is going with you and when?"

"Rai certainly going, I just don't know when. What about Jaylah, Daddy?"

"I already talk to Tasha, and I'm taking Jaylah. She told me she can't handle all the responsibilities." He paused. "Oh, and I forgot to tell you. She's been blowing with that one nigga that she fucks with now."

My eyeballs widened. "Really, blow? She clowning." *Damn. I haven't been gone that long and the hoe blowing shit up her nose already.*

"Yeah, she is. That's why I'm taking my baby girl along."

"I know you is." I smiled.

My daddy answered the phone vibrating in his pocket. "Okay. I got Jayah with me, so I'm just gonna bring her." He turned to me smiling.

My daddy said he needed to stop pass his place to grab something. He told me to come in because it was going to take a few minutes. He walked in the direction of the backyard. I followed directly behind him, walking into the back.

"Surprise!" Everyone screamed out. I was shocked. In front of me stood all my family and friends. Even Cheno was in attendance. For what, I don't know, but he could have left for all I cared. It was my day, so I wasn't even gonna show out and entertain the foolishness. I kept my cool.

"You like it, baby?" My mother greeted me with a hug.

"Yes, Ma. I miss you." I kissed her cheek, happy to see her.

"Do you really like it, sweetie?" My dad asked.

I smiled. "Yeah, Daddy. It's beautiful." They had the massive backyard decorated to my likings. "Y'all have it set up real well. I had no idea that you was gonna do this. Who helped you?" I probed.

"Rai, Tee, Driano, and Crazy P." He said. They all walked up.

"Happy birthday, you look very pretty." Rai gushed.

"And I'm glad that you are back to usual," Tee added, hugging me. The others hugged also. Out of nowhere, my granny and cousin Tamera emerged from the sliding doors and walked up to me.

"Happy birthday, baby. I miss you." Granny hugged my neck tightly. "Yo' cousin begged to come. I hope you don't mind."

"Yeah, we getting to old to be beefing over minor shit," Tamera said, amicably.

Like hell I mind. I decided to put our differences aside. After all, she must have wanted to dead the beef between us, begging to come to my party. Besides, I had bigger fish to worry about than having any animosity towards my blood, so I spoke. "What up?"

"Cuz, all that shit we been through was nothing, and we both need to get pass the bullshit. We family and we need to act like it." She said, sincerely. I'd looked at her like she was speaking a foreign language. Ever since I could remember, there was always beef and we stayed battling. "I know you don't care too much about me. But I just came to show my respect because I know you've just went through a tragedy, and I don't wish anything like that on my worst enemy."

"Fam, I really appreciate you for being the bigger person out of our pointless differences. I needed this, fo' real." I hugged her, but not for too long because I knew me and Tamera would never be anything but cousins that never really got along. I really did appreciate her coming to squash the beef. If it was left up to me, we would have never reconciled our hateful relationship. A prideful arrogant chick like me wasn't bowing down to no bitch, family, friend or foe.

"Yeah, I'm glad you doing good after all that has happened."

"You know the kid ain't gon' stay down for long," I said, laughing as D'vena and Daijah started approaching me. Everybody was on some rekindling shit.

Vena sounded off apologetically. "Jayah, we so sorry. I just don't know why I did some crazy shit like that. But I do know you fam, and we always will be family, so can you forgive me?" She took a deep breath. "And also, Cheno didn't know what was going on. He was drunk as fuck. When he woke up, he was mad at us and kept talking about you."

"That's tight. I do forgive y'all." I embraced them. "But what really got me is Daijah fucking on J.P., and he got a baby by her blood sister and he got Herpes."

Daijah sighed hard and long. "Jayah, this how it goes." She began as we stepped away from the crowd. "I been fucking with J.P. since I was 13. He didn't start messing with Tee until I was 15. I was sneaking around with him anyway, so I really couldn't do shit about it." She lightly huffed. "But me and him had fell out a little bit before him and Tee started messing around, 'cause I had given him Herpes. I got it from Big Tommy." She said, quickly. I was damn near out of air in my lungs when she finished, but every bit of it had registered in my brain.

"Big Tommy?" I yelled, surprised as fuck.

"Yeah, man." She nodded, embarrassed. "He didn't make me

fuck him, I just wanted to. He was giving me that amazing cash. It was an offer I couldn't refuse. I found out that he gave me Herpes and I gave it to my supposed man." Tears welled up in her eyes. "It was all hard for me to do. J.P. figured hell, he got it anyway, so why not keep fucking with me."

"Big Tommy, bra?" I asked, still thunderstruck.

"I was fuckin' him and J.P. simultaneously. You ain't never noticed every time I'm around he walks away?"

I shook my head no. "Damn. That's fucked up. My daddy will be so mad if he knew."

"I know," she muttered. "That's why you not ever telling, right?"

"I ain't gon' say shit. That's on y'all." I assured her. "But let me go over and holla at Cheno."

I strolled over to him, covering his eyes from behind.

"Guess who?" He turned around and grabbed me.

He smiled, gleefully. "Happy birthday, baby girl, and I'm sorry."

"Sorry for what?" I squinted my eyes, confusedly.

"For what I did." He chimed, genuinely.

I waved him off. "Man, forget that," I blushed. "They told me the whole story. You cool, just don't do that shit again." I sounded.

He pulled me into his chest. "Okay, baby. Damn, I miss you so much, and I been going too crazy." He laughed, planting a wet kiss on my forehead.

"Really! It's cool though, just forget all about it. Okay?"

He licked his sexy lips. "So, what's been up with you, shorty?"

"Hanging in there. You?"

"Well, you know I'm gon' stay good. I been back and forth to the N.Y., 'cause Shawn been in the studio with Diddy recording his album like crazy."

"What? He signed him?" I asked, genuinely excited for the nigga.

"Yes, he did. I'm his manager."

"What, that's crazy. I know Rai happy about that shit. She ain't told me."

"I know. Did she ever tell you that Diddy was looking for y'all? He ready for y'all to become models for next year's Sean John collection?"

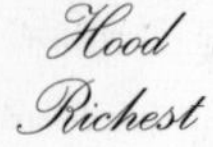

"Really, do he?" I asked, super excited at getting' that going..

"Yeah, I tried calling you to tell you that, but you never answered my calls."

"Oh really?"

"Yeah, really," he replied.

"Well, being honest, I have been thinking about moving to New York anyway. I got to get away from this city before I kill all these clowns."

"You so crazy, but come outside. I got something to show you."

I walked behind him as he guided the way. Once we reached the front, all I saw was a champagne pink Lamborghini Gallardo with a shimmering black one parked directly behind it.

"Oh. My. God!" I screamed, hyped. "Cheno, I been wanting one of these forever and a day, this is so crazy! I just can't believe you got this for me!" I squealed in amazement.

"Happy birthday." He laughed at my reaction. "But Jayah, I didn't get this for you. Diddy himself made sure you got this. He asked what he could do to persuade you to model his line. At first he said a Benz, then a Lexus, then a Range, but I told 'em that was nothin' to you 'cause you been pulled out them make of whips already." He cracked a smile. "So, what do you say?"

"I mean, I love the car, but you know I don't work for folks. He mean, and you know how I get, I follow no orders."

"Yeah, Jayah, this ain't like that though. And this is the meal ticket. Fucking with that nigga, you will get a lot of clout. You ain't gon' only have clout in Miami, but you will be known worldwide. Maybe one day you can own your own fragrance, shoe line or whatever you want. Dealing with him, you can be an actress. Everything you wanna be."

"You're right. I'm just gon' need time to think about it."

"Think long and hard, because I'm up out of here before the Fourth of July."

"Okay, but do I still get to keep the car?" I asked, eager to know.

"Yeah, that's yours. The black one is mine. It's just an incentive gift." He said as we walked back inside the party.

My daddy asked me if I was ready for the slideshow on the monitor.

"Yeah, I'm ready," I replied.

"Okay, have a seat right here."

I was sitting there watching my slideshow of when I was a kid with my family and friends, when some crazy shit just came across the screen. It was me on there, butt naked, having sexual relations with Jay Jay. It was shocking, because I didn't even recall having sexual performances or nothing with this man. I didn't quite understand how that happened. I pinched myself, because I thought I was dreaming. Everybody was sitting there just as stunned as I was. Nobody budged and the tape was steady rolling. The last frames said it all. Payback's a bitch, I got money now you fucking whore!

Oh my God he set me up! That was his whole plan, to get me to take ecstasy pills and fuck me when I wasn't in control. I couldn't believe he had revenge out on me, embarrassing me in front of my daddy, my mother, my granny and everybody. All I could do was run inside and bolt upstairs into my old room. I grabbed my Mickey Mouse pillow and flopped down, sinking comfortably into the bed. My granny and Dad chased right behind me.

"Jayah, who is that boy?" My granny asked from the door entrance.

I mumbled an answer. "This boy named Jay Jay that I used to mess with while I was in high school, but I never did anything at all with him. I don't even remember that day."

"What the fuck you mean Jayah you don't remember?" My daddy questioned me.

"Daddy, I don't remember that day! I don't remember doing nothing with him! We never did anything! I have kicked it with him a few times, but it was never anything like that."

"Have you ever been off them pills or drank around him?" My daddy asked.

"Yeah, I used to take ecstasy pills and drink, but I don't remember that," I pouted.

"Well, that's it right there, silly. He got you while you was high and drunk." Daddy was mad, but he was at ease, too.

"Yeah, Jayah, that's it! He wanted to get you, so he got you drunk and high to the point where you didn't rememember. He tried to expose you."

"Dang, y'all, what if he puts it on the internet?" I whined. "Dude really tryna assassinate my character."

"Man, I'm gon' handle this, and you better believe that shit." My daddy assured me and took off.

"Yeah, that's some fucked up shit," my granny added.

I whimpered. "Granny, I need a big favor from you." I squeezed Mickey, frowning. "Can you please go and explain everything to Cheno? I know he's like what da hell!"

"I know baby. I'll talk to him for you so don't even worry about it." She said, walking out the door.

What a fucking surprise party. I burried my face in my satin pillow.

Chapter Twenty-One

Payback is a bitch!

I arrived at the Mango Tropical Café Bar 15 minutes before 11. I pulled up right in front. Money was at the front door waiting on me. I grabbed my Carlos Falchi clutch and walked in as he greeted me.

"Hello, beautiful. How are you doin'?" He smiled.

"I'm a'ight, but I'm gon' really be alright after we get this clown."

"Yeah. So, what the fuck happened?"

"I told you. He had me drinking and taking pills, recording me doing it to him. That part I don't even remember." I cut my eyes. I tired of telling the story and still reeling from the embarrassment it caused me.

"Aw, well I got my peoples working on it now." He nodded. "That nigga got me fucked up thinking he gon' try and play my baby like that." We talked for about five minutes and I took off.

Wow. That's what I'm talking about. I got all kind of niggas that want to off niggas for me. Jay Jay a clown, all because he wanted to play get back, over some shit I did in high school. Him and everybody else knows that I ain't fucking with no broke niggas, so if that was his intentions on hurting me, he can forget about it. It was nothing compared to losing his life.

I couldn't answer my phone fast enough to catch the caller. The person just left a voice mail, and I decided to check it later and called Tee instead..

"Sup, babe?" She answered.

"What's up, man? Where you at?"

"About to meet J.P. so I can get my daughter."

"What now, when that happen?" I asked, shocked.

"Honey, this his second time watching her," Tee said. "But he started getting lil shit for her when that shit had happen to D-Nice."

"Aw, I was gone off them beans all day and night," I giggled.

"You was, though."

"Yeah, I was. But I'm back, and I'm better than ever, okay? I'm reloaded. The heats loaded. Okay, now we rolling." I laughed. I had to spit that line.

Tee laughed. "You silly, girl. So what everybody doing about Jay Jay?"

"Daddy and them couldn't find dude, but Money on it now, too."

"Who is Money?"

"Girl, the one nigga that I met in the club when I beat Chassidy up."

"Oh him." She sighed. "Jayah, I really don't like him. I'm really not feeling him at all. It's just something about him I don't like."

"He cool though, Tee." I told her.

"Okay, so why he don't never like coming around?"

"I mean, I can't answer that, but I can say that some niggas just like hanging around they own people."

"Well whatever, I will holla at you when I get home."

"Alright sis, love ya."

"I love you too, babe." Tee said hanging up the phone.

I was riding around town thinking about everything. The good, the bad, the sad, the terrible things that we'd did. I realized at that very moment that it really was time to reposition myself. Relocating was not bad, especially if wonderful opportunities are thrown at you. Actually thinking about it, it really was a great opportunity for me. I never dreamt of becoming a model. However,

I always felt like a star. I didn't need the world to let me know that I was fabulous. But, it was funny how life just throws shit in your direction. It's just on the person if they catch it or not. *Hey, I guess Cheno would like the idea of me modeling. Then again, maybe not, because he hadn't called me since the incident that happened at the party.*

So me, being the person I am, went to his house. It was a little after midnight when I arrived. Parking on the street was my best solution, because I didn't want him to hear me when I came in. Yeah, I had a key. He didn't give me one, but I had one made one day when he had me grab some shit at his house. What a mistake. Niggas are so stupid at times, they should know by now how women are. I unlocked the door and went straight in. There were no signs of him downstairs, so I ascended the staircase. He was sleeping in his humongous bed. He had Louis Vuitton detailing the room, from the pillows, to the sheets, drapes, and the big boy comforter. An enormous 72-inch flat screen was hanging down from the ceiling. He wasn't gon' play when it came down to his shit. He always said he had to have the best of the best.

My eyes slowly drifted over to him, and I was admiring him totally. He didn't snore or anything. He was lying there in a deep sleep. For a while, I just stood, observing him, wondering how our baby would look. Then I finally got underneath the covers with him. I forgot that he was a light sleeper. He woke up looking at me. I guess he thought he was dreaming, but he spoke to me.

"How you get in here, Jayah?" He whispered.

"I got a key," I said, as if he gave me one.

"Damn, I didn't know that. But what up?" He said in a flat tone.

"Did my granny explain to you what happen?" I asked, sadly.

"Yeah, she did."

"So, why didn't you call me?"

"For real, Jayah. I been here all day just clearing my head. That's it."

"About what?" I wanted to know.

"Man, about it all," he huffed.

"What is that supposed to mean?"

"Shid. What it sound like? I been thinking about you a lot, of course. But, I also been thinking about the game, and if I should let it go for this music shit. I know Shawn raps his ass off, but ain't no telling if the world gon' like him. Maybe I should just stay here."

"Man, you the same one telling me that it's time for a change. Now you don't wanna move and shit, scared to take a chance. That nigga tight. I know he gon' blow. So, you shouldn't even trip about that." I paused. "And what have you been thinking about me for? I hope it ain't nothing bad." My eyes wandered around, avoiding looking directly at Cheno.

"Nah. It's good shit. I was just thinking about how me and you should just start all over, become a family, maybe start our own family."

Damn, that's crazy how I was just thinking the same thing. Maybe it's meant to be. My thoughts of the future was interrupted by a phone call.

"What's up?"

"Oh my God, oh my God!" Rai said screaming, yelling and crying simultaneously.

"Hello?" I jumped up, completely on edge.

"Jayah, they killed her. Jayah, they killed her," Rai couldn't seem to get any other words out.

"Killed who, Rai? What are you talking about?"

"They killed Tee and the baby is...is…shoo – "

The phone dropped from my ear and Cheno picked it back up.

"Hello?" Cheno said, raising up.

"Man, who is this?" Rai asked, still crying.

"This Cheno, Rai what's going on?"

She could barely let the words out. "I'm up here in front of J.P. and SaNara's house." She sniffled, crying hard. "And when she pulled up, she found J.P. and Tee in the car dead, and the baby shot."

"What? Not Tee and J.P. dead? And the baby?" He dropped his head into his chest.

"No, the baby is at the hospital now. She got shot in the arm."

"What!" He yelled. "So who did this, what happened? I just can't believe this shit here." He slowly shook his head.

"I know, just get over here. Both of y'all, now," Rai cried out. "The police still got the bodies out here investigating."

We wasted no time rushing over there, hoping that things were indeed a lie. I arrived at the crime scene and saw Tee lifeless body. J.P. head exploded from the impact of the bullet, his brain fagments were everywhere. We couldn't even identify his body. It was something that I just didn't fathom. It really didn't sit right with me at all. One hundred thoughts raced through my head. *What was he doing in her car? Who was this for? Him or Tee? Who did this? Whoever did this is gonna die! I mean they're gonna die.*

I just sat there in disbelief. *My sister, my best friend is gone. I couldn't think straight. I didn't think this would happen to Tee! I thought it would have been me before her! She got a baby!* I tapped Rai on the shoulder. "Rai, where is the baby?" I whispered, tears streaming down my face.

"She at the hospital. They said she gonna make it." Rai wiped her eyes, but the tears wouldn't stop rolling.

"Oh, have anybody talked to Driano?" I slowly paced back and forth.

"Yeah, he was here at first, but yo' daddy had to escort him away from the scene because dude was going nuts, man. Him and P was going crazy, talkin' about their killin' everybody. Yo' daddy and them went to your granny's house."

"Well, let's go over there, Rai."

When we walked in the door, my granny started talkin'.

"I knew it." She shook her head. "I knew it was about to happen."

"What are you talking about?" I asked.

"Check yo' voicemail child." Not knowing what she was talking about, I pulled out my phone.

"Hey, Jayah. This Granny. Call me, I had a dream somebody had gotten killed. It's a girl face I kept seeing. Baby, call me back. I hope you okay." I dropped to my knees. I didn't know what to do.

"Damn. A premonition?" My daddy said.

"It was! It was Daddy." I burst out into tears again. "Why Tee? I just don't get it." Cheno grabbed me, trying his hardest to console me. I cried hysterically, slobbering on his shoulders. My cell phone rang, Cheno answered.

"Yeah, bitch. That's why your right hand gone, and being honest, I wish it was you. But trust, you're next," the stranger said, not realizing it was Cheno.

"Man, who the fuck is this?" He asked, enraged. The caller hung up. Cheno didn't tell me what the caller said.

"Who was that?" I asked.

"Man, nobody." I could read in his eyes that something wasn't right.

"Oh, okay. Whatever, Cheno." I said. "Daddy, have you talked to Ms. Laura and the twins?"

"Yeah. They had to go to the hospital with the baby," he said.

I just couldn't take it. Everybody was crying hysterically. I would have had an anxiety attack if Cheno had not left with me.

I cried the entire night. Cheno held me for dear life, allowing me to feel comfortable. He said nothing.

We watched the sunrise together. Neither of us got any sleep, and when we finally decided to try and doze off, Cheno phone rang.

He answered. "Hello?"

"Man, Cheno, what up, bra? This R.P. man." I could hear him clearly. "Word is J.P. owed the Cubans a half of a million and they wanted that back. Early yesterday, J.P. told them that they wasn't getting shit. They supposedly thought that they were killing him and SaNara, knowing that she had involvements with him. They also knew that she did handle his money sometimes, so they thought it was her and ended up killing Tee. That's some fucked up shit, man. I'm gon' kill them fuckin' Cubans."

"Look, don't be tryna do no crazy-ass shit like that, bra. We gon' get 'em, and you better believe that whoever it was gon' die. That's word to my life."

"A'ight, bra. I'ma stay cool." I heard the click as R.P. hung up the phone.

We lay back down and fell asleep until the afternoon. We got dress and met everyone over Tee's mother house. When we got there, the baby was lying down on the couch. She was fine, Boo Boo Kiddie had got grazed in the arm and she was looking so precious. I cried when I saw her, knowing that she would have to grow up without a mother and her father, even though I knew Adrian was gonna take good care of her. Still, that shit just cut me deep. *Fuck the world*.

♛ ♛ ♛ ♛ ♛ ♛ ♛ ♛ ♛ ♛ ♛ ♛ ♛ ♛ ♛ ♛ ♛

The funeral was held at our church. Both families agreed to have the funeral services together. When we pulled up, it was 10 in the morning. There were people there before the families arrived. Service didn't begin until noon. People made it there early. Folk made sure they were getting seats. Both Tee and J.P. had to have closed caskets because of the terrible wounds. It was really sad, but the preacher was good and got us through it. Once we left, the outside looked more of a festival than a funeral. That just showed how much they were loved, and folk's really showed mad love to both families.

Later on that night, everybody went out to Club Fierce. Everywhere you looked, someone had on shirts to honor J.P. and Tee. One thing I knew, that they would be forever missed. And God took them away for a reason, which I would never understand why, but it wasn't my place to ask questions. I got myself together and knew there wasn't no need for me to keep crying and weeping on the shit, 'cause I couldn't bring her back. My theory was just to fuck everything, live life to the fullest and follow my heart.

The the club collected more people. It have never been that packed in a club, at least that I've ever seen. My daddy and Big Tommy slithered their way through the amped crowd, approaching me. They had me follow them to the bar in the center of the club. They guided the way, and I slid onto the barstool slowly bobbing my head to the smooth beats.

"Jayah, watch this." My daddy spoke, smiling and taking a seat beside me.

"What?" I asked, concerned.

"This lil skit that's about to come on the monitor."

I cut my eye at him suspiciously. After a few minutes, I grew irritated. Then it finally appeared across the screen. Shocked beyond words, there he was, Jay Jay. The fucking clown on the monitor was fucking another man. Enjoying himself? He certainly was. I didn't understand how they had accomplished this, but I knew I was happy. I was surprised at his boldness, but so happy he was on the set of the club scene that night. I thought I'd gotten embarrassed, shid. Embarrass is an understatement for what he was feeling, I know.

I cracked up laughing and shifted my head in my dad's direction. He was pointing at Jay Jay rushing out the club, humiliated. Most of Miami was in attendance, if not all the people that truly mattered. There was no way of covering up that shit. Dude was getting fucked and was happy, like a bitch would be.

"So, what y'all drug him up?" I asked, doubling over into laughter.

"Being honest." He chuckled, sipping on his drink. "Sweetie, it was easier than we thought. Dude was really a homo thug." He cracked up.

"Are you serious?" I asked, mouth open wide.

"Yup. You know Tommy nephew Tre be fucking all the fag-ass homo niggas," he spoke with disgust in his eyes. "So, we asked the lil nigga to see if he could get Jay Jay and we would pay for his surgeries to become a girl."

"Really?"

"Let me finish telling baby, how the shit played out." My daddy paused and began demonstrating how it went down. "Okay I told him who the nigga was or whatever. He was excited. Tre made sure we was gon' pay for his transformation if he got the shit on tape. We got the tape the very next day. I knew that would make you feel better, so I decided to have it played in the club. What better place?" He shrugged.

I jumped on my daddy, happy as shit. The nigga basically raped me, and he was a fuckin' faggots! *Hell naw, that's why everybody knows you're gay now, bitch.*

The shit was funny. Rai and I laughed for days over that shit. Jay Jay's face was never seen in Miami again after that night. I was trying my hardest to get over Tee's death so I coped with it by partying daily.

Chapter Twenty-Two

Tryna make it!

It had only been a few weeks since Tee and J.P. deaths, but things between me and Cheno was great. The two of us were trying to make our relationship work, and forget about the fucked up situation. From time to time, we just sat and reminisced on all the fun times we all shared together.

Rai and I grew closer and we were together every day. Tasha, on the other hand, was starting to become a fuck up. The bitch had start messing around with some blow head nigga name Tawny, and word was floating around that she started fucking with that shit hard. That was crazy to me. I couldn't believe she was that naïve and allowed a nigga to persuade her into indulging in some addictive drugs. That was on her ass, though. I had different shit on my mind than to be worried about a grown-ass woman that knew the difference between right and wrong.

Cheno and Shawn were in the studio like crazy, tryna get some shit together for Diddy. They were making sure they were gon' have perfection in their work. They knew Diddy wasn't gon' play with them unless they brought their rap game hard.

I still wasn't sure if I wanted to do the modeling thing for him or not. And he really wanted us to model his clothing line. On several occasions, he phoned us, offering us a contracted position that had many zeros in the good deal. He promised that we would be the lead face of Sean John, even taking up other jobs as far as everything his enterprise produced. Surprisingly, he was a cool dude, but I always had plans to get money myself. I just didn't know if I wanted to be in the public eye like that. *What will them hoes do if I get in the entertainment business? Ain't that something, I know I will be shutting hoes down, no makeup, no weave, a natural beauty. Me and Rai would be the best of the best.*

It was almost 4 when I pulled up at the shop in my Lambo. I spotted Candace with her hoes attached at her hip. I strutted in that shop looking too cute. Donned in a Christian Audigier dress with a huge, outrageous butterfly and skull design on the front. Purple python Christian Louboutin platform pumps decorated my feet. Everyone greeted me as I made my way through.

"Sorry about your loss." It seemed like I'd heard that one hundred times within the first five minutes.

I would simply say, "It's cool. God got her now, she home." And that would be it. Fee called for me to get my hair shampooed and I was underneath the dryer before you knew it. That's when Anne walked in and came right up to me.

"Girl, what's up?" She said, excitedly. I knew she knew something.

"Nothing just getting my hair did up."

"Oh, well, I don't want to be the one to tell you this." She puckered her lips and gently shook her head. "But Adrian and SaNara are back together, and I guess they gon' have the kids grow up together thinking that they are their parents."

"What? Are you serious?" My hearted dropped. "What you mean?" I said as tears ran down my face.

"I mean." She shrugged once. "Adrian is back with SaNara and her son gon' think that Driano is his daddy and that Tee baby gon' think that SaNara and Driano are her mom and dad."

My heart returned, pumping heavily. "Fuck no! That will not happen. What the fuck you mean?"

She nodded. "Girl, yes. I guess they decided that Tee daughter will be staying with Driano since she's so used to him."

"Yeah, that's true. But if he on that, he will never see Boo Boo Kiddie again. If that's the case, me and Cheno can take her. What the hell! Tee didn't even like that hoe come on now." I sighed.

"I know that's why I had to tell you girl." She shook her head, feeling my pain. "But I'm sorry about the whole ordeal. Shid. I hope y'all work it out."

"Thanks for letting me know, girl."

Once Fiona called me to her station to finish my hair. I was too anxious for her to finish me up. I paid and dipped out the door with the frantic sound of my heels clunking against the ground. I popped in my car and phoned my daddy, telling him to meet me at his place. I hung up and rocketed to my dad's crib. I arrived 20 minutes later and darted inside his house, telling him everything.

"I know, baby. Calm down. If that's what he wanna do, just let it be. He just want Boo Boo to be raised with a family, that's it."

"That's it?" I roared. "That's it, Daddy?" I went nuts. I had never been so angry in my life. That was one thing that me and my daddy totally disagreed on. I didn't know if I was taking it too far, but I knew I was going to get my baby.

That's fucked up! Who the fuck they think they are?

I called Rai as I was leaving out the house. I told her to meet me like now, and she did just that.

She popped out the car and asked what was wrong with me. I told her 'bout Driano and SaNara's plan for Tee baby to grow up thinking they the parents. Rai also flipped out.

"What the fuck! Hell nah! Both of them bitches got me fucked up. I know Tee rolling around in her grave. She don't want her baby over there with that bitch."

"That's all I'm saying, Rai." Tears fell from my face.

"Don't cry, Jayah." She wiped my tears. "Let's go over there."

"Let's go." I said. We hopped in our whips rushing over there. We jumped out the car and walked right inside.

"Man, what the fuck?" I cocked my head back. "Put Boo Boo shit on, and that's that." I yelled.

"What's wrong, Jayah?" Driano asked, like he didn't know.

"What the fuck you mean what's wrong? Clown-ass nigga. This is what's wrong," I said, pointing at SaNara."

"Calm down, this is the best way. Everybody think so Jayah."

"What?" I screamed. "Fuck everybody! That's my right hand, and I know what it is and how she would feel about this bitch being around Boo Boo, nigga," I glared into his eyes. "Give me my niece, and we'll holla at you. Fuck that."

"Yo, let me call your daddy, Jayah. We can get this straight."

I stared at him, dumbfounded. Rai injected at that point. "There's nothin' to get straight." She paused briefly. "Man, look A. Fuck the bullshit. Give us Boo Boo Kiddie and you can call Jay your damn self. You don't need us to wait for you to call. We don't like being around this bitch, simply." She snickered. "I should beat yo' ass again." Rai said, pointing in SaNara face.

"Y'all need to get over it and grow up. Me and Tee wasn't even beefing anymore. Actually we had gotten cool."

"Cool! What the fuck you call cool?" I looked at her, waiting for an answer. She said nothing, "'Cause I know my bitch wasn't on no sucka-ass shit like that. Believe me. She don't like your bitch ass."

"Okay, Jayah. Yo' daddy on the phone." Driano said, as if I was 'posed to change my mind

"Fuck that. Tell him I'll call him after I get my baby." I pushed the phone away from my ear.

"Rai, grab Boo Boo Kiddie some pampers and some milk and we out."

Without stalling, we grabbed Boo Boo and took off. I couldn't believe how everybody thought it was the right thing to do. *The bitch was just wanting to fight Tee, but now she wanna raise her baby girl. Not neva! What the fuck! Over my dead body!*

Everybody kept calling my phone. I wasn't answering. *All these bitches can go to hell*. My inner voice kept the same thoughts going through my mind.

I went over Cheno's house, 'cause I knew everybody would have been tryna go to my place and want to solve the problem. In my world, problem been solved.

Soon as I walked inside the house, Cheno seen the sadness in my eyes. I picked Boo Boo up from her car seat and laid her blanket on the loveseat, gently laying her on her stomach. She squirmed around for a minute. I placed her pacifier in her mouth, softly patted her back and she went back to sleep. Cheno immediately asked what was wrong.

Tears instantly feel from my face as I kicked my heels off and plopped down onto the couch. "Them clowns tryna have SaNara raise Boo Boo Kiddie, and that ain't gon' happen. I will raise her my mothafuckin' self rather than have that hoe around." I sniffled. "It's mighty funny, all of a sudden she want to be with A now. She is a clown man. I swear to God, she lame."

"Well, Jayah I really don't know what to say. Just do whatever you think Tee would really want. Think it over long and hard."

"You right, babe, I will think it over and make sure you set the date for us to leave."

"Whud, you ready?" His eyes bucked.

"More ready than I ever been." I gazed into his eyes. "I think the world ready for a naturally beautiful face. What you think?" I said, smiling.

"Yeah I think so, baby. So you gon' do the modeling thing?"

"Yeah, and hopefully a lil more."

"Like what?"

"I don't know yet. Maybe a film director or something major, I don't know." I shrugged. "I guess whereever life places me. I'm just gon' allow my Heavenly Father to handle that, and whatever is whatever."

"Okay, just let me know what's on yo' mind and I'm behind you one hundred and ten percent." He kissed my forehead and headed upstairs.

I sat there with tears falling down my face. It was so confusing to me. I didn't know what I was gonna do. I laid my head down on the armrest, drifting off to sleep. Someone stood over me and shocked the hell out of me. It was Tee.

"Jayah, I know you might be scared, but know that I'm in a better place. And I'm here to let you know that everything is gonna be fine. Let them raise the baby. You got a whole life ahead of you, and I don't want you to miss out on a great opportunity. They already settle in and believe me, A is only being with her 'cause I gave him my consent. I really think they should raise the kids together. When they kids grow up, they can tell them the truth. When they're old enough to understand everything. Believe me, I love you and everything is fine."

"But Tee…" That was all I could say because Cheno started talking, awakening me from my dream.

"Baby, Tee is not here. What are you talking about?"

"Babe, she was just standing right here talking to me." I nodded, profusely.

"You tripping." He looked like I had been hallucinating.

"No, I really saw her, and she told me that she want the baby to be raised by SaNara and Adrian."

"Okay." He replied.

"Baby, I'm serious." I looked at him sternly. "She must have wanted to let me know that, so she came in my dreams."

"I'm glad to hear that. So what you gonna do?" He asked.

"Take her back to her mom and dad. That's how it suppose to be."

I hopped up quickly and took the baby to her family. I walked in with a smile on my face and handed Driano his daughter. I could see on his face that he was relieved about my decision. I quickly whispered in his ear, "This is what Tee wants."

"I know. She had to let me know that before I even made a move," he replied, grinning. Before I left, I gave SaNara a hug, 'cause it surely takes a strong woman to raise another female's seed. "Yo, anytime y'all need time to y'all self, call me and it'll be my pleasure to get Boo Boo." They thanked me and I walked out.

I called and let Rai in on everything that was going on. She understood once I informed her on the present status. Rai was ready to hit the club, like always, and I was on it also after I got finished talking to my daddy. I told her to meet me at my crib in an hour and I headed to my daddy's place.

Pulling up in my daddy's driveway, I sat there looking at the life that I had been blessed with. But, then I thought if it actually worth losing Tee, her daddy, the killing, watching people get killed. All sorts of things flashed in my brain. In truth, I really didn't think it was worth the headache. So, it was definitely time for a change, a big one. I walked in the house only to see my daddy on the couch crying. That was weird. The nigga never cried unless it involved me.

"Daddy, what's up? What happened?" I asked.

He looked at me like he'd just saw Jesus. "Jayah. It's you, baby." He grabbed me, hugging me for dear life.

"Yeah. Who else would it be? What you talkin' about?" I slowly patted his back, hugging him back.

"Crazy P and them just called and said that it was a shootout at your house, and that a girl and two boys was shot. Nobody knows the status on it." He exhaled in relief. "I was just about to walk out the door, but you here, baby. You here." He picked me up, kissing me all over my face. My body instantly weakened and I dropped to the floor. "Daddy, Rai. Rai is at my house! I can't believe this, Daddy. Not Rai, too. Daddy, what's going on? Somebody is trying to kill me! I know it, what, what's going on? Man, let's go see what's wrong with Rai. I can't lose another friend, Daddy, that's something I can't do. Oh my Lord, why is everything going so wrong!" I yelled on my knees.

"Jayah, I don't know, but I'm gonna get down to the bottom of this shit." He roared in anger, lifting me up from the floor. "Who want you dead? Who is tryna do this?" Daddy screamed out as my phone rang.

I retrieved my bag from the floor, fumbling through it, tryna find my phone. I answered, but the caller hung up. The phone rang back. I answered quickly.

"Baby, Jayah, where you at? They just told me you was dead." Cheno sounded off.

"Dead? Who said that? I know Rai ain't dead, I know she's not!" I cried out.

"What are you talking about, baby?" He asked.

I responded, heart heavy and aching. "Something happened at my house, and I guess three people got shot. I know for a fact Rai is one of the people. She was the one person that I know was at my house."

"Are you serious?" He asked, shocked.

"Yes, I'm over my daddy's, and we 'bout to see what's going on, so I will get with you."

"Okay, baby. Call me soon as you get there."

Arriving on the scene was like watching "CSI", it was uniformed people everywhere. My daddy pulled up quick and I popped out, seeing the corners bringing one body out in a black bag. I just didn't understand. I asked if I could I see the face. That shit was a surprise. The body belonged to Money. He had a single bullet implanted in the dome. I started crying hysterically. How Money got killed in my house? *Where is Rai? Who is the third person? What happened?* I didn't understand. At that moment, my mind went blank and I passed out.

Chapter Twenty-Three

Confused!

Hours later, I woke up with Cheno by my side. He had a single tear streaming down his face. He tried not to let me observe the pain he held inside, but his eyes allowed me to see the agony. He must have felt the pain within me. He eventually broke the silence, taking a deep breath and holding his head down.

"Jayah, bra, Shawn and Rai got shot."

My eyes widened. "What? What do you mean Shawn? I thought Shawn was with you?" I asked, confused.

"Nah, I ain't never say that. He was with Rai."

"Will they make it? Baby, just tell me they will live. I can't take this. Just tell me, Cheno tell me!" I screamed, completely hysterical.

"I don't know. They in surgery now."

"Oh my God, what happen? Do anybody know who did this? I got to go." I tried to snatch out the needles in my arm.

He jumped up grabbing my arms. "Baby, stop. Please. That's all we waiting on. That's it, Jayah." He gently kissed my hand. "They in there getting operated on right now."

"Baby, where did Rai get shot at?" I asked, heaving.

"In her stomach and arm. Shawn got shot in his back twice and in his legs twice."

More tears fell from my eyes, like it was a rainstorm. *They got shot over me. That was supposed to be me. The person was looking for me.*

After a few minutes, I calmed down, but I had questions. "Baby, so how did that boy Money die? Was he with them also?"

"Nah, word is that the nigga was waiting in your house and hit Shawn twice in the back and twice in the leg, then Rai pulled out her strap and blasted him with one hot one to the head."

"Okay, so how did two get shot?"

"I don't know,."

My mind raced. I was puzzled. "It gotta be some details left out. But what did the nigga Money wanna kill them for?"

"No." He gestured his head from side to side slowly. "Baby, he was in the house waiting. I guess thinking you was gonna be the one coming in."

"But I never did anything to him! Why me? Why try and kill me?" I lost my breath. I couldn't breathe. It was hurting to talk. The pain went to my throat. At that moment, my daddy made his entrance with that infamous killer instinct plastered on his flawless face.

"Baby, you okay?"

"No. Daddy, who want me dead? Who?" I cried out, feeling more protected, 'cause I knew if anybody could keep me from out of harm's way, it would be my father.

"I don't know, but who is Money, Jayah? Where did you meet him at?" My dad asked.

"At the club that night we got into it with Jay Jay girl Chassidy. That night daddy."

"Okay, so did you bring him to your house?"

"Never daddy. I know the business we're in, so why would I bring a stranger to the house?"

"Right, but I'm gon' be out all day tryna find out what happened. 'Cause I'm thinking that all this shit is connected." He nodded, agreeing with himself. "I got to get down to the bottom of this before I move out this fuckin' place." He said. "And Jayah, you gotta let me know what you gonna do, 'cause you can never stay here. I won't leave you in this hell hole without me. So, either you're comin' along, or you going far from this place, at least for a while." He said. "I'ma holla, I gotta see what these streets talking 'bout." He stormed out the room all crazy.

Bad Boy here I come. I prayed and wished that Shawn and Rai was going to be alright, really not knowing their condition because they were still in surgery.

* * *

A few days had passed and I was still on pins and needles. There wasn't a word on Rai and Shawn's recovery. I wound up staying at Cheno's house. Dude wasn't allowing me to leave his sight for shit. Literally, he would sit in the bathroom with me. All the while, my daddy was still in the street, not sleeping, searching for a leak in the mysterious events that had occurred. Cheno stayed close to me, and we would talk for hours, ranging from the past to the present to the future.

Another week had passed, and I had to grab some clothes. I had worn everything that was at Cheno's crib. He wanted to go, but he had other things to handle before he got out of the game.

"You sure you gonna be cool, baby?" He asked, pondering on whether he should go with me or not.

"Yeah, I'm straight. I'm just running there to get me a few items, then I'm gonna head to my daddy place. Maybe check up on Tasha."

"Okay, I love you." Cheno said, kissing me on my forehead.

My once beautiful house looked so weird, I guess because the tape was still up surrounding the entire place. My house just didn't feel like home at all to me anymore.

I entered my home and everything was like I left it. I bolted upstairs to gather my clothes so I could dip out quick. I was in my closet trying to figure out what I was taking and what I was leaving. I looked at my Chanel fit that I wore when me and Cheno had our first date together. It brought back so many memories. It was crazy though, because my whole intentions were to fuck with dude, get his money and then holler at the next nigga. But it didn't happen that way. That's why I should have known to live day to day, to roll with the flow. I never know what God has planned for my future. One thing I knew was he planned for Cheno to stay in my life. Contemplating about it just made my heart glow. I was thinking about all the crazy acts that we performed and it was well worth it to prove our strong love for each other. As I was in my deep thoughts, somebody quickly appeared with the barrel of a gun pointed to the back of my head.

"Yeah, bitch. You thought it was over. You thought you was safe, huh?"

I couldn't speak. All I could do was stand there frozen as she ranted and raved. My mind sat thoughtless. I knew my time would come one day, but never once had I sat and thought my loathing and jealous cousin Tamera would be behind the dire happenings in my life.

"Bitch, you hear me. You thought you was a glamour doll or some fabulous hoe. You thought you was the princess of the ghetto, huh? You thought you were the superstar of the hood! But guess what, bitch? You 'bout to be dead, just like you supposed to been long time ago! All the people that died are because of you! Tee died 'cause I couldn't get to you. Somebody always tryna protect your ass! Like the dude that we shot up. If only he had let the bullets hit you, he would still be here. But nah, mothafucka's wanna play captain save a hoe. I've been playing your ass since day one. I never liked you, and you gotta be a fool if you really thought our relationship could be anything other than an adversary on totally opposite sides. You thought it was all good and we was cool. Fuck you, bitch! I never liked you, and never will. How you think, your lil porn video was debuted at your surprise party?" She laughed, deviously. "Is there anything you wanna say before I kill yo' hoe ass?"

My words staggered out my mouth. "Why did you have to kill Tee and have people set my peoples up though? I really wasn't that hard to find, I know."

"Oh, bitch, that's irrelevant. I said all that needs to be said. Besides, you 'bout to visit Tee, Rai and the other fools. Ask 'em when you get to Hell." I could tell in her stern voice that she had no remorse. "Fuck you, I've always hated your booshie slut-ass and often dreamt about this day anyway. Oh, and bitch, you fucked with the wrong one. This one for Ashley bitch."

Pop! Pop! Pop!

Chapter Twenty-Four

The beginning to a never ending!

I was relieved. It wasn't me that had been hit, it was Tamera. The bitch was profoundly jealous of me after all the years that'd passed. She really hated me to the point of death. I mean, the bitch was saying some shit that I didn't even remember. It was wild. Come to find out, she and Money had set me up from jumpstart. Rumor has it, that they were dating for a year and that's when she came to the conclusion that she wanted me and my family dead. Plans were to kill my daddy first. Money had sent some of his contract killers down to do the job, which that failed and they got fucked up. Then they really took shit to the next level, going for the head. *Damn. May my sister Donteice rest in peace*. That's one thing I'm salty about. I still can't believe that my sister dead. That sick bitch got that shit off fo' real.

All Tamera needed was help for someone to facilitate of her secret movements. Her and Ashley was tryna conquest shit like I was from a tangible rival of some sort. And Money's clown-ass was the one that indulged in the act with the clown-ass bitches. Hell, they wanted us badly, but the bitches fucked with the wrong

bitch, believe that shit. They may have killed a few and wounded a few, but all parties involved with them are dead, and this bad bitch still standing.

I guess the saying is true, when it rains, it pours. But, I surmise when the sun shines, it shines brightly, huh?

Strutting down that runway in a classy colorful new Sean John dress was glory to my life. I seen so many celebrity faces. At that particular instant, it all made sense to me. It was obvious that I was also supposed to be in the limelight. And that day was the day that got me noticed. Don't get me wrong, I always was center of attention, 'cause I was the hood's richest girl and ain't have to touch a piece of dope. But now, I'm the center of attention from a whole different perspective. I'm the beautiful new celeb face, the it girl in ways beyond my imagination.

I was finally finished with my first runway appearance and Diddy approached me, acknowledging my excellence.

"Great work," he congratulated me, adding a pat on the back.

"Oh, thanks, it was nothing." I playfully waved him off, cracking a slight smile.

"I know, every time you came down in the different outfits, you looked better and better, girl. You did ya thang out there."

"Well, thanks. What's next?" I blushed, excitedly. I couldn't believe Diddy thought I did my thang.

"Oh, you and your girl are definitely keepers. We have a lot of upcoming projects underway.Yo, you girls are beautiful, and from the looks of it, y'all look like y'all been modeling for years. So yeah, that's what's up. This just the beginning." He smiled and hugged me before peering off into the crowded showroom.

Oh, I forgot to mention, Rai was released from the hospital a few days after Cheno killed my cousin, Tamera. Let me recap how this bitch tried to play the game. Hatin', envious hoes, I tell you. I once heard that jealousy a mu'fucka, and it'd have a lot of these muthafuckas hatin'.

Tamera told me everything before Cheno killed her. I couldn't do or really say much, 'cause she caught me slipping. I didn't bring my pistol along or nothing. I was enraged, but there was nothing I could do.

"I hate that you have everything, and that people always protects you." Tamera said, sounding like the jealous bitch she was.

"Okay, so you did all of this for that?" I eyed her with my

arms crossed.

"Yup, I was damned to be like my momma and allow you to be the center of attention, like your mother was in our family for years."

"I can't believe you have that much hate in your blood to do all this shit, for what though, really?"

"First off, I killed Donteice because I knew you loved her and that you would hurt from the whole ordeal. That's exactly what I wanted before I killed you. And it's fucked up how I'm your blood and you showed that bitch more love than me. That's why I killed her first, and we had to kill J.P. so people would think it was 'cause of him. Like he had beefed with somebody and they were coming back for revenge. I killed that dude that you was in the car with on accident. I really wanted you at the time. But like I said before, mothafucka's always wanna protect yo' ass. And the situation with Rai was simple. Money thought that you was the one coming in the door and shot her, and then that boy, but I guess somebody shot him."

Yeah, she was right. Rai had shot his ass clean in his skull. I don't know who the fuck he thought he was. I was pissed because Tee told me not to trust his glummy ass. Shit happens though, that's how I look at life. Although, I couldn't believe the hoe actually tried to kill me, my own fucking blood. Envious because I didn't fuck with her on a friendship level was what it all boiled down to. I mean, a fight that ain't shit. We could have fought every day, but nah, the hater wanted me dead and killed people to try and succeed, but it was totally unsuccessful. Hell, if she would have been real, she could have hung with no problems. Fuckin' nah though, the bitch was fake as plastic. It was that simple. She was a fraudulent, clown-ass bitch.

After Cheno shot her, I checked myself, making sure I wasn't hit, and I ran over to him, and jumped right into his embrace.

"Baby, I love you. I love you so much." I screamed, kissing him everywhere on his face.

"I love you, too, Jayah. I told you ma, that I'll never let anything happen to you as long as I'm here on this earth."

"I know, but how did you know it?"

"I felt something in my body and I just followed you here."

"All that's so sweet baby, this bitch was 'bout to off me." I laughed in utter relief.

"Not neva. As long as I have air in my breath, believe me,

you'll always and forever be straight."

"Thank you." I said, kissing him passionately on the lips.

♛ ♛ ♛ ♛ ♛ ♛ ♛ ♛ ♛ ♛ ♛ ♛ ♛ ♛ ♛ ♛ ♛

Rai and I were in the back after the runway appearance, preparing ourselves for departure, when my daddy came out of nowhere.

"Good job, ladies." He applauded.

I turned around swiftly, recognizing the voice instantly. "Hey! DADDY!" I gushed. I hugged him, almost squeezing him to death, and planted kisses all over his face.

I hadn't seen my daddy in what had seemed like forever. The last time seeing him was when we were at the airport leaving for New York. Him, Amelia and Jaylah was on their way to Africa. Didn't seem like that was four months earlier. I didn't even know he was coming. It was truly a surprise. And that was the greatest gift ever, because I never went a day without seeing my daddy unless he was locked up. And still, even when he was in jail, we chatted every single day, someties several times during the day. It was an unbreakable bond. But sometimes, when you grew up, business can cause changes in a relationship. Hell, I was still on a getting money mission, but this business consists of hard work and a distance between personal and business life. Forever, my dad will be my heart and soul. He made me into the woman I had become and for him, I'm grateful, and wouldn't change a thing in my life.

Adrian and SaNara moved to New Jersey. Main reason was for the great change, and also to be closer to me so I could see Kiddie anytime. They are happily engaged and are due to have their baby boy next year sometime. Yeah, Driano was finally having a baby of his own. He was excited, but it was all the same to him, because he said he would always treat all his kids the same. I sort of think that him and Kiddie would have that Jay and Jayah type of bond. He had enough money, so he could just sit back, kick up his feet and relax. Living life comfortably and enjoying the glamorous life with his family.

Big Tommy and Crazy P are still living in Miami. They had decided that they were never moving. It was the name that they had established years ago as true gangstas, meaning they still wanted to live chaotically. Even though they had money on top of money, they wanted it all. I believe will always have Miami on lock. My granny still lives there, too, in that same house sitting in the middle of the war zone. It's known that she will never leave the hood either. For some people, that's the only way to breathe

For Tasha, last I'd heard she was blowing her fucking nose off and was starting to shoot up dope with that nothing-ass nigga. Luckily, her kids are living with Tasha mother. I guess Tash will do it until she can't do it no more. I send her mother money every month for the kids and bills, just off the strength, because I know it's hard raising children, especially if they are not yours.

My father, baby sister and Amelia are residing in Africa, and that is their place of happiness. My daddy now treats Amelia how a wife should be treated. They visit us often to see if I'm straight. You better know I'm good. I'ma stay good.

Cheno and I moved into a huge house and we are together and plan on having a family of our own in the near future. Shawn and La'Rai are also holding down a serious relationship and happy, residing in a massively expensive loft in downtown Manhattan. Yes, Rai still is infected with the virus and Shawn still isn't. Thanks to Valtrex, he will never be. Shawn is the big and rolling hot artist for Bad Boy Records. He meant business once he stepped in the studio and into the booth. He made the number one spot on the billboard charts for six weeks in a row with his hit single, "Swagg".Cheno is his manager, so you know me and Rai make sure we stay boppin' in all his videos. And we are living it up New York style and hanging out with all the celebrities at all the classy and polished events. That's the way it is. Hey, you think Jayah Carter was the shit then, Jayah sets a whole new standard for Hood Richest in the NYC! Holla!

Triple Crown Publications

Order Form

P.O. Box 247378 Columbus, OH 43224

Name	
Address	
City	
State	Zipcode

QTY	TITLES	PRICE
	A Down Chick	$15.00
	A Hood Legend	$15.00
	A Hustler's Son	$15.00
	A Hustler's Wife	$15.00
	A Project Chick	$15.00
	Always a Queen	$15.00
	Amongst Thieves	$15.00
	Baby Girl Pt. 1	$15.00
	Baby Girl Pt. 2	$15.00
	Betrayed	$15.00
	Bitch	$15.00
	Bitch Reloaded	$15.00
	Black	$15.00
	Black and Ugly	$15.00
	Blinded	$15.00
	Cash Money	$15.00

Shipping & Handling

1 - 3 Books	$5.00
4 - 9 Books	$9.00

$1.95 for each add'l book

Total $_______

Forms of accepted payment: Postage Stamps, Personal or Institutional Checks & Money Orders. All mail in orders take 5-7 business days to be delivered.

Triple Crown Publications

Order Form

P.O. Box 247378 Columbus, OH 43224

Name	
Address	
City	
State	Zipcode

QTY	TITLES	PRICE
	Chances	$15.00
	Chyna Black	$15.00
	China Doll	$15.00
	Contagious	$15.00
	Crack Head	$15.00
	Crack Head II	$15.00
	Cream	$15.00
	Cut Throat	$15.00
	Dangerous	$15.00
	Dime Piece	$15.00
	Dirty Red	$15.00
	Dirtier Than Ever	$20.00
	Dirty South	$15.00
	Diva	$15.00
	Dollar Bill	$15.00
	Ecstasy Flip Side of the Game	$15.00

Shipping & Handling

1 - 3 Books $5.00

4 - 9 Books $9.00

$1.95 for each add'l book

Total $________

Forms of accepted payment: Postage Stamps, Personal or Institutional Checks & Money Orders. All mail in orders take 5-7 business days to be delivered.

Triple Crown Publications

Order Form

P.O. Box 247378 Columbus, OH 43224

Name	
Address	
City	
State	Zipcode

QTY	TITLES	PRICE
	Flip Side of the Game	$15.00
	For the Strength of You	$15.00
	Forever A Queen	$15.00
	Game Over	$15.00
	Gangsta	$15.00
	Grimey	$15.00
	Hold U Down	$15.00
	Hood Rats	$15.00
	Hood Richest	$15.00
	Hoodwinked	$15.00
	How to Succeed in the Publishing Game	$15.00
	Ice	$15.00
	Imagine This	$15.00
	In Cahootz	$15.00
	Innocent	$15.00
	Karma Pt. 1	$15.00

Shipping & Handling

1 - 3 Books	$5.00
4 - 9 Books	$9.00

$1.95 for each add'l book

Total $_______

Forms of accepted payment: Postage Stamps, Personal or Institutional Checks & Money Orders. All mail in orders take 5-7 business days to be delivered.

Triple Crown Publications

Order Form

P.O. Box 247378 Columbus, OH 43224

Name	
Address	
City	
State	Zipcode

QTY	TITLES	PRICE
	Karma Pt. 2	$15.00
	Keisha	$15.00
	Larceny	$15.00
	Let That Be the Reason	$15.00
	Life	$15.00
	Love & Loyalty	$15.00
	Me & My Boyfriend	$15.00
	Menage's Way	$15.00
	Mina's Joint	$15.00
	Mistress of the Game	$15.00
	Queen	$15.00
	Rage Times Fury	$15.00
	Road Dawgz	$15.00
	Sheisty	$15.00
	Stacy	$15.00
	Stained Cotton	$15.00

Shipping & Handling

1 - 3 Books $5.00

4 - 9 Books $9.00

$1.95 for each add'l book

Total $________

Forms of accepted payment: Postage Stamps, Personal or Institutional Checks & Money Orders. All mail in orders take 5-7 business days to be delivered.

Triple Crown Publications

Order Form

P.O. Box 247378 Columbus, OH 43224

Name	
Address	
City	
State	Zipcode

QTY	TITLES	PRICE
	Still Dirty	$15.00
	Still Sheisty	$15.00
	Street Love	$15.00
	Sunshine & Rain	$15.00
	The Bitch is Back	$15.00
	The Game	$15.00
	The Pink Palace The Set Up	$15.00
	The Set Up	$15.00
	Trickery	$15.00
	Trickery Pt 2	$15.00
	The Reason Why	$15.00
	Torn	$15.00
	Vixen Icon	$15.00
	Whore	$15.00

Shipping & Handling

1 - 3 Books $5.00
4 - 9 Books $9.00
$1.95 for each add'l book

Total $_______

Forms of accepted payment: Postage Stamps, Personal or Institutional Checks & Money Orders. All mail in orders take 5-7 business days to be delivered.